THE ESCAPE ARTIST

Jonathan Holland was born in Macclesfield, Cheshire, in 1961 and educated at the universities of London and East Anglia. His work first appeared in *First Fictions: Introduction 11*, published by Faber and Faber in 1992. From 1985–9 he taught in the south of Italy. He now lives in Madrid.

GW00724665

THE ESCAPE ARTIST

Jonathan Holland

... 'We'll have a talk. You can tell me what you've been doing in Petersburg. How about it?'

'My dear Maxim Maximych, I've really nothing to tell. Well, goodbye. I really must be going – I'm in a hurry.'

Mikhail Lermontov, A Hero of our Time

faber and faber

LONDON · BOSTON

To my parents

First published in paperback in 1994
by Faber and Faber Limited
3 Queen Square London WC1N 3AU

Photoset in Palatino by Parker Typesetting Service, Leicester
Printed in England by Clays Ltd, St Ives plc

A CIP record for this book is
available from the British Library

ISBN 0–571–17101–X

My name is Marc.

There's something not nice about an outsider like me. We're the ones who don't say anything, whose answers, when we speak, are cautious and fearful. Where the corners are, that's where we are. People quickly grow bored of us, realizing that the depths we wish to imply in ourselves are not in fact there.

Outsiders are cautious and fearful because they're ashamed. They're – we're – ashamed of their confusion, of not participating in life, of not being able to feel. The world of surface and light is the only world they trust. What lies deeper down is simply too dangerous, too frightening. And what can happen is this: given sufficient time, the heart itself becomes a stupid object of surface and light, and outsiders become terrified exiles in the foreign country of themselves.

All I do is watch. An outsider never grows up, but remains permanently locked in the delocation of adolescence. I watch the others as they line up with me for their food, wearing their silly white uniforms, licking their moustaches. In my mind I watch them as they stupidly cry at night, howling the names of old loves. I watch them as they fight, and dream, and make plans for the future, just as though they were outside, in the world. I watch it all, happy in the knowledge that in here their passions mean nothing. Because we'll be in here for the rest of our lives, now.

Watching them is the only thing that keeps me sane. That, and the other crucial difference between us. Which is that whereas they feel trapped, I feel safe. I feel as though I've escaped. Watching, I'm one of them, but I'm not one of them. Because for an outsider, detachment and involvement, out there and in here, are the same.

Doesn't that sound grand? It isn't. It stinks. But a bit of self-mythologizing always goes down well, so I've written the story of how I came to be here. I'd been planning it for a long time, but what with one thing and another, I never got round to it. It's not the truth, of course – what is? – but it's as close to the truth as I can get it, given that I was out of my head for much of the time.

Living through it all again has been strange. Watching myself across time, crawling across my own history like a fly across a dead man's lip. A failed grammar-school boy, fortunate enough to have the words to describe it. Can that nasty character really have been me? That nasty, dislocated lump? Can it?

I don't know – but anyway, this is the story of how I learned to see killing and dying as a sort of game, and of how I managed to break my way into jail.

I

We were on the Costa Brava again, having just driven four hundred uncomfortable miles in order to remove ourselves from the increasingly intense, dusty heat of Madrid in late May. But as far as I was concerned, we could have been anywhere in the world. What mattered more than where we were was where we were not: and we were not, I reflected with satisfaction, in Whately, Lancashire, England.

'Right, everybody. Prepare yourselves for the fleshly equivalent of Stirling Castle.' Donald peeled off his T-shirt, armpits stained ochre, and laid it on the sand beside the previous day's copy of *El País*. 'There you are,' he said. 'One magnificent Scottish ruin.' He flexed his biceps repellently.

'My *God*,' drawled Michael. 'Those hair-graced nipples. That blinding Scottish whiteness, despite years of exposure to the sun. Somebody tie me down.'

'Ach, fuck off.'

Brian gingerly knelt and laid out his towel. I watched him carefully. One reason we'd come away was because Brian had felt he needed a break: two weeks before, after a lengthy illness, his wife had died.

'Oh, Brian.' Chantelle picked up the newspaper and fanned herself with vigour. 'A brown towel. How totally *sweet*.'

'Brian's a brown individual,' growled Donald. 'Am I right in this, Brian? Brown, the colour of sombre dignity?' He studied his Ducados for a moment before clamping it between his lips, eyes screwed up, and lighting it.

Brian dabbed at his liver-spotted forehead with a tissue, occasionally peering at the tissue as though to see whether anything had come off. I'd expected some reference to Carmen's death in the Beetle coming down, but he'd made none, and whatever turbulence there was behind those pale, watery eyes was clearly being held back.

'Speaking of sombre dignity,' Michael said, 'check out Donald's shorts.'

Printed on to the front of them was the face of Lenin.

'There's a story to go with these shorts,' Donald said.

'Music?' Chantelle said quickly. 'Michael's got some Juan Luis Guerra, if anybody could get into that . . .' Michael fished about inside his shoulder-bag.

'*Merengue*,' he said. '*Very* sexy music for sexy Australians like Chantelle.'

'Go on, then,' Donald said. 'Bang a bit of that on, then.'

Several seconds later, our little patch of sand was alive with bouncy, summer music, manufactured to make people dance and consign their sorrows to oblivion. The words, I presumed, dealt with love and the distress it causes. Since I'd been in Spain only four months, I couldn't say I understood many of them.

The five of us spread towels, settled in the scalding sand. The conversation grew disjointed and abstract, passing from the subject of cellulite, to that of my own short-sightedness, to the fact that cows can only see in black and white. We became mindless in the heat, and lost the ability for speech. Words passed between us, but little was said.

I lay on my stomach, my back prickling, and looked across the bay to where the pale concrete buildings of L'Estartit shimmered. It was remarkable that Auntie Beryl didn't know where I was at this moment. Not only that, she couldn't even picture it in her imagination. She'd never been abroad, her existence having been played out in a miserable fifty square-mile patch in the North of England.

I felt in my shorts pocket for the letter I'd started to write her on the train from Whately to Manchester on New Year's Day. I kept it with me at all times, adding to and subtracting from it at those moments when my resolve would weaken.

I have decided, *it said*, to take a break. I have come to the conclusion, at the age of twenty-four and with another hellish Christmas over, that I must now take my life into my own hands for a little while, something which, if you think about it, you never allowed me to do. It's time for me to receive an education. I'm sure Dr Minshull would have approved my decision. I'll pay you back the money when I see you again.

'Have you seen this?' Donald said. 'The Serbs have bombed a shopping centre in Sarajevo. Innocent people dead. Human beings, every man-jack of them.'

'That's terrible,' said Chantelle. 'Where *is* Sarajevo, anyway, exactly?'

'That kind of thing's just too *big* to understand,' Michael said. 'Like the stars. Like the grains of sand on this beach. How many grains of sand do I have in my hand, Frank?'

'How should I know?'

'Well, say a number,' Chantelle urged.

'Twelve,' I said.

'There are more than twelve grains of sand in my hand,' Michael said. 'I have a Math degree and I can confirm that there are more than twelve grains of sand in my hand at this time.'

'Well, you said say a number . . .' Such literalness of mind was Auntie Beryl showing in me. 'This is lovely,' I said. I had to get off the subject, quickly. 'Just the five of us, lying on a beach.'

Later in the afternoon, the news about the bombing in Sarajevo would become an improvised sun-hat for Chantelle. Now we were again with only ourselves, and the blue sky with its big orange hole, dancing behind our closed eyes. Each time we came to L'Estartit, this descent into silence was quicker. The dose of excitement on arrival was no longer sufficient to keep us buzzing for more than a few minutes.

'Ah . . .' Chantelle murmured and stretched. Sand fell from

7

her. 'It's like they say. The best things in life are free.'

'Hey,' Michael replied three minutes later. 'Don't be bizarre. The best things in life are the most expensive.'

'Millions of people would give their right fucking arms to be where you are now,' Donald reminded us. 'Never forget that.'

It was true. For the others, there was nothing extraordinary about these escapes from Madrid. But I was still new enough for them to give me more pleasure than I'd ever had. It was unbelievable that I, Frank Bowden from Whately, probably the whitest-skinned person in Spain and certainly the most self-conscious person in the universe, should be doing these things.

Meeting up at the Café del Nuncio in Calle de Segovia – the sensuous exoticism of the words – at 4 o'clock in the morning, the pavements still shiny after the street-cleaners, just as the clients from the night before were preparing to go home to bed or to go on somewhere else. Drinking a cup of milky coffee and then climbing into Donald's infirm VW and driving out of the city under the street-lamps of wide, anonymous highways. Pausing at somewhere in the middle of nowhere for another dose of caffeine, the hulking shadows of mountains in the distance, watching heavily constructed women dressed in black and toothless, grimy-faced men gibber away in the half-light. The pleasure of anonymity, of just passing through. Arriving in L'Estartit, checking into the Miramar *hostal*, a Blackpool name in a Spanish location, whose owner Chantelle and Michael referred to as Freddy Krueger, since she resembled the film character of that name: coming down here to the beach to catch the last of the sun and skim stones across an idle, empty ocean, to recline under a parasol with a fat novel and a ham roll.

It was, I thought, as though I were taking part in a film I'd never seen before. At moments like this one, I least doubted my decision to come away, to leave everything behind me.

Donald was twice removed from his homeland, twenty-five years before having left Scotland for England and later England

8

for Spain. As messy and oblivious in his emotions as he was in his appearance, he'd recently divorced for the third time. He'd met Conchita, the saxophonist in a band called Alfonso Brown and the Del Fuegos, in 1969 in Wardour Street in London, a city which, like so many, I had read and dreamed about without ever visiting.

He'd come to live in Madrid on Conchita's account, and had founded the Albion Academy of English after attempting and apparently miserably failing to produce and market a wine called *Sangre de Jesús* – Jesus' Blood – with an eye on the immense Catholic market. The way Donald explained it was hilarious, making me wish I had his ability to see his own life as a humorous subject. His marriage to Conchita had survived eleven years, but they'd lived together only three months, the inevitable result of what Donald termed the 'Catholic love trinity' – Donald had loved Conchita, but not as much, apparently, as Conchita had loved her mother, whom Donald deeply despised even now. He'd been in Madrid for twenty-one years and was full of plans for the future, none of which, it was suspected, would ever be realized. 'You know what was so great about the sixties?' he asked me once. 'It was a dreaming time. Everything was possible, and nothing was real. It was paradise for a kid on the streets back then.'

His stories about those times, usually recounted with a bottle dangling from his hand and fiercely driven through to their conclusions, could be dull. But we loved him for them. It was as though he wished to assure you that he was a man whose interesting history compensated for his higgledy-piggledy present.

Smoking and spirits had acted on Donald's vital organs much as rust had acted on his VW Beetle. 'Half my money goes on drink and the other half on limiting the bloody damage it causes.' He quoted with glee an expression his dentist had used, referring to Donald's mouth as the oral equivalent of Pompeii.

There had been a scare in Valencia only three weeks after I'd arrived in Spain. We'd been savouring the details of the divorce when suddenly Donald had emitted a peculiar sound and his head had dropped into his paella. The lives of all of us, dependent on him as we were, had flashed before our eyes. The diagnosis, a fluttering heart, had not modified his habits in the least, and he himself made a bigger fuss about how the leg of a prawn had got into his eye.

'Donald,' I asked him in the hospital, 'do you drink on account of a love of life or a hatred of yourself?'

He'd appeared taken aback. I did not generally give the impression of being an articulate person, as Auntie Beryl had never tired of reminding me.

'Frank,' he said, 'in an indecent world, to be an oenophile is the only honest option for the decent man. Now fuck off.'

I dutifully looked up 'oenophile' in the dictionary. It meant 'lover of wine'.

We dined that evening in a chaotic seafront restaurant on the Passeig Maritim. Fishing nets hung from the whitewashed walls. Elegant, compactly formed waiters barked orders at one another; bored children ran around. Two smooth-faced German people sat at the next table, their jaws rotating in unison.

Before coming to Spain, I'd been unacquainted with seafood. On the steel plate in front of me lay several different species, among them lobsters, clams and mussels: words I hardly knew in English, let alone in Spanish. These were practically the only occasions in Spain on which I ate what Auntie Beryl would have called 'proper' food, and it was pleasant to stroll back to the Miramar in our shirtsleeves, lightly perspiring under a clipping of moon, with the chirruping of crickets and the gentle aroma of the sea, and the midges the worst problem we had.

In Whately, corpulent women like Auntie Beryl would be lying asleep in beds in small, stale rooms with net curtains, the sounds of snoring issuing from their open mouths. If they were dreaming, it would be about getting new wallpaper up in the back room, about a nice summer frock from Marks and Sparks they'd had their eye on. England was reality. Spain was not.

Ahead of Brian and myself, Donald was recounting to Chantelle and Michael a homosexual experience he'd undergone in 1966 on the Northern Line between Balham and Tooting Bec. He hadn't, he confided, found it as disagreeable as expected.

'Well, you can forget it, I'm afraid,' Michael said lightly. 'I'm saving myself for some teenage action later. Yeah!' He gave an athletic skip and punched the air. Donald protested that Michael had got the wrong end of his stick, thereby provoking further innuendo.

'A most pleasant evening,' murmured Brian.

I involuntarily jumped.

'It certainly was. As always.'

'I do feel most grateful to you all, you know . . .'

A tall, gentle man in his late fifties, he had a perpetual cold, the consequence of an accident on Exmoor thirty years before, when he'd fallen asleep at the wheel of his Mini Minor and driven it into a tree. Brian was the opposite of myself in that he was anxious to return to England, to his native St Ives, where his sister, Gladys or something, lived. The one thing Brian hadn't got used to after thirty years abroad was not having a vegetable patch to tend.

'You're all young people,' he went on. 'Yourself, Chantelle, Michael, the students . . .'

'I'm not particularly young,' I said. I couldn't remember how old Brian thought I was. He plucked absently at his shirt collar.

'Oh, but in your attitude you are. To have come here, like this, to have thrown up everything you had in New York . . . you're very brave . . .'

Suddenly I felt uncomfortable.

Since the details of my former existence were of interest only to psychiatrists, I had felt it necessary, on arriving in Spain, to invent a small history for myself. This had originally been for the benefit of Donald at my job interview, but I'd overdone it slightly, word had got around and now not only the people I was here with but also most of my students, my landlord's family and even Freddy Krueger were under the impression that I was a reformed drug addict who'd come to Spain after several years in New York, during which time I'd worked as an assistant to the internationally renowned photographer Robert Mapplethorpe, most famous for his beautiful pictures of the naked bodies of big, beautiful men.

I'd read about Robert Mapplethorpe in an old newspaper in the Whately library a couple of days before leaving, read about all the famous friends, the sex and the drugs, thought him a wild and cool figure – though the article, unfortunately, had been his 1989 obituary. It could only be the absolute impossibility of my having invented something so preposterous – an obvious virgin with prematurely receding hair, mild but persistent halitosis and pre-scription spectacles – that had convinced the others of its truth.

'We must appear rather an odd bunch, don't you think?' said Brian. 'What must people make of us?'

'We're misfits, aren't we?' I said. 'As in the film of the same name.' While I did feel uncomfortable, I did derive a small excitement from being thought other than I was. I managed to muddle through most awkward spots. 'I've thought about this, Brian. You're our Clark Gable. Chantelle's our Marilyn Monroe, Michael's Montgomery Clift, Donald's Arthur Miller and I'm Eli Wallach.' I'd seen the film twelve times, during my years at VideoWorld in Whately's Churchill Shopping Precinct.

A car careered past, its window open, the sudden windy rush of music causing both of us to step into the ditch and a stone to lodge itself in my sandal.

'I must say I'm a little worried, Frank,' Brian said. For a second, he appeared lost in frenzied internal debate.

'Worried?' I stood on one foot and beat my sandal against my thigh.

'Well, it's not actually a terribly easy thing, losing your wife after thirty-eight years of marriage.'

I wasn't very good at this sort of conversation. I wondered why Brian had chosen to talk to me about it rather than to any of the others, and then realized that it didn't have to be me, that it might as well have been any of them. That he just wanted to talk.

'Carmen was the only thing keeping me here, you know,' Brian murmured. 'And the job, too, I suppose. We never had children or anything . . .'

It wasn't necessary to speak, so I didn't. I hadn't met Carmen. Donald had: he'd called her someone you could imagine being good for a bit of a tumble thirty years ago. That recollection seemed inappropriate at this point. I wondered how I'd feel if someone I'd been close to for many years died. Only Auntie Beryl really fitted into that category: in which case what I'd feel would be relief.

'Sometimes,' Brian said, 'I picture a summer evening in England. Cream tea on the lawn. Tiny little sugar spoons. The buzzing of wasps. The lowing of cows. Don't you ever think of these things, Frank?'

'Not really,' I said. 'A broken bicycle being thrown off the tenth storey of a block of flats. The stench of cat piss in the lift. Badly spelled graffiti on concrete. A polystyrene Spud-U-Like tray in a smashed-up telephone box. Prams containing deathly white babies.'

But Brian's mind had drifted, whether towards Carmen or himself with a trowel in St Ives among the hydrangeas, I didn't know. The back-porch light of the Miramar twinkled across the bay: Chantelle's voice twinkled along with it, wondering whether Brian and I could get into a nightcap.

TWO

Breakfast was at midday, in the shade on the red-tiled *terraza* at the back of the *hostal*. Donald generally started the day with a strong spirit called *orujo*. When he'd suggested I try the same thing, I'd almost passed out and had to return to bed. He followed this up with two cups of coffee and three Ducados. Chantelle, bright-eyed in her pink bikini, popped segments of a mandarin orange into her mouth, allowing them to rest for a moment on her tongue before swallowing. The rest of us slobbered over *café con leche* and brioches from deafening cellophane packets.

'Well, what am I going to do today?' Even at breakfast, Michael gave off the aroma of scent. 'Nothing,' he said, replying to himself. 'Absolutely nothing, apart from dabble in my art. *Michael's Book of Influences.*'

Considering the nature of his social life, and the hours at which he led it, he seemed remarkably alive. I'd heard Michael and Chantelle getting back at about 4 o'clock, whispering as loudly as most people shout. He stretched his tanned, bony limbs and then set about rubbing Ambre Solaire into his bald scalp. His baldness was a mystery which he didn't care to talk about.

'Come off it,' Chantelle said. 'You'll have half a novel finished by lunchtime, I bet.'

'I might go swimming today,' Brian put in. 'Or then again, you know, I might not.'

'How's the novel going, Frank?' Michael asked me. He was perhaps the person who had been most impressed by my connection with Robert Mapplethorpe, repeatedly enquiring as to what Robert was like in the flesh. My answer to that was 'very nice'.

'The novel's fine,' I said, although it didn't exist.

'What's it about?' Donald wondered.

'Frank's very private about his art,' Michael assured the others earnestly. 'You can't just ask him what it's *about*. I wish I could be private about my art. It's so *artistic*, to be private about your art.'

Michael was the first American I'd met. You didn't get Americans in Whately: you got Whatelians. Although it couldn't be said that he was good-looking – 'facially dispossessed' was the term he used to describe himself – parts of him did remind me of the actors I'd seen in films. His confidence, the languid way he had of arranging his body: it was as though he were perpetually aware of a camera trained on him. He wore a crucifix earring and circular metal-rimmed spectacles which he didn't need.

His background was the sort of background you envied if you had a background like mine. It was ironic that he should 'adore' me for having 'hung out with Mapplethorpe', but then fictions like mine create irony at every turn.

Michael had apparently already known passion, and continued to know it several times each night. After graduating, he'd obtained a grant to go, strangely, to 'Leicester, England', where he'd met a man called Roy, a garage mechanic – although when pressed for more details, Michael seemed uncharacteristically reluctant to reveal them. I wished to know more about his legendary night-life, which involved making the rounds of Madrid's many gay bars and sweat-shops, places with unusual names like 'Very Very Boys' and 'Ficty Ficty'. He would fence expertly my goggle-eyed enquiries as to the details of his sex life – although he had revealed that he squirted eau de cologne on to his anus each morning – merely asking whether I'd read Joe Orton's diaries, which I duly did.

Donald found it beyond comprehension that there could still be Americans who came to Europe to 'be writers'. When I said I

15

didn't understand why it should be so strange, Donald looked at me, and said, 'Oh, Frank.' Michael's reply was that it was not the Hemingways, the Fitzgeralds, the Millers who were his heroes, but the creator of the Nancy Drew mysteries.

While I'd been working at VideoWorld, I'd read a book called *The Plague* by a Frenchman called Albert Camus. There is a person in it who repeatedly starts to write a novel, but who is unable to get past the first paragraph, which he rewrites obsessively, uselessly polishing it, scared to continue. Nevertheless, he'd got further with his novel than I had with mine. Michael was similar with his own writing: he possessed the will to begin, but not the dedication to finish, the ticket but not the destination.

Fear of what came next was a failing I'd observed in the lives of many people at one time or another. I was guilty of it myself.

There were not a great many people on the beach that Saturday. It was still too early in the summer. As we'd done before and would do again, we busied ourselves in purposelessness. Chantelle took photographs, using a Polaroid camera her Italian businessman friend had given her. Whereas Michael felt that from certain angles he looked better than from others, I was aware that I appeared unpleasant from most angles. Nature had not made me a beach creature, and it was now too late to think of becoming one: my flesh was irredeemably pallid, my stomach irretrievably protuberant, my knees irrevocably knobbly.

When she tired of taking photographs, Chantelle went swimming in the nude. I didn't know why she felt she had to do this. She returned with a pink shell and a bloodied big toe, which Michael kissed better before writing out the first words of his new novel in her blood. Donald lay bone rigid, complaining that we shouldn't have let him at those mussels last night: Brian did likewise, flinching occasionally, perhaps dreaming of an afternoon in 1961 when he'd driven a Mini Minor into a tree.

This is paradise, *I wrote*. This is the sort of life you can't imagine, Auntie Beryl. The sort of life you don't believe people should lead. 'Idlers', you call them, and then you press your lips tightly together. People talk about getting away from it all for a few days: well, if this is getting away from it all, then I'd be happy to do it for ever.

A bead of sweat dripped from my nose and on to the page.

At 2 o'clock, Michael and Donald reluctantly agreed to visit the bar. They returned with unpleasantly dry bread rolls containing *chorizo* sausage and sweating cheese, and a bottle of warm Coca-Cola. At this hour, the few people dotted across the beach generally trudged back to their holiday homes or hotels for lunch. Looking about me as I worked to dislodge a lump of crust from my palate, I could see no one except for a single man, a hundred or so yards down the beach towards L'Estartit village, lying on his side.

The thin sound of his radio crackled across the sand.

A friend of Chantelle's joined us for lunch. It was unusual to come to the beach and not come across a friend of Chantelle's, a Ramón, a Javier, a Diego: her ability to converse in Spanish, indeed her ability to converse at all without becoming tongue-tied, left me feeling envious. Diego, whose T-shirt had apparently been sprayed on to his pectorals, was carrying two inflatable beach mattresses, so the others spent much of the afternoon taking turns on them. Giggles and squeals came from the heads bobbing about in the sea, wafted towards us on the cool, lethal breeze.

'Come in, Frank,' Michael gasped. 'The water's lovely.' He shook himself as a dog might, flecking my back with drops of salt water.

'I can't swim.'

'I'll teach you.'

I shook my head. Swimming, like driving, was an activity for which life with Auntie Beryl had not prepared me. Among the others were a desire to take risks, the ability to hold a conversation, and the capacity for true friendship and love. These were elements of the education I'd decided to give myself. These were the reasons I was in Spain.

Late into the afternoon, Michael spoke of the first paragraph of the latest instalment in his *Book of Influences*.

'This is going to be a *radical* book,' he informed us. 'Love, death, betrayal, history, memory. The ancient values are in danger of eradication. The world needs a new high priest of literature.'

'Jesus H. Christ,' Donald said. 'What the fuck have you been reading this time?'

'*Time* magazine. This has to be the adjective of our era, wouldn't you say, Frank?'

'What? "Time"?'

'"Radical". The need to define our values by pushing our behavioural patterns to new extremes. Testing our limits in order to seek out the truth. Or something.'

'Oh, yes,' I said. 'Definitely.'

'Writing, of course,' Donald said, 'is a leisure pursuit like any other. There's no more sense to writing a novel than there is to having a wank, except – '

'Wanking doesn't make you go blind,' Chantelle and Michael said in chorus.

Donald grunted.

'You keep on with it, Mikey,' Chantelle said. 'Don't let Uncle Donald put you off. I *like* hearing about love and death and all that stuff. It's fun. It doesn't have to mean anything.'

'How pleasant,' Brian murmured from under his sun-hat, 'to be so young.' He sneezed. The hat fell off.

The sun commenced its slow daily death. Michael and Chantelle pulled on their T-shirts: cautiously I removed mine. The conversation turned to what people would be doing over the summer. Michael said he'd like to revisit Tangiers, Chantelle that she'd like to cross the United States on the back of Diego's Harley-Davidson. My own intention was to stay in Madrid and try to write the book which everyone thought I was writing.

None of these things, I suspected, would happen.

'Right,' Chantelle said. 'I don't know about you lot . . .' She stood up and clicked off the cassette player with her heel. 'I hope you're not thinking of leaving that pile of tissues there, Brian. They constitute a threat to our fragile ecosystem.'

'I'm sorry.'

'That guy's been lying like that all afternoon,' said Michael. 'I've been watching him.'

'Maybe we should go and see if he's all right,' Donald suggested.

'Any excuse to socialize,' said Chantelle. 'You can't just go up to someone on a beach and ask if they're all right.'

'He may be ill,' said Brian, shading his eyes. 'He may have sunstroke. It's foolish not to sport some kind of headwear.'

They could have gone on like this all afternoon. It was something to talk about.

'Hey!' Michael suddenly shouted, causing Brian to drop the armful of tissues he'd gathered together. 'To hell with it. I'll go and check him out.'

We watched him lope off across the sand.

Donald said, 'Just watching the bugger gives you three heart attacks.'

Michael slowed down and stopped. He fell to his knees.

'What *is* he doing?' Chantelle said. 'Saying a prayer?'

Then Michael was on his feet again, walking slowly towards the man.

'Mikey?' Chantelle shouted. 'You all right?'

He stopped and turned. 'No, I am fucking *not* all right.'

We got there as rapidly as we were able, pulled along by the urgency of Michael's voice. By the time we were close to him, he was squatting in the sand, looking back at us over his shoulder, his eyes wide, his mouth hanging open.

'Oh my God,' Chantelle said. 'Oh, Jesus God. I don't – I can't – I'm going to –'

She took a couple of paces back and put her camera to her eye, pointing it at the dead man. The camera flashed.

'Chantelle, what the hell –'

'Just don't *ask*!' she shouted. 'OK?'

'Christ –'

The camera flashed again. Chantelle slowly lowered it and stared at the dead man. Dumbly I followed her gaze.

The sand on which he lay was stained a dark red. It glistened stickily on his neck, slowly turned solid in the hair on his chest. The secret, spilled treasure of his life.

I leaned down to turn off his radio. The disc jockey's voice was spoiling the moment. I closed my eyes. This was just the sort of terrible, magnificent experience I had dreamed about having as a part of my life.

The rush of waves, scrambling for the shore.

Michael was still on his knees, sobbing, shoulders heaving. 'There's a fly walking on his lip,' he said. 'A goddamn *fly*.'

Chantelle went to him and put an arm around his shoulders.

'He's dead, Mikey.'

'Dead.'

'Somebody tell him to stand up. Don't just stand there, Frank.'

'Somebody call an ambulance,' Donald said, empty-voiced. But we didn't move: not because an ambulance would have been useless, but because we were petrified, magnetized.

The mysterious body. Lying in the cooling sand. The sunset.

Donald exhaled deeply and squatted down beside the corpse. He put his ear to its chest.

'Looks like he's had his throat cut. Looks like some bright spark went and took a knife to his fucking throat.'

Brian arrived, wheezing. He stood with his hands on his hips.

'I'll stay here with Donald,' he gasped. 'You go back to the *hostal*. Go on, Chantelle. Michael. Donald and I can sort it out. Now go on. Go *on*.'

In the high-ceilinged entrance hall of the Miramar, a pair of flies chased one another around a light-bulb at impossible speed, unaware that one of their number had been seen, minutes earlier, scrutinizing with its thousand eyes the lip of a dead man.

Freddy Krueger had been informed after seeing Michael's tear-stained cheeks. The shock of finding the body seemed to have affected him particularly badly.

'*Qué pasa, hija?*'

'There's a *cadáver* on the beach, señora,' Chantelle explained.

'*Un qué?*'

'*Hay un cuerpo muerto. En la playa.*'

The colour of the landlady's crumpled old face altered and she started flinging her arms about, bemoaning the condition of the Spanish tourist industry. She expressed the wish, after the manner of Auntie Beryl, that her poor brother were still with us. Then she left us to go and lie down in her room.

'His *throat* was cut.' Michael sat, feet wide apart, his track shoe rapidly tapping the floor, and stared out like a bad passport photo of himself. 'He was just *lying* there.'

'What happened, though?' Chantelle wondered. 'I didn't see anybody near him or anything.'

'He just looked so *dead*.'

'Are you going to carry on saying that all night, Mikey?'

'I guess so, yeah. For the rest of my *life* I'll probably carry on saying it. Oh, man . . .'

'It was like something out of a film, wasn't it?' I ventured. I didn't often speak, and when I did, people were always a little surprised to find me there.

'Pardon me, Frank. That's a real dumb thing to say.'

'That's the whole point, Frank. It *isn't* a film.'

It would, as usual, have been better to keep my thoughts to myself.

'I wish it were a film, though,' Michael said. 'Don't you? I cannot *believe* this . . .' He went to the window and reached up to switch on the rotating fan.

'The mysterious body,' I insisted. 'Washed up on the shore.' I wanted them to admit it. You didn't find bodies on beaches, not in real life. Everybody knew that.

'You're a cool guy, Frank,' Michael said. 'I don't suppose death has much of an impact on you. With all your friends dying of overdoses or AIDS. Well, you're lucky. Or maybe you aren't.'

'I suppose I am,' I said, not understanding him. Try as I might to spot glimmers of sarcasm or irony when Chantelle and Michael spoke like this, I couldn't see them. Since we shared no common history, they took me at my face value, as I took them at theirs.

'It'll be the police and everything, won't it?' sniffed Chantelle. 'Oh, *God* . . .' She pushed her hair back with one hand and absently felt about in her beachbag with the other. When it emerged, it was holding a hand mirror.

'Wouldn't he have shouted or something?' Michael said.

'His face was a bit puffy. He must have been dead quite a long time . . .'

It was probable that he had died messily, in a kind of bloody orgasm, his body twisting and bucking as the liquid spurted from his neck. Meanwhile, a hundred yards away, we had been lying inert, insensible.

'He might have been brought to the beach first.'

'There wouldn't have been the blood.'

'No. Knocked out. Or chloroformed. A handkerchief soaked in chloroform. Then he might have been brought to the beach to have his throat cut.'

'With a sharpened screwdriver. By a maniac. Oh, Jesus.'

22

'What sort of person,' Chantelle wondered, 'would spend time sharpening a screwdriver, anyway?'

'What *is* chloroform?' Michael asked vaguely.

I knew. I'd read books. 'It's an anaesthetic.' In a moment of divine inspiration, I'd once told Dr Minshull that my ambition was to lead my life soaked in emotional chloroform.

In the absence of facts, the imaginations of Michael and Chantelle went haywire, excited by possibility. I could picture them later, settling down together over cocktails to create the goriest, most effective story for the folks back home, just as though they were writing a film script. It was true: their emotions were influenced by Hollywood, as everyone's are. Why wouldn't they admit it?

'You're both talking just as though it were a film,' I said. 'You really are.'

'Just think,' Chantelle said. 'It could have been *us*.'

The next thing was the sound of sirens and the scrunch of gravel, as though the police believed that by imitating television they could scare away the horrible truth. Donald came in, looking about a hundred years old, followed by Brian and two members of the Guardia Civil. Brian went upstairs to alert Freddy Krueger; Chantelle whispered something to Michael, and they both slipped away. 'We have to talk, OK?' Chantelle explained. 'We're both hysterical.'

'They don't know anything we don't know,' Donald acidly told the policeman. 'They're young and it's got to them. Don't you worry.'

The policeman who spoke to us was courteous. His colleague leafed through a tourist brochure with one hand and with the other absently picked at his right ankle, occasionally examining his fingernails.

'Before we commence,' the courteous one read from the back of an envelope, 'I should want to express my hope that you will not give the blame for this terrible event to either Catalunya or

23

indeed to the nation of Spain.' He looked at his colleague, who nodded curtly and went on picking.

'*Hablamos español*,' Donald said with evident irritation.

The policeman seemed relieved. I didn't yet speak Spanish well, but I could understand the general sense. This was not, the policeman told us, a terrorist assassination. It matched no terrorist patterns. His belief, offered with a sneer which suggested that he believed such murders justified, was that it must be a drugs-related or homosexual killing.

We were then asked to make a statement. Donald and Brian recounted what we'd seen, stating that it had been Michael who had first realized that the man was dead, and that there had been a fly walking on his lips. Neither of them mentioned Chantelle's photograph.

'It was getting towards sunset,' I said when it was my turn, 'when we discovered the corpse. The man's blood appeared to be a – a visual echo of the sky. It possessed a kind of terrible beauty. The expression on his face was almost that of relief, as though in his final moments he had experienced joy at being able to escape from the woes of this world. Cast off the terrible yoke of his existence.'

I was pleased with myself for having said this in Spanish.

'Actually, Frank,' Donald interrupted me, 'I think they're more interested in whether we saw anything. And I can recommend you a good Spanish course, if you want.'

'That's what I did see,' I said. 'I'm only trying to help.'

'Well, he's not writing it down. So save it for your novel, eh sunshine?'

After making the statement, we bickered over the details among ourselves, acting as though we'd been witnesses to the crime rather than merely discoverers of the corpse, participants rather than spectators. The policeman yawned and read the statements back to us. They sounded strange, as though these could not be *our* actions, as though such an event could not have taken place in *our* lives.

*

24

What we should do, Chantelle suggested after we'd showered and had some time to ourselves, was go somewhere loud, busy and full of people, like Geneva. 'To pretend that nothing has happened' was the way she put it. We left Brian reading *Middlemarch*, climbed into the Beetle and drove into L'Estartit village.

Geneva was a discobar. Everybody danced and seemed to behave in ways not normal to them. The music, Michael informed me, was called rap. There were other types of music which were called hiphop and rave.

'How come you don't know that, of all people?' he asked me. 'A guy like you?' The ultraviolet light made spots of my jacket appear white, which was unusual, since by day it was an entirely black jacket.

In the absence of other things to talk about, we talked about our discovery.

'Just think,' Michael said. He flicked his crucifix earring back and forth, looking about him. 'None of these people know what we know.'

'They're lucky.' Chantelle's eyes widened. 'God, I hope they find out who did it. I couldn't stand it, not knowing who did it. Like, *To be continued*.'

'I've seen millions of dead bodies in the movies,' Michael said. 'But this guy was just so *still*.'

'Isn't there a difference,' Donald asked, 'between seeing a dead body in a film and in the papers? Because if you can't see it, then you should try.'

'What's the difference? They're both as horrible as each other.'

'Maybe he was here last night,' Chantelle said. 'Sitting where you're sitting, Frank.'

'Thank you.'

Suddenly Donald perked up. 'Did I ever tell you about the time I headbutted David Hemmings? That was before he was famous, of course.'

'Donald? Please? Apart from who's David Hemmings, what

does that have to do with anything?'

'David Hemmings in *Blow Up*. I'm just trying to change the fucking subject for one second, before we all top ourselves. Anyway, did anybody know that the very first death of all was a murder? Cain and Abel? No, I don't suppose you did. You lot probably think the first murder of all was on *Kojak* . . .'

I wanted to know why Chantelle had taken those photographs of the dead man. But nobody else mentioned it, so I thought I better hadn't either.

In the Beetle going home, all of us squeezed up together, I reflected that the conversation between us had rarely flowed as it had tonight. We'd never have been friends if we'd met in England. We'd just been thrown together. But now we had something apart from our foreignness, from Spain and from one another, to share. Dark and unpleasant though it may be.

I closed my eyes and fantasized about one day removing my socks and climbing into bed with the woman I called the Hola Woman, about putting my arms around her soft, enormous body, about telling her all these things. It would be necessary to invent a little. An event like this needed to be embroidered upon to achieve the proper effect.

I turned and looked at the faces of the others as they blinked out into the darkness. Nobody said it, but everyone was thinking it: something had changed, and things could go anywhere from here. Matters felt suddenly brittle and a little dangerous. This was exciting: this was why I'd come to Spain.

I couldn't sleep that night for all the peculiar images swooping around my mind, many of them unpleasant. 'You want to watch that imagination of yours,' Auntie Beryl had said, after I'd called her a disease-ridden rhinoceros from hell. I'd do it, I thought: I would. I'd write the novel which the others believed I was writing. Frank Bowden's *The Beach Killing*. Like Stephen King's *The Shining*, or whatever it was. Perhaps I could make this particular fabrication real. Live up to the notion they had of me.

Then I thought about the Hola Woman and, as usual, ended up making love to her in my mind. I generally wore my Sony Walkman when masturbating, listening to Meat Loaf's 'Bat out of Hell'.

It must have been about 3 o'clock when I was roused from a sweating doze by a tap on the door. I only hoped it wouldn't be Donald, come to crack open a bottle of wine and talk about how shitty it all was, when you really thought about it.

It was Chantelle. She looked the worse for wear, as though she'd cried. She was barefoot, her toes turned slightly inwards, wearing a pair of jeans cut off above the knee and a T-shirt bearing the forlorn inscription: 'Where's the Party?'

Her teeth stood out, bright in the darkness.

'Chantelle? Are you all right?'

'Do I look all right?' she whispered.

'No.'

'Couldn't sleep.'

'Neither could I.'

'Well, then.'

We looked at each other for a moment. A different person would have recognized a sexual opportunity in that look, and reacted to it. But unfortunately, I was not a different person.

'Tell you what,' Chantelle said. 'Pull on a pair of trousers and we'll go and sit on the back porch.'

I hesitated.

'Oh, come on, Frank. I don't bite. The air'll do us good.'

Nobody ever said no to Chantelle. It was clear that her parents had never said no to her, perhaps because of the combination of a winning, open smile and a fragility which made you think she'd have a nervous breakdown if you refused her anything. Donald had become irritated with her a couple of months before when she'd asked him to drive fifteen miles through the Sierra Nevada to buy her a hamburger. He'd told her to grow up, that people wouldn't forever be at her beck and call. Then he'd driven off into the night.

During my troubled teens, I'd opened a magazine in Bill Podmore's barber shop in Canal Street. In an attempt to move into the seventies, he had changed the sign outside the shop from 'W. Podmore, Barber' to 'Billy's'; underneath, it now said 'Unisex Hair Salon for Men and Women'. Inside, nothing had altered – it was still shelves of Brylcreem and the powerful odour of hair alcohol – but on the table inside the entrance there was an old copy of *Vogue*, the best Bill Podmore could do by way of creating a small island of glamour in his matt brown world.

There'd been something noble about this doomed attempt of Bill Podmore's to change the way the world saw him. I'd never thought such a thing possible before.

I'd looked at *Vogue* and entered a different world entirely, one more to my tastes than the real world. Wealth and happiness, and bright colours, and the feel of quality. By the time Billy had finished clicking his scissors niftily about my earlobes, I'd fallen in love with the image of a woman called Jean Shrimpton. As you do, I wrote poems to her:

> Jean
> Do you know what true love means?
> I don't. But you can show me any time
> Under a bright blue sky, if you want to
> Jean.

Boyish, delicate and freckled like Jean Shrimpton, Chantelle had apparently almost blinded herself at age seven back home in Melbourne, trying to remove her own freckles with vinegar.

Her eyes were clear and green, of the sort that would glint if eyes actually did glint. I'd often wished to describe them to Chantelle herself, but had always found myself unable to. I was no David Bailey to Chantelle's Jean Shrimpton, and my own body, unlike hers, scarcely constituted a sexual invitation. Quite the opposite, in fact.

Chantelle bought a can of Coca-Cola Light from Freddy Krueger's drinks machine and we went to sit barefoot on the back-porch step of the Miramar, gazing down across the ruffled sand to the sea and its vast triangle of shimmering moonlight. From the village there came the faint, hypnotic thudding of rap music: from Chantelle, the aroma of sun-tan oil, a hot presence.

'Lovely and warm,' she murmured. She pushed her hair back and raised her face, greedy for the breeze. 'Night wind. So pure. So ecological.' Then she clapped her hand to her mouth and opened wide her eyes. 'But there's *death* on it now.'

'Anything in particular you wanted to discuss, Chantelle?'

'Maybe not. Maybe I just wanted to sit here for a while and talk with someone. I couldn't sleep.'

'Did it have to be me?' I asked hopefully.

'Not especially. God, I'd give anything to be back in Paris again . . . Brian says we should get back to Madrid tomorrow morning. If we don't want to be hounded by the media.'

'I suppose he's right . . .'

'I am so *bored*, Frank,' Chantelle suddenly blurted out. 'Bored, bored, bored. It's *bad* for me. I require constant stimulation if I am not to fall prey to self-destructive tendencies.'

I knew what she meant there.

Reflectively Chantelle started to trace patterns in the sand with her elastoplasted big toe. 'You're a very cool guy, aren't you, Frank? I mean, to look at you, you wouldn't think . . . but it's like, you're *interesting*. You've *lived*.'

It would have taken a person of greater integrity than I possessed to shatter an illusion from the lips of Chantelle Ray. I remained silent while Chantelle no doubt pictured me doing things I had never done, assimilated me into the trendy black and white world depicted in the photography books she bought. There's Frank, his dark curls trailing back in the wind as he races his Harley-Davidson across the Mojave Desert; there he is again, raising his glass to camera as he stands leather-jacketed among the ruins of the Berlin Wall; there again, seated across from Robert Mapplethorpe as Robert lights a cigarette and compliments him on yet another marvellous idea.

29

'Listen, Frank.' Chantelle's toe stopped its circling. 'You know the photograph I took? Want to see it?'

'That was weird,' I said. 'Why did you do that?'

'I don't know . . . I just did it sort of *automatically*. You want to see it, Frank? Only one came out.'

I found it oddly exciting. Entering into a little private conspiracy like this.

'Just look at it. Please.'

That was him: his oddly angled face. His open mouth was a funny shape, as though someone had stuffed an invisible potato into it. The photograph was warm between my fingertips.

'He was actually quite good-looking, wasn't he?' Chantelle said. 'You can imagine him actually being quite good-looking, underneath it all.'

'Why did you do this?'

Chantelle stood up, put her hands on her hips and clicked her tongue.

'Listen, Frank,' she said. 'I don't make a habit of going to guys' bedrooms at four in the morning, you know? I have something to *tell* you.'

She reached down and took the photo from me, turning it distractedly in her fingers.

'Me and Michael met him last night,' she said quickly. 'And something happened.' Chantelle eyed me in a challenging way. 'Maybe you don't want to *know* what happened. Maybe I shouldn't tell you.'

'I do. Of course I do.'

'Well, you know how I get bored? Me and Michael were in this bar last night, and we're just sitting there having a quiet smoke and a cocktail, and then all of a sudden, this guy's getting thrown out of the bar.'

'*This* guy?'

'*This* guy, yes. This actual guy.'

She was talking as though she'd met James Dean or somebody.

30

'He was so drunk, Frank. He couldn't even stand up properly. He was just wearing these really grubby baggy trousers and an absolutely *filthy* T-shirt. Ugh.' Chantelle shivered. 'So he just stood there swaying, and then he collapsed on the street. So Michael said, we can't just leave him lying there, he'll get killed, run over by a car or something . . .'

'Go on.'

'Yeah. Well, to tell the truth I wouldn't have minded leaving him there myself, you know? But Michael said we should at least get him to the edge of the street . . . So there we were, pulling him to the edge of the street, and people are *looking* at us, imagining we're his *friends*. I didn't want them thinking that, Frank. You can imagine. So I took some photographs of the guy, so people'd think I was a journalist or something . . .'

'What does it matter,' I asked, 'what people who don't know you think about you?'

'Oh, it matters, Frank. It matters. You know that.'

And I did.

This was Chantelle's ambition, to be a photographer. Unfortunately, she knew a fair amount about the subject, and three or four times had come close to inadvertently exposing my Robert Mapplethorpe fiction. She'd shown us photographs she'd taken during the year she'd lived in Paris, living out her own particular fantasy, pictures of crinkle-faced old men playing *boules* in the street, or of fat old ladies selling onions. 'I've seen these pictures a million times before,' Donald had told her cruelly. 'There's a big difference, darling, between wanting to be a photographer and wanting to take photographs.'

It was a distinction I didn't believe Chantelle understood. But if she didn't want to understand it, then the best of luck to her.

'So after a few minutes,' she continued, 'the barman comes out and throws down a piece of cardboard. "You foreigners," he said' – and Chantelle's imitation of a Spanish accent was exciting to me – '"why you dreenk so much? You so good for business, you bad for business." And on the card it said, "*I have no money. I*

31

am HIV positive. I must get back to England." Just those three sentences. You can imagine . . .' Chantelle repeated the sentences, counting them off on her fingers.

'Anyway, I jumped back about fifty yards. It was like, I'd *touched* him, Frank. A guy with AIDS! So Michael got all uppity with me. He said that I was stupid, and just because somebody was HIV positive, it didn't mean they had AIDS, and to catch it I'd need to have slept with the guy without a condom on repeated occasions. It's like, I'm a bit innocent that way . . .'

I watched her. She was talking exactly as she would have talked if there'd been no one in the room, as if she were practising in front of the mirror before going on to the stage. She was playing the part of Chantelle, portraying an idea she had of herself, performing. They probably hadn't met the guy at all. It just wasn't the sort of thing that happened.

'This guy just smelt of sick and beer all mixed up. But Michael was being really kind of *gentle* with him. I said, Michael, I think we've done the Good Samaritan bit now, let's go, but Michael said we had to wait till we knew he was all right. I should just have come back here, but Michael had the keys to the Beetle . . .'

Perhaps I was going to hear something appalling. I wanted to hear it. I didn't want to hear it.

'. . . so anyway, the first words the guy said when he came round were, "Don't go." So I got him some water, and we waited a bit longer, and then we got hold of him and took him down to the beach. He clearly hadn't showered in *days*, Frank . . . How can people let themselves *go* like that?'

'I suppose they can,' I said. 'If they're extremely unhappy.' At any rate, that was how it had been with me.

'Yes. Well, they shouldn't.'

'Let themselves go?'

'Shouldn't be unhappy. So anyway, we were sitting on this wall and the first thing the guy said when he could speak properly was, "I haven't slept with anyone in three fucking years." Then he started crying. "Don't cry," Michael says. "You just talk, and we'll just listen." "Maybe it's four years," the guy says, and I'm thinking, God, we'll be here all night . . .'

I was starting to think the same thing myself. Further down the beach, there was a dim yellow light and a low rumbling, presumably the lorry which came every night to smooth the sand and give the following day's tourists the impression that they were the first people ever to set foot on it.

What Chantelle said next brought me back to earth.

'He was trying to escape from his real life, he said. He said he'd come to L'Estartit because there was a lot of stuff he wanted to get away from. His marriage. He said he always came back here, because at least he knew a few of the barmen. He said he always hoped he'd have a good time, meet a few people, but it always went wrong, because he was afraid of people. He said he wanted to go back home feeling *human* again. Not like some ugly sewer rat. That's what he said, Frank. He wanted to escape.'

'It looks like he succeeded,' I said. 'Better than he wanted to, probably.'

'Then he just really opened up. He said that sometimes he thought he was gay, and sometimes he thought he was straight, and sometimes he thought he was bi. There was just all this *confusion* inside him. But it didn't matter anyway, he said. He said it was like asking a blind man his favourite colour. What he really was, was a pissed-up English sewer rat who had AIDS and no money and no friends and no personality. A twenty-first-century Englishman, he called himself . . .'

'What was his name?'

'I don't know. I'm *glad* I don't know. Maybe Michael knows.'

'What did he mean about having no personality?' This was something I'd thought about myself. At times, I'd wished not to have one, to be freed from the burden of having one. I wouldn't have wished a personality like mine on my worst enemy, which was why it was pleasant, in a slightly troubling way, to know that Chantelle and the others believed I wasn't who I was.

Chantelle appeared nettled at having had her recital interrupted. 'I don't know what he meant. I suppose he meant he had no personality. So anyway, then he went off to the toilet. It's like, he was so depressed. I thought he was going to *kill* himself, Frank. You can imagine. Michael said that all the guy needed was to sleep with someone. "Sex is salvation . . ." Michael's been through it himself, not sleeping with anyone for a long time. . . What's the longest you've gone without sleeping with someone, Frank?'

The answer was 'about twenty-four years'. But since it was a favourite pastime of Chantelle's to ask me direct, 'grown-up' questions which showed her knowledge of the workings of the world, and because she probably believed that I had an exotic and creative sex life, I told her with a smile that it was none of her business.

'You're just cool, aren't you, Frank? Behind those specs? It's like, you don't say much, but I bet you have all these *thoughts* . . .'

'Go on.'

'Well, the next thing is, Michael says we should toss a coin to see who sleeps with the guy.'

'You what?' Exotic and creative though my supposed sex life was, this was a little beyond the pale.

'Yeah. And I'm like, what? This guy was in no condition to sleep with *anybody*. But Michael's a Twangy, so he can just do it like that.'

'A what?'

'A Twenty Guy a Night Guy. So Michael starts saying how he only thought the idea up out of the goodness of his heart, how he wanted to save the guy's life, how he sees it as an act of *redemption* or something, and I'm saying, Michael, this guy *smells*, he's utterly without *charm*, and Michael's like, "It's OK, I have condoms" . . .'

'So what happened?'

'We tossed a coin. And Michael said heads, and it was heads. And that's it.'

'That's it?'

'The last I saw of Michael, he was just walking towards the toilets. To where this guy was . . . then we met up an hour later and drove home . . . then today, God . . . you can imagine how I felt when we *found* him . . . and how *Michael* felt . . .'

'And what did Michael say? You don't think Michael . . .'

'I don't know, Frank. I just don't want to know anything.'

Chantelle's sharp glance suggested that it would be better not to pursue that particular line of enquiry. She ran her hand quickly back and forth through her hair, causing her breasts to bob vigorously.

'Does Michael know you're telling me this?'

'Of *course* not.'

'So why are you telling me?'

'Because you're experienced,' Chantelle said simply. 'Because a guy who's had a life like yours would understand. You do, don't you? You must understand why I wanted to take that photo? I mean, with you and Robert Mapplethorpe and every-thing . . . it's *nice* to be understood, Frank. It doesn't happen often enough.'

I looked at her, and at the photograph sticking out of her shorts pocket. Chantelle was afraid of something, afraid of what-ever it was inside her that had made her take it. For the first time, her own mortality had been made apparent to her.

'I mean,' she muttered, 'a photograph normally catches the fleeting moment. But death is the permanent moment. It's the medium denying the message.'

I lost her at this point, apart from sensing that she was using big, abstract words to conceal big, concrete, frightening emotions.

'That's what Robert Mapplethorpe used to say,' I said. Chan-telle's eyes opened wide.

'Did he really? Oh, that's *great*, Frank.' She slid the photo out again and tilted her head to one side, eying it critically. 'It's quite like a Diane Arbus. Except that in a Diane Arbus, the subject is generally still alive. But that's only a small technical difference. Andy Warhol painted soup cans, didn't he? A soup can's never even *been* alive . . .'

I drifted as Chantelle continued her performance. From inside the *hostal*, there came the sound of a television being turned up too loud and quickly turned down again.

'I've never known love. I've never met the right man. I'm not a sack of potatoes. It always just feels so empty, so distant, somehow. . . Just to find someone who really *understands* . . .'

Perhaps it was where we were, on a Catalan beach at night, conversing in low, intimate voices: when Chantelle said that, I felt a rush of warmth in my lumbar region. I wanted to hold her. It was unusual for me to want to hold people.

It wasn't that I could have been the right man. Not for Chantelle, not for anyone, apart from the Hola Woman. Not Frank Bowden, for God's sake. But I still had that uncomfortable tingling, and I wanted to be rid of it.

'So what kind of person do you think killed him, Chantelle?'

'Hey, Frank. He might not have *been* killed.'

'His throat was cut. What sort of person?'

'A real sicko. Like a Hannibal Lecter. A serial killer.'

'Somebody alienated from society, maybe. Somebody who lives unto his own laws and who doesn't give a damn about *anything*. An outlaw. An escape artist.'

'What are you saying? Do you think Michael did it?'

I didn't know what I was saying.

'Well, *I* certainly didn't do it,' Chantelle said. 'I'm essentially well-integrated, despite a perfectly normal post-adolescent propensity to mild depression.' A big, slow yawn filled up her small body. 'You're *weird*, Frank. But I suppose that's your appeal, in a nutshell.' She stood and walked a few paces, walked back again, and sat down. Her fingers picked at the plaster on her big toe.

'Did Robert Mapplethorpe really say what I said?'

'What?'

'About the medium denying the message?'

'Yes . . .'

'Listen, Frank. Would you mind sleeping with me tonight?'

'Chantelle . . .'

'Not *sleeping* sleeping . . . just lying in my arms for a while? Friendly?'

She brought her knees up to her chest and hugged them to her. 'I just feel so *bad* about finding that guy today.'

'Perhaps another time? All right?' I heard a silly crack in my voice. I wasn't the sort to leap into bed with people, however much I might want to. One day, I intended to be that sort of person. But not yet. Things would go wrong. There would be misunderstandings on my part.

'All right, Chantelle?' I said, and my bloody voice cracked again.

She was on her feet once more, looking out to sea. Absently, she passed her hand across her left breast. 'There's no one else I can ask,' she said. 'Please, Frank. I'm scared of the dark.'

That was it exactly. She didn't know how true that was.

But paranoia and sexual attraction go hand in hand, and I thought I could see a faint smile on her lips.

'Talk to your Italian businessman, then,' I said. 'Talk to Pino.' I stood and stretched. I must have been sweating, because sand clung to me. 'I might wait here a little while. What time is it?'

'Around six, I guess. We're going in an hour. Is that a no, then, Mr Cool?'

'I suppose so.'

'Well, you can consider yourself truly honoured that Chantelle Ray has tried to seduce you.'

'Oh, I do. Goodnight.'

I wandered down the sand. Was she watching me? I straightened my spine, held in my stomach.

I was not tormented by Chantelle's request. She could as easily have asked someone else. Her words were just part of the free and easy atmosphere of our beachy days. They meant nothing. Everything was play. Brian confiding in me, the dead man, Chantelle's performance. Play.

The sand still retained some heat from the previous day. There was only the lazy slapping of the waves and the first suggestion of today's sun over the horizon. I cast about, trying to establish the exact spot at which we'd found the corpse, sensing the beginnings of an obsession.

There was a sneeze some yards away to my left. A stooping shadow.

'Brian?'

'Just taking a little air,' he called back. 'Couldn't sleep.' He produced a short, high-pitched laugh. 'Ridiculous. At my age.'

'I couldn't sleep, either. Chantelle couldn't, either.'

'I'll just be getting along to bed, then. Early start.'

'Sleep well.' My head was full of thoughts that needed shaking out. I slid off my shirt and trousers and jogged out, splashing, into the huge, warm ocean.

FOUR

The principal reason for the shabbiness of the Albion Academy of English was that its owner, Donald, never had any money. In the gloomy reception area there was a map of the world which garishly proclaimed the existence of Malaya, Ceylon and Tanganyika. In the Children's Activity Room – instigated at the suggestion of Pilar, the plump secretary with scarred cheeks, after a bored, hysterical child had blacked her eye – it was figures such as Rupert the Bear, Dougal and Zebedee who held sway. The influence of modern technology was nowhere in evidence, and a visit to the lavatory required an iron will and steel-clad respiratory apparatus.

Another problem was competition. All over Madrid, old schools were closing down and new ones opening almost weekly: the Cambridge Institute, the London Academy, the Cambridge School, the Oxford Academy . . . the permutations were endless. On being called to interview, one candidate had apparently gone to the Albion School by mistake and been offered a job there instead.

'You'll feel at home,' Michael had told me on my first day. 'It's so *English* here.' Donald had replied that the most English thing about the Albion was that it was completely out of touch with the mood of the nineties and was badly in need of some new blood. He was a modest emperor.

'Since I know no other way,' he'd recited without zest at my interview, 'I'll be honest with you. You're entering a school which is plummeting towards oblivion. The free market, etcetera.'

A dense, sour aroma filled the room, which Michael and

Chantelle called Donald's 'opium den'. This was the only job interview I'd had during which mention hadn't been made of relevant experience, which was lucky, because I had none.

'The world has become disgustingly professional,' Donald went on after coughing for a while. 'Now the fact is that this school was inspired by an ideal, dreamed up in less materialistic times. Happier times. This school is my gift to the youth of the world. I suppose a guy like you has heard of George Whitman?'

I shook my head.

'George is the guy who runs the Shakespeare and Co. bookshop on the Left Bank in Paris. He gets kids in there to work for him, pays them nothing and lets them sleep upstairs. Yanks, mostly. Kids who are travelling in order that they might worship at the shrine of experience. So I thought, why not do the same in Madrid? Let's face it, only about one per cent of the kids who come abroad to teach English actually *want* to teach English. Most of them are here because they want to have a bit of fun while they're finding a direction. They're in limbo. The last thing they want's a fucking *job*.'

That was my situation. But it was more than a bit of fun that I wanted. It was a whole new life. I was here to discover myself, as it were: not that that had anything to do with Donald.

'This is the system. I pay you an absolute pittance, you come in and teach about fifteen hours. You don't work Fridays. The rest of the time you're to get out there and live. You can sleep in the school, if you want. You can smoke dope in here, but nothing harder. But if I look at you and I think you're not looking after yourself, so help me God you're out on your arse.'

He leaned across his desk and peered at me, a great soft vein network underneath a weary mass of grey curls, crinkled skin under his eyes. The aroma, I decided, was probably alcohol.

'There are bags under your eyes too, sunshine. Get out into the sunlight. Get out into the mountains. You're not to stop at home reading books, you're not to go to the cinema. No substitute for life. You look older than most of the kids we get in here. What age are you?'

'Twenty-seven,' I lied, confident that the Albion Academy lacked the means to check this.

'And you've spent the last five years in New York, working in photography.'

'That's right.'

'Are you a loser in life? Is that how you'd describe yourself?' Donald looked almost hopeful.

'No,' I said.

'Well, our motto here has always been, let's have fun while it lasts. If you're after anything permanent, then I suggest you apologize for wasting my precious time and piss off. Speech over. Any questions?'

'Yes,' I said, and Donald appeared slightly surprised. 'Why is it called the Albion?'

'The Albion? Reminds me of a pub back in Kilmarnock. Happy New Year.'

Having overcome my initial nervousness, with the assistance of Pilar, I quickly found that it was not necessary actually to teach the students anything. They simply wanted to chat: they were unreflective, enthusiastic people with a great deal of energy, and quite unlike those who had filled my days before then – white, gawky, misshapen men and women in shell-suits, with red Ford Fiestas and yellow teeth, who were obsessed with money and the domestic security they believed it offered. English people. I fantasized wildly to my students, and they lapped it all up: incredibly, the idea of Frank Bowden was exotic to them.

Those were the days when I was still under the impression that a proper job might be worth doing, still thinking under the malign influence of Auntie Beryl. I hadn't yet assimilated the basic principle that job satisfaction decreases proportionally to the amount of job you had to do. There was a crudely scrawled graffito in the lavatory – *'Let's get it over with then'* – which was the unofficial working motto of the Albion staff: the walls were a multi-lingual word salad of such graffiti, penned by teachers and students down the ages. *'Why did man invent God'*? Chantelle had written in an especially bored and inspired moment. *'To get him out of bed on Sundays'*.

One Sunday morning during the Christmas break I'd woken up, still drunk, at 6 o'clock under a lamp-post in the Street of the Flying Fish. There was dog excrement on my trousers. It was a wild situation, vastly different from the repressive order of my life in England, against which my imagination had always struggled.

I'd realized that I was happy, that I would never have it as free and easy as I was having it now. I said as much to Michael, who was stretching and rubbing his eyes a few yards away.

'It's a great life!' he shouted, and his voice reverberated among the buildings. 'No anxieties, no responsibilities, no ambitions to make you worry about not having achieved them. Freedom!' The words had tumbled from him as I'd looked on admiringly. 'We're killing time, all the time!' He'd run up to me and put his arm around my shoulder. In my ear he'd whispered, 'Welcome to paradise, Frank.'

'In the Albion Academy,' I added, looking over my shoulder in case anyone came into the lavatory, *'there is no God and it's always Sunday.'*

It was late on a Saturday night, a week after our return from L'Estartit. The narrow streets of Chueca were alive with hooting cars, roaring motor bikes, squealing people, the stench of black tobacco. A fire engine, siren blaring, was being held up by an elderly lady wishing to reverse her Panda out, in turn almost crushing the legs of a young couple sprawled across the bonnet of the car behind, their limbs wrapped round each other, a razor-blade's width away from making love.

I sat on a fire hydrant, feeling ill and sweating buckets. One day, I too would be part of this exciting, incomprehensible world. But it's a hard business, escaping from the way you are, and tonight I was my usual depressed, thoughtful self.

Finding the corpse, Chantelle's recital, the fact that nobody in England knew where I was, and nobody here who I was: seven vodka and tonics had brought these matters home to me with unpleasant clarity. Sometimes, when you're unable to recall a particular word, or resolve a particular conundrum, you joke that you won't be able to sleep until you've sorted it out. This was just how I was feeling about the beach killing. In its arbitrariness and bizarrity, it presented itself as a puzzle to be solved, a new item of understanding to be had. My connection with the event was exciting, dangerous, a little wild: three adjectives which did not generally apply to to the life of your average Whatelian. I wished for more.

The event had been given space in all the Spanish papers. I purchased them all, struggling through the articles with a donkey's vocabulary and the patience of a saint. I'd stood outside a television shop on Santa Isabel and stared at multiple images of the beach at L'Estartit as people like ourselves, but apparently happier, had tossed beach balls to one another. The *Daily Mirror* had dedicated a few inches to it, but the only magazine to use a picture was *Interviú*, which had obtained a fuzzy photograph of the man Michael and Chantelle had met, skinny and gormless, holding a greyhound in his arms. The greyhound's name was Stanley.

LA MUERTE TRAGICA DE UN VERANEANTE

The tragic death of a Holidaymaker, a Summer Person. His name had been Derek John Platt, a thirty-five-year-old car mechanic from Macclesfield. It was strange to see the word 'Macclesfield', there in *Interviú*. His car had been a metallic blue Peugeot 205, hired from Europcar. He'd visited Spain each year for several years and had been an *aficionado* of greyhound racing. As far as the press were concerned, the last person to have seen him alive had been a barman in L'Estartit.

It was all a little pathetic. He was just an assortment of facts. It

43

seemed that there had been nothing in the least suspicious or scandalous within miles of the life of Derek John Platt.

When you brought the photograph to your face, and stared at the eyes of the dead man, you saw an emptiness there, the foreknowledge that something spectacular and awful was one day going to happen to him. What Chantelle had told me confirmed this. Here we were dealing with a man the nature of whose death would more than compensate for the evident banality of his life, whose picture could only ever appear in the papers as the result of his dying.

It was a shame that Derek John Platt was dead: if I'd been there that night with Michael and Chantelle, I'd have spoken to him, tried to understand him and have him understand me. We might even have become friends. There'd have been something between us.

Finally the fire engine was able to pass, its siren still stupidly blaring, intermittently cutting out all other sound. Donald emerged from the bar we'd been in. The ripped poster on the door said, in English, *'Nightmares in a Damaged Brain, Tonight, Live at 24 o'clock'*.

'Did you hear that band, sunshine? They're doing old Sinatra numbers with electronic blips and new words. "You are Hypodermic". "The Methodology of Self", for fuck's sake.'

'I don't get it,' I said.

'You all right? You look as though you've lost a fiver and found sixpence. Nice use of idiom there, from Donald.'

'I'll be OK, thanks. I think I'll be getting back home now.'

'A novel to write?'

'Yes.'

Donald's right foot slipped off the kerb and he said, 'Christ.' Then, 'Now, repeat after me, sunshine. I'll live this life to the full if it kills me.' I repeated the sentence as requested. 'See you Monday.'

He stumbled away.

I pulled a notepad and pencil from my pocket.

The tragic collision between the need to control and the need to be loved, *I scribbled*. To be understood is not to be free. To have someone believe they understand you is to be wrapped in the chains of their incomprehension. This has to be avoided. Freedom is control. Escape is all. What is it like to kill, to be killed? Are these the ultimate freedoms? The ultimate freedom is to kill the one you love.

That would go down a bomb over the Quaker Oats and PG Tips.

'Eh, English,' a large youth with a leather jacket and a large scar said. '*Qué pasa?*' Quite a lot of his teeth were missing.

'I'm writing a book,' I said, too drunk to feel threatened.

'*Cojonudo*. This world needs more artists, man. You like the Pleasure Fuckers? My brother play *la batería* for the Pleasure Fuckers.'

'Really?'

'I an artist, too. I an artist of *love*, man. I give my love for *free*, man.' He puckered his lips and rubbed his groin. He appeared miraculously solid, somehow. He seemed to be composed entirely of himself. I bade him goodnight.

Hoping to come across street episodes that would serve in my novel, I took a circuitous route back home through Lavapiés. The plaza in Lavapiés was a rendezvous point for the dispossessed of Madrid: by day it was full of gleaming-eyed old men and women proudly watching their grandchildren at play, sitting cackling on benches and bollards. At night, these were occupied by dull-eyed drug addicts, prostitutes and beggars whose heads lolled forwards and then jerked backwards as they sought to prevent themselves from sleeping. It was common to come across a dirty syringe lying in the gutter, and more than common to feel obliged to give money to a rough-faced, twitching *vagabundo* or to be approached by the fat, greasy-haired girl with the high voice: '*Señores, una ayuda, por favor . . .*' These were the people who yelled things at you as you passed, and although you didn't

45

understand what it was that they were yelling, it sounded like abuse.

There was more life in that square in one hour than there was in one year in Whately, and more death also. It was a location of extremes, and fascinating for that.

Back at the San José *hostal*, I was fumbling for my doorkey when the Hola Woman said, 'Hola.'

'Hola,' I said. Once, drunk, I'd said 'Hola' to her and she'd replied 'Hola'. Since then, we'd continued to say 'Hola' to one another, our relationship never deepening.

What the hell, I thought: I'm drunk, I'm lonely. I asked her whether she had a light, as though it were my intention to smoke my key.

'*Sí*,' she said. '*Tienes tabaco, guapo?*'

Guapo. Handsome. She clearly had a sense of humour.

The Hola Woman already occupied more space in my mind than she was aware of. I'd glimpsed her from my balcony one morning shortly after my arrival, pushing aside her curtain and leaning out into the street to water a plant on her window-ledge. She'd been wearing a pink nightgown: I saw plumpness, an exploding mound of shining black hair and a swollen pair of breasts. Right, I'd thought. One day, when I'm drunk, I'll ask her for a light. With that simple request, Frank Bowden's first grand passion would explode into being. I'd returned to bed that morning with my dreams in my head and my Filth File – a twenty-page document containing, in alphabetical order, a list of intoxicating things I'd spotted – 'Chantelle Ray's giggle', 'Esperanza Feijoo's black bra strap' – in my hand. For the first time, I'd arrived at the Albion late.

I'd begun to watch her. She often sat late into the night on the front doorstep of the house adjoining the *hostal*. I estimated her age at between fifty and fifty-five. She always munched from a pack of sunflower seeds and sometimes she wore a Sony Walkman. It was hard to place her. Was she a prostitute? How could she be, looking so brilliant-eyed? Was she married? Single?

Happy? She didn't form part of the life of the street, which consisted primarily of cackling, critical eighty-five-year-old widows with varicose veins and dysenteric poodles. She was never to be seen during the daytime at all, in fact. What was coming through those headphones? Meat Loaf? Julio Iglesias? Nightmares in a Damaged Brain?

Slowly, quietly, I constructed my version of her, a version which was now under threat from her physical presence.

'I haven't got any,' I said.

'Haven't got any what?' She was wearing a tight-fitting red and black striped woollen dress which gave her the appearance of a bumblebee.

'Cigarettes. I thought I had some. I wouldn't have asked you for a light if I had – if I hadn't –' my Spanish blew to pieces in this syntactical minefield. 'I just wanted to say "Hola". I have to go now.'

'American?'

'English.'

'English? Really?' Now we were going to have a conversation in which she'd tell me she had a son in England. Margaret Thatcher and football hooliganism would also be mentioned, these being the subjects which first occurred to the minds of Spanish people when they heard the word 'English'.

'You want some *pipas*? How you say *pipas* in English?'

'Sunflower seeds.'

'I study the English a little,' the Hola Woman said. 'I listen to the English.' She removed her Sony Walkman and put it on the step beside her. 'I have a son in England.'

'Do you really.'

'You are lonely,' the Hola Woman said, shifting matters on to an altogether different level. 'I can see. You are confused.' The huskiness of her voice had no doubt been brought on by half a century's tobacco consumption and screaming at members of her family. 'You have problems with your girl?'

'You might say that,' I said. 'I haven't got one. *Adiós.*'

47

She merely nodded and patted the doorstep. She explained that she was almost deaf in her right ear.

As I numbly walked over and sat down beside her, I was dizzied by a severe attack of Hemingitis. Hemingitis was a disease named by Donald, provoked by Michael: it was named after the American writer Ernest Hemingway, who never wrote a novel set in America. The story of his life was the classic case history of the disease. The way Donald described it, early symptoms consist of pretending to be Superman or a cowboy, after which most people shake it off. The unlucky people, according to Donald, the lucky ones according to me, are those who read a lot, moving from Salinger Syndrome, through Hessitis and Kerouac's Condition to Sartritis, by which time you're smoking too much, spending thousands of hours in cheap cafés, requesting bad wine and pretending to read unreadable books.

Living abroad automatically lowers your resistance. Yourself becomes no more than a memory. You believe yourself to be a character from the head of one of these myth shapers, or even one of the myth shapers themselves: not only are they writing *about* you, you come to realize, they are *writing you*.

All of us suffered from Hemingitis to some degree. But I suffered from it most strongly. After all, I'd been Robert Mapplethorpe's assistant.

I spent most of the night drinking Bull's Blood and smoking black tobacco in the cool Spanish shadows with the dark-skinned whore they called the Hola Woman. I looked up at the moon, proud and cold above this dirty city, and then I put my arm around the Hola Woman's waist and I squeezed and her heat ran up my fingers and into my heart and the world felt like a good place to be.

Her name was not the Hola Woman. It was Africa. And her surnames were 'Lechuga' and 'Fernández', Spanish for 'lettuce' and the equivalent of 'Smith'. So her name was 'Africa Lettuce Smith'.

We hit it off so well that we introduced ourselves only at parting. She had plump, jolly cheeks and thick eyebrows which, she told me, were dyed black. Her upper arms trembled when she laughed, which was often. She offered me sunflower seeds and wondered whether I wasn't the same person she'd seen standing on his balcony each morning in his underpants, trying to watch her breasts. It was pointless to deny it.

'If someone said that a pop group was playing old Frank Sinatra songs,' I asked her, 'and one of the songs was called "You are Hypodermic", and it was a joke, would you get the joke?'

It took about ten minutes to get all that across, but it didn't matter.

She thought for a while, her hands cupped behind her knees. Wrinkles of concentration appeared in her forehead.

'No,' she said. 'I wouldn't understand that at all.'

It was exciting to be communicating, however uncertainly, with someone so different from me. Someone who had nothing to do with the rest of my life. Even on that first night, I found that I was revealing myself, instead of just listening as I normally did, afraid that the fiction which was keeping me employed and keeping me in Spain would be exposed if I opened my mouth. Plump and thin, dark and white, fertile and arid, instinctive and forced, Spanish and English – taken together, I reflected as Africa taught me how to shell *pipas* with my teeth and tongue, we made something whole.

At long last, real life was happening.

FIVE

Several days later, we were all dragged out of class to be interrogated again by the Guardia Civil. The sight of a brown uniform standing in the entrance to the Albion caused patches of sweat to appear on Donald's clothing.

'Are you sure you saw absolutely nothing which may be of use to us?' the policeman enquired, incredulous that a man could have had his throat cut a couple of hundred yards away without our noticing.

I looked up to see Chantelle and Michael exchange a brief glance, but I didn't say anything. They'd both been less effervescent since we'd been back in Madrid. I'd seen them in the staff room, talking in low voices and smoking cigarettes, neither of which activities you'd generally have associated with them.

'If you keep asking bloody questions,' Donald muttered, 'we'll feel obliged to invent something for you.'

This wouldn't have been too hard. I'd spent the night before mentally planning the novel Frank Bowden's *The Beach Killing*.

The policeman apologized. Donald showed him to the door.

'Let's call them and say we remember something after all,' suggested Chantelle. 'Let's say we saw Frank with a razor-blade in his hand and blood all over his Dr Scholl's.'

'No,' I said. 'Let's tell them you and Michael saw him the night before and tossed a coin to see who should have sex with him. Let's say that *you* two killed him, Chantelle.'

That shut her up. It was safe, though – Brian was having a sneezing fit, and I'd spoken too quickly for Pilar to understand.

'Cancel this afternoon's lessons,' Michael said when he arrived. 'Go on.'

'I can't do that, you foolish bloody American. Tomorrow's the last day of term.'

'All the more reason,' Chantelle said.

'Do it, Donald. We're all nervous wrecks. My hands are trembling, look.'

'I certainly don't feel up to teaching,' Brian said. 'The older I get, the more the heat affects me.'

'Go on, Donald,' we whined.

'Oh, all right then. You tell them, Pilar.'

'I certainly will not tell them, Mr Brightwell. You can fucking well tell them yourself.' Being Donald's secretary brought its linguistic benefits.

'Oh, for Christ's sake . . .'

We huddled together in the staff room and tried not to giggle as Donald turned away twenty-four chattering children with the excuse that we were all sick that day.

'How can they *all* be sick?' we heard Carlos Santa Cruz wondering. He had a very deep voice for a child of eight.

'They just are. They ate something. Mussels.'

'Is Chantelle sick?'

'Yes.'

'Is Michael sick?'

'Yes.'

'Is Frank sick?'

'Yes, yes. They're all sick. They're *all* sick.' He raised his voice, and Chantelle giggled. 'Now,' Donald said in rapid English, 'piss off home, Carlos, all right? See you in September.'

'Right,' he said when he came back. 'Anybody fancy a swift *aperitivo*?'

We gathered in Los Fernandos, the spit and sawdust bar owned by a family in which the grandfather, son and grandson were all called Fernando.

'Ugh,' Chantelle said. 'I always smell of cooking fat after I've been in here.'

Once again we discussed the beach killing. Donald ordered

two stodgy platesful of *patatas bravas* to lend spice to matters.

'It would appear, then,' Donald said, glancing through *El País*, 'to have been an existential killing. "*No terrorist group has claimed responsibility*".'

'They've agreed it was a killing, then,' I said. I felt vindicated.

'A what killing?' Brian said to Donald.

'A killing without motive. A killing which shows how meaningless it all is. Which shows up how we all pretend we can't kill each other and how the fabric of society crumbles if we stop pretending. America's full of them. A Yank called Ressler called them serial killers. Now every town has its own serial killer. They're all the rage over there. Right up there with Coke and Big Macs. Illiterate drifters going barmy. A bit like you lot, now I think of it.'

'Ooh!' Chantelle growled and flexed her claws. 'I'm an illiterate drifter going barmy.'

Donald enjoyed having an audience. 'Oh, yeah. The Yanks love them. Lots of spondulicks in criminal insanity. Films, books, video games. "Simon Miller, Serial Killer. Can *you* track him down? For children of all ages." Killing for kicks. Death addicts. They haven't arrived in Europe properly yet. They will soon, when all the barriers are down. They'll kill in one country, then hide in another.'

'Actually,' Michael said, 'not *all* Yanks love them, Donald, you old Celtic racist pig.'

'I wonder why people feel the need?' Brian wondered. 'They should give them all a trowel and some rhubarb seeds.'

'It's psycho this, psycho that in America these days,' Donald mused. 'Psychokiller. Psychocomputer. Psychobutter. The last gasp efforts of a civilization in a self-conscious spiral of terminal decline to entertain itself. Hollywood absorbs our darkest nightmares and sells them back to us in dayglo colours at five dollars a throw. Right. I've finished. Applause.'

We applauded. Donald mopped his brow.

'Psychobutter!' squealed Chantelle. 'Isn't that *fab*ulous? I love him really,' she told us.

I watched and listened, hoping that someone might say something to help me solve the riddle of Derek John Platt's death. Inspired by years of watching the type of entertainment Donald had been describing, I'd spent the previous afternoon sitting in my favourite spot in Madrid, on the edge of the shadow of the statue of Alfonso XII by the boating lake in the Retiro Park, notepad and pencil in hand, making a list of possible explanations together with marks out of ten for their likelihood:

DJP cut his own throat	2
DJP victim of mad, unpremeditated killing	8
Suicide made to look like murder	4
One of us did it	0

But this last possibility was by far and away the most stimulating.

'Serial killers must be amazing people,' I said to get the ball rolling. 'The outlaws of the new millennium. The tragic collision between the need to control and the need to be loved sort of thing.'

Instead of provoking lively debate, this caused everyone suddenly to reach for their beers and sip. If I didn't keep my big mouth shut, they'd all end up thinking that it had been me who'd killed him.

'Well,' Donald said. 'That's it. The summer stretches before us. You're free again. That's official, and this round's on me.'

As Michael was pretending to fall off his seat, a small, authoritative voice cut in.

'Señor Brightwell?'

We all turned.

'Yes, Carlos?'

'You said you were all sick, Señor Brightwell, but you are all here. You are eating *patatas bravas* and drinking beer.' Carlos pointed at the table and gazed at us defiantly, his other thumb through the shoulder-strap of his enormous Snoopy haversack. 'You are not sick,' he declared in perfect English, 'and I am going to tell my father.'

'*Un momento*, Carlos,' Pilar said. '*No importa que –*'

'*Sí, importa.*' Carlos and his two cohorts slipped away. Donald made as if to get up, but Pilar put her hand on his shoulder.

'It doesn't matter,' she said. 'I'll buy them all a *batido* after the holidays.'

'Fuck,' Donald said, and slapped the table with his palm. 'Fuck, fuck, fuck.'

'Listen,' Chantelle said. 'I think we all need a great big party. I'll have one of my famous parties next Friday, OK? Anybody doing anything else?'

Nobody was doing anything else.

On the last day of term, solitude and boredom took me to the Palacio de las Comunicaciones to see whether any mail had been redirected to me. I couldn't remember what had possessed me to leave a *poste-restante* address with the Whately post office. The only mail I'd ever received at home was official. I'd probably done it in a crazed fit of anticipated sentimentality.

Apart from a reminder from the library that Camus' *The Outsider* was six months overdue, there was a letter with a Manchester postmark. I suddenly became possessed by the irrational fear that it might be from Auntie Beryl herself, and considered, as I made my way to the school, throwing it away unopened. The last thing I wanted to read was an inexhaustible litany of complaint and recrimination, interspersed with recommendations for a new brand of haemorrhoid cream.

The letter was not from Auntie Beryl. It was from someone called Graham Pond.

I'm sending this to the Whately address in the hope that it will get to you. If it doesn't, then at least I'll have fulfilled my duty. I'm afraid to say I've got bad news. I don't know if you'll

54

remember me, but I was there at Alan's twenty-first in Hull, that day when you had one of your turns. Your Auntie Beryl was taken ill a week ago and Maureen said we should bring her over here to rest up. So I drove to Whately and fetched her over here. She seemed to be doing quite nicely for the first three days, but then yesterday morning Maureen came downstairs and found her just lying there on the floor in front of the telly. We called for an ambulance, but unfortunately she died on the way.

I took the letter into my classroom, told the students to get on with some pair work, and read the rest of it. I couldn't for the life of me remember who Graham Pond was, or what he looked like. No doubt he was part of the family, but I couldn't remember which part. The subject of the family had never held much interest for me. I knew what would follow, though. Recriminations.

She'd been worried sick about you since your disappearance, Frank, as I'm sure you can imagine, although actually you probably can't, or you wouldn't have gone gallivanting off in the first place. She was spending whole days sat by the telephone. It wasn't a particularly responsible act on your part, after everything your Auntie Beryl did for you. And I won't even mention the thousand pounds you stole from her. She'd been on blood pressure tablets for the last three months and her insomnia had got worse, and apparently she'd taken to going round to the neighbours' houses at all hours, asking if they'd seen you anywhere. I hope you're satisfied with yourself, Frank.

Auntie Beryl was full of talk about getting the police involved, but Maureen and I were adamant that it was your responsibility to get in touch with her, not hers with you, something you seem to have neglected to do. And if you do get this, let's not have any excuses about the postal service in Spain, either. My friend Peter Pickles has been doing business with Barcelona for years and says that these days, Spain's ahead of us in many respects.

The situation is the following. We've fixed up the funeral for Saturday June 20th at 11.30 at the crematorium in Whately. We'll expect to see you there. If you need money or anything to get back, then you've got my number at work. I know you've had your fair share of troubles down the years, Maureen and I appreciate that. But we think the time has come for you to show a little respect where respect's due to the woman who treated you like her own son. She devoted the best part of her life to you. If you decide not to return, then we shall take this to mean that you've decided to make a thorough break from the family and we shan't consider it our duty to disturb you any longer. Hoping you're in reasonable health, both physically and mentally.

I folded the letter and replaced it in the envelope.

Auntie Beryl's dead, I thought. Auntie Beryl's dead. My understanding of the event refused to go any deeper than that, just three short words bouncing around inside my head, with no meaning attached to them.

'You have the face white, Frank,' a student said.

'I've had some bad news,' I said. 'An artist friend of mine from New York has died. Shot dead on the highway by a Hell's Angel in downtown Minneapolis.'

'Really?'

We devoted the rest of the class to talking about my artist friend from New York.

The names Graham and Maureen Pond meant nothing to me. However much I thought about it, I couldn't remember who they were. They were merely part of the family horde who'd paraded facelessly through my childhood and adolescence. This made their implication that I'd been instrumental in Auntie Beryl's death, and even the news of the death itself, a little unreal.

It would have been easier if I'd received the letter after the funeral had already taken place. I couldn't go back, I knew that. Not yet. If I did, I'd never get away again. It would be best to remain silent.

Anyway, I didn't feel sad about Auntie Beryl, who'd been prey to heart trouble for the past five years. I couldn't see her death as anything more than a fortuitous escape from her own unhappiness, not all of which had been caused by me, thank you very much. You only had to look at her to know that unhappiness was her natural condition.

There was death everywhere, it seemed. I felt imposed upon by death. Since I was an orphan, death had long been part of the air I breathed. In a few days, I thought, the full impact of this would hit me. Auntie Beryl has died, Auntie Beryl has died, I kept thinking. But these words concealed something either too immense or too meaningless for my comprehension, and so I never, in fact, managed to understand them.

SIX

Africa was on her threadbare old sofa, her feet curled up under her, smoking one of the three cigarettes she permitted herself daily. We'd only been together a matter of days, but already I was surrounded by the trappings of domesticity.

The television, its sound turned down, showed an excitable, smooth-faced young man opening a briefcase full of money. A couple hopped about and hugged one another, delirious with gratitude. I changed channels. A red car hurtled across the desert. *'Las apariencias no engañan'*, the slogan said. Appearances don't deceive.

In my hand I held my letter to Auntie Beryl. I'd felt the need to continue it even though she was now dead.

'Go on,' Africa urged me. 'Read it to me. You'll feel better afterwards.'

I'd held off telling her until now, aware that the full impact of what had happened might suddenly hit me when I heard myself recounting it and cause me to become upset. If I didn't want to crash into the chaotic mess of feelings I'd once been, I had to keep a safe distance from them.

'I'm not sure I want to,' I said. 'These are my deepest thoughts. Nobody knows these things about me apart from you.'

'Shut up and read.'

'"Dear Auntie Beryl,"' I read aloud. '"People like yourself are not a good advertisement for humanity. You should have made more of your life. Your death has made me understand that we only have one crack at the whip and that to repeat the same acts, day in, day out, as I'd have ended up doing if I'd stayed in

Whately, is not truly to *live*. That is why I have come away. I know that these are harsh words, words I have never felt able to express to you before, feelings which I am only able to express now that there is the necessary distance between us. Only now am I emerging from a twenty-four-year confusion."'

Africa looked up at my pause.

'It all sounds very grand,' she said. 'The parts I understand.'

'Well, it is.'

'Was this woman really as bad as that? That you had to run away from her?'

'I think so, yes.'

'Why are you reading this out to me, Frank? Why aren't you just telling me?'

'It's easier for me like this. If I read it out, it's like I'm not talking about myself. I'm talking about a different person.'

'But you are talking about yourself.'

'No. I'm talking about the old me. The one I've escaped from. Can I carry on, please?

'"Both of us are now free. Free of the terrible boredom of lives led according to other people's expectations, free of the routine of putting on a tie each morning at seven-thirty, working all day and removing the tie each night at eleven o'clock in the miserable knowledge that you'll be putting it on again in eight and a half hours, free of going to sleep and dreaming about putting on a tie at seven-thirty . . ."'

'What's all this about ties? "Tie" is *corbata*, isn't it?'

I ignored this.

'"Unhappy people prefer not to dream, Auntie Beryl."'

'What does that mean?'

'What it says.

'"I was thirteen before I realized that you were not my mother. Knowing that made my adolescence extremely difficult, not only for myself but also for those around me, as I struggled to comprehend her absence. As I explained to you a million times without being understood, such things can leave a child feeling extremely dislocated. The traumas, the depressions, the violence, the psychiatrists, the baked beans up the walls. And then I realized that, as the result of not being able to have children yourself, in your mind at least, you'd actually *become* my mother . . ."'

'What are "baked beans", Frank?'

'A small white vegetable in tomato sauce, sold in a tin,' I said.

'"I was the son you never had: you expected me to perform that false role, expected me to behave like your son to a far greater degree than my mother would ever have done. You didn't know what being a mother, and being a son, actually *meant*. Really I should have been forging my independence from you, adjusting to the lack, discovering a role I wrote for myself. I'm not saying you weren't acting from the correct motives. I'm just saying that you got it all horribly wrong. You never for a single moment in twenty-four years paused to think how *I* might feel: you were so wrapped up pretending to be my mother. But you weren't my mother. You were acting."'

'Poor woman,' Africa mused, which was hardly the point.

'How much of this are you understanding, Africa?'

'The words, or the meaning?'

'Both.'

'About sixty per cent,' Africa said after judicious consideration. 'Perhaps more of the words than the meaning.'

'That's not very much, is it? Sixty per cent?'

'Sixty per cent is a lot to understand about a person,' Africa said, 'actually. Is this what they call *psicología*?'

'Sort of.'

'You aren't going back, then?'

'That's right. Soon I'll be happy inside myself. Then I'll begin my new life.'

'You won't go to the funeral of your own stepmother?'

'You'll understand, Africa. In time.'

'I don't think I will.' Africa rearranged her bulk on the sofa and tugged distractedly at her necklace. 'That's the sort of thing I can't understand.'

The life story of Africa was a fit subject for a novel. Indeed, she'd once been interviewed by a Spanish magazine for an article called 'Widows of the Franco Years'. Africa admitted that not a syllable of what she had told *esos jodidas gilipollas* – those fucking wallies – had been the truth. Her husband, Alfredo, had been a playboy of his time, given to going on week-long benders and to knocking about with other women; he'd also had financial concerns which Africa had never been able to get to the bottom of, but which had offended the Falange.

'One night there is a knock on the door, and there are two men in black coats. I am in the back room there, putting Marta and Paco to sleep, and I come through and they are standing there with their hands in their pockets and Alfredo is looking as white as a wall. So I say *qué pasa?* and they say they come to ask my husband if he wants to go for a stroll with them. *Dar un paseo.* So I start screaming and I hit one of them on the head while the other one, he takes Alfredo's arm and he takes him to the door, and I scream at him and I tell him he mustn't go, *joder*, but he says it is better if he goes, with Marta and Paco standing at the bedroom door, and he is right, and I give him a big kiss, it is horrible to kiss someone when you know you never kiss them again, and then he is gone.'

Alfredo had not been seen again. Africa had been three days short of her twenty-second birthday.

'Is that true?' I asked her.

'Of course it's true. But there is no point in complaining.'

I felt dry and unhappy on realizing that, as far as I was concerned, this slab of tragic life was little more than a story, a word-picture of a world which I could never hope to understand. We'd only known each other a week, and yet already there were whole areas of each other's lives which were inaccessible to us.

Her story sounded remote and exotic, like the product of

imagination: Africa herself felt like nothing so much as the product of my own imagination, a private escape from the rest of my life, as secret as a debasing fantasy. Aware of my own fabrications, I had to work hard even to believe what she was telling me.

But there would always be those first evenings, when Africa had still been the Hola Woman.

'Come and see me again,' she'd said as we'd bidden one another goodnight on her doorstep, cigarette butts and the husks of sunflower seeds strewn over the yellow-lit pavement. The following night, clutching a carton of Ducados, a bottle of La Rioja and two hundred grams of sunflower seeds, I'd settled down to listen to her stories about the *años de hambre* – those not so distant days in Spanish history when peasants by the thousand had been forced into eating boiled grass and weeds and the cats and dogs they found lying in the gutter – when the gruff man with the knotted leg from the minimarket down the street had interrupted us.

That was it. Being with her was like going to the cinema. The warmth and comfort. The suspension of reality. The shock of returning to the cold light of day.

The man from the minimarket was still wearing his green-streaked apron.

'You got half an hour, Africa?'

'Half an hour? You'll be lucky.'

'I won the *lotería*.'

'*Date un paseo, hijo*,' she told me, and winked. So at least one of my questions about her had been answered. She later explained that she didn't do as much as before, but you had to keep the wolf from the door, and if there were people who needed comfort and who had a little *dinero* to spare, then she wasn't the one to deny it to them.

'Bless them all,' she said. 'I always know just when they will come. There is Arturo from the undertaker's on Mondays and Wednesdays, there is Roberto from the bar on Fridays, he always argues with his wife on payday, and I still get the odd few who are doing it for the first time, though less now. Young people these days, they do it among themselves.'

I no doubt blushed. No one knew better than I that not to have lost your virginity by the age of twenty-four stuck you firmly in the statistical minority. Not only not to have lost it, but not even to have come close.

For a long time now, I'd been happy to make love with thousands of women, real women, fabricated women, composite women, in my mind, and the sex manuals said that there was nothing wrong with that. But there was. It was not part of my new self. I hadn't come to Spain to be a wanker.

'Do you want to make the love?' Africa asked with disquieting forthrightness.

'Me?' I said, as though she'd singled me out from a large gathering. 'Who with?'

'*Tonto*, with me.'

'I'll have to think about it.'

'You think about it, then.'

'I've thought about it,' I said.

Africa's flat was two or three murky brown little rooms with a wobbly tiled floor and a stubborn odour of drains – an odour which, I knew, would linger in my memory long after the images had gone, much as the odours of my father – his breath, his skin – had lingered after his death when I was five. In the living room there was a tall, glass-fronted oak dresser, once full of silverware and porcelain which Africa explained she'd had to sell. An unframed print of Goya's *La Maja Desnuda* was tacked to the wall: Goya had painted it, Africa tantalizingly explained, for his personal pleasure. It had never been intended for exhibition.

'I look like that once, Frank,' she said. 'I look like the Duchess of Alba.' She placed her hand behind her head and leaned back, heavily writhing, and my lumbar region shivered. There was a small black and white television set, under which lay a pile of sensationalist magazines – *Hola*, *Diez Minutos*, *Lecturas*, full of half-truths about the lives of the rich and privileged.

'The skirts of the famous blow up in the breeze,' Africa explained. 'People like to see that. There's your Princess Di, look. You need a drink.'

She went into the kitchen and returned with a bottle of Larios gin. I sat down in the armchair, positioning my body so that the steel spike jutting out from it would not break my spine. When I next looked, half an hour later, I was surprised to see that half the bottle of Larios had gone.

'Listen,' I said. I'd been thinking. 'When we –'

'*Sí*?'

'Well – will I have to pay?' I shifted and winced as the spike drove into my spine.

Africa smiled broadly. Her chubby cheeks rose.

'How much money you have?'

'Not a lot.'

'Well, we'll see.'

'No. What I mean is, I *want* to pay. I'm not ready to be in love yet . . .'

'Who said anything about love? If you want to pay, pay. I no need the money. *No importa*. You pay me in *pipas*, if you want.'

I *had* to pay. To pay Africa would give me control over the situation. Payment would absolve me of responsibility towards her, allow me to keep the statutory distance. I'd be able to leave her at any time I wanted. I had it all planned out: it was no good my entering into a relationship with someone and then losing control. Anything might happen if I lost control. Things might become overcomplicated.

Africa came to sit on the arm of my chair, causing something in it to split.

'Everybody pays in the end,' she murmured, and laid her hand on the nape of my sticky neck. 'Even the Duke of Alba pays, in the end.' She wore a rich, enveloping perfume and her breath gave off sunflower seeds: her large, soft body emanated a continual flow of hotness. 'Anyway,' she said, 'you are paying for my dreams.'

'You what?'

'I tell you one day. I have my reasons. I am not only an old whore, Frank.'

Her fingers played lightly through my hair, something which hadn't happened since Bill Podmore's.

'Are we going to do it now?' I asked.

'Why not? You English men . . .'

'Right *now*, though?'

In the bedroom, after a shaky start, we made love under the compassionate gaze of the Virgin Mary, Africa having turned her photographs of the dashing, mustachioed Alfredo and their two children to the wall. I perspired heavily, frantic and agitated, feeling myself to be slippy like soap in the bath, banging my head repeatedly against the bedstead and dislodging my false tooth.

In films, these things didn't happen. It shouldn't be like this. But Africa calmed me, treating my body with an intimacy and interest it scarcely deserved, moving over it with surprising lightness and what was obviously a great deal of expertise, chiding me softly when I clutched her too tight. 'But there's a hell of a lot of you to touch,' I said.

Africa guided me into her when I lost my way, and all I could feel was her hotness, all I could smell was Y by Yves Saint-Laurent, mingled with other, more bitter, more exciting smells. Little strings of soft Spanish words came from her, but I was in no mood to translate them just then. I was behaving like an out-of-control road drill.

When it was over, I sobbed slightly as I lay there, foolish in Africa's body, giddied after my retreat into this world of unfamiliar sensations and thoughts, and I realized that I would never again be able to live without having something like this in my life.

'There is a middle-aged couple in this street,' Africa murmured, 'who make the love every Friday night at nine-thirty. Imagine that. Then afterwards, they weep together for an hour . . .' She reached across for her cigarettes, lit one and lay back. Her heart pounded against my side.

'This will kill me,' she said.

'I love you,' I said into her ear, and wondered what on earth had come over me, to be saying those words. Later on, I understood that I was saying them in order to make the moment perfect, but when I spoke, I genuinely believed I was saying them because I loved her.

Then I found my false tooth, tangled up in Africa's hair, and I grew embarrassed.

'I must make quite a difference from the man with the knotted leg,' I said.

Africa replied that I didn't love her. I'd be surprised, she said, how many people said they loved her, the man with the knotted leg not excepted. 'They love me for a second, and then they go back to their real lives.' It was just that I wanted somebody to love.

'You are so lonely,' she said, and blew on my brow to cool it, stinging my eyes with her smoke. 'You are so lonely you could find love in a stone.'

'God, Africa.' I had to stop myself from crying again. 'That's beautiful. I must write that down. "Love in a stone."'

'No, *hijo*. No. Just *feel*.'

I left 3,000 pesetas on the bedside table. There'd always be those first evenings, when Africa was still the Hola Woman.

SEVEN

'I'll tell you what Chantelle's parties are like,' Donald said. 'They're like a Henry Miller book. They're big, they're sexy, and they go on too fucking long.'

Chantelle lived in a vast, expensively furnished apartment with parqueted floors and no ducks on the wall above a boutique in the Barrio Salamanca. She shared it, on an arrangement which Chantelle revealed 'suited them both wonderfully', with an Italian businessman whom none of us had ever met. The businessman, who worked in dairy products, spent the weekends in Turin with his family, no doubt ignorant of Chantelle's troubled depths.

It was Chantelle's custom to photocopy about a hundred invitations and share them among us, to be distributed as we saw fit. This meant that Michael would slip one into the back pocket of every young 'hardbody' he saw in the street, and that they fell out of Donald's trousers in bars, later to be happened upon by total strangers.

I was never quite sure whom to give my invitations to. Drunk, I'd once presented some to three overbeautiful and underdressed teenage girls on the Metro; they had giggled but hadn't turned up, perhaps suspecting that I was playing some kind of bizarre foreign joke.

On this occasion I'd handed out none, because Chantelle had stencilled, in bold black lettering diagonally across the backs of the tickets: '*A Commemoration Party for Derek John Platt*'. When I asked, Chantelle replied that she thought it was a nice idea, and that was that.

'People are just so horrid,' she said. 'Aren't they, Frank?'

'Are you horrid, Chantelle?'

'I don't *want* to be . . .'

I arrived at the party at about midnight, having walked most of the way so as to kill time and come across vignettes for my novel. There'd been a vignette outside the VIPS restaurant on Gran Vía: five small Peruvian boys having a competition to see who could look most like Arnold Schwarzenegger, whose portrait, at a hundred times life-size, hung over the entrance to the adjacent cinema. Further down the road, an old man wearing heart-shaped sunglasses had furtively presented me with a flysheet for a strip- club, believing that I was the sort of person who would enjoy watching impoverished Latin-American women remove their clothing.

I took the shaky old lift to the sixth floor. There was evidence that someone had recently broken wind inside it. I felt weary and battered: the previous evening, Africa had fallen asleep on top of me and I'd lacked the heart and strength to remove her.

Chantelle's apartment had taken on a life of its own, become a welter of strange faces, sounds and smells. Stimulating and intimidating, it drove you into corners. The bass guitarist from Nightmares in a Damaged Brain I recognized, and a whiteface I'd seen miming to Beethoven with a dustbin lid in the Plaza Santa Ana. People spoke animatedly, experts in small talk, moving their arms about and reacting to one another as if their conversations actually meant something.

It was hard to make out anyone I knew. I slid my way circumspectly between bodies, apologizing: thank God, there was Pilar, lumbering about with a dish of peanuts. And Donald, his arm around the shoulders of a girl at least thirty years his junior, and Chantelle, as discreetly as she could manage taking candid photographs of her guests.

The television set was on. A man with curly blond hair was bobbing his head up and down between the legs of another man.

'That's an Almodóvar movie,' Michael said.

'Hello, Michael.'

68

'*Labyrinth of the Passions*. *Fabu*lous. Go on, Frank. Tell me you've met Almodóvar. Go on.'

'I've met Almodóvar,' I said.

'Oh, my *God*! I just *knew* it. Frank knows Almodóvar. Excuse me, I'm a little hyper tonight.' Off he bounded.

I went into the kitchen. I'd decided that I was going to get very drunk indeed, since on occasions like this I was even more fed up of being myself than normal. To be blind drunk was the only state of mind that was anything like the one I experienced after sex with Africa, when I said goodbye to myself for a short while. I wanted more.

Chantelle must have raided both her Italian businessman's drinks cabinet and his bank account, since the table was groaning under the weight of bottles.

'Brian. Surprised to see you here.' He was stooped, Kleenex in hand, peering into a bowl.

'Ah, Frank. I was just establishing whether this is, ah, fit. For human consumption. I've been here since seven o'clock, actually.' He prodded a lump with a fork. 'This punch certainly is an odd colour.' He swayed slightly and said, 'Oops.'

'Go on, Brian. I will if you will.'

'Oh, all right, then.' He moved his jaw about and swallowed. 'Mmm . . . I'm afraid this tastes rather as if someone had spent a penny into it. Spot of bother at the Albion, I believe. Have you heard?'

That was exactly what it tasted like. I determinedly drained one plastic beakerful and then filled another. There was a fat, purple-faced man in the corner who gave the appearance of being the sum of his bodily functions. It was probably the same one who had broken wind in the lift.

'Donald received a telephone call from the father of that child,' Brian informed me. 'The small one.'

'Carlos Santa Cruz?'

'It seems that he won't be enrolling his son for the forthcoming academic year.'

69

'That's not such a great problem.'

'But he has also threatened to call other parents and advise them to do the same thing.' Brian stooped still lower and murmured, his breath smelling strongly of pickled onions, 'Evidently this Mr Santa Cruz is a person of some influence in Madrid. Opus Dei, someone said.'

This meant that the number of enrolments was going to be small, since Donald was reliant on word of mouth and devoted a round o per cent of his budget to advertising.

'You'll be all right, won't you?' Brian said. 'If we have to shut up shop? I mean, you've got your writing, haven't you?'

'I'll go and mingle,' I said. 'Cheers, Brian.' When I was drunk, I had to be especially careful not to let the fiction slip. It was an effort I didn't feel up to making.

The living room was fuller than I'd seen it before, a dark, breathing block of sound and motion. Teeth in a head thrown back in laughter, a fist raised high. I marvelled at these people, who were mostly Spanish – at how they could be so spontaneous with one another, how they could gather one another up like that and spin around so freely. How they *enjoyed* one another, tied together simply by being human. Some of them were dancing, and over by the television a group of them were singing a trivial old Spanish pop song,'*Las Chicas Yé Yé*'.

I wondered whether any of them had ever felt the need to invent a past for themselves, and doubted it. They seemed so happy. Such gaiety, which came so naturally to them, would have seemed hysterical and forced in me. Had Africa been there, I reflected, and had she been thirty years younger, she would have been there with them, jumping up and down and singing '*Las Chicas Yé Yé*'.

Then I saw something which almost made me drop my punch.

The whole of the wall behind the sofa was covered with photocopied reproductions of the dead face of Derek John Platt.

Chantelle was next to me. She stared at me, eyes wide, and then held out to me the cigarette she was smoking.

I took it from her and inhaled deeply, enjoying the fact that Chantelle's spittle was mingling with mine. Then something unusual was happening to me, as though a pocket of air had slowly opened up inside my brain.

The same face, repeated, repeated, until it meant nothing.

'It's good gear, isn't it?' Chantelle shouted over the music. 'My God, Frank. I don't believe this. You're *smiling*.'

I didn't say anything.

'I've been a very bad girl, haven't I?'

'Certainly looks like it.' I inhaled again on the cigarette. It was pleasant, having something unusual happen in my head after all these years, a slight mental reorganization.

'I did it yesterday. I was bored out of my tiny little mind. I just had all this *time*, and I got stoned, and I started thinking about exhibitions, and I went to the school and I photocopied them and I came back and put them all up. With *glue*. It took *hours*. I can't take them all down again without ruining Pino's fucking wall . . .'

'God, Chantelle . . .' I realized that at some point I had descended to my knees.

'It's an expression of my inner life.' Her voice came from above me. 'Does it shock you, Frank?'

'Chantelle, could you just help me up?'

'Does it *shock* you, though? It's *meant* to shock. It's like that *Piss Christ* thing. It comprises a radical challenge to our middlebrow bourgeois assumptions. The whole thing just upset me so badly . . . Did Robert Mapplethorpe really say that?'

'What?'

'What you said he said. I can't remember what it was. Frank, what *are* you doing down there?'

'This stuff,' I said, holding up the cigarette she'd given me, 'is great.' Someone stumbled past, accidentally kicking me in the kidneys. Or possibly deliberately. But I didn't care. Chantelle helped me to my feet.

'Didn't it upset you, too?' she said.

'What?'

'Derek John Platt.'

'Yes. But I haven't gone and redecorated my house in the death style.'

'Just *stare* at it, Frank. You can get lost in it . . .'

While Chantelle was busy getting lost in it, Donald lurched past, struggling with his flies. 'The death style,' he said. 'I heard that. A very striking modern phrase. Catch you later, sunshine.'

I wanted to say something to him. But there was a time-lag between my head and my mouth, and nothing came out.

Chantelle was gone. I went over to the sofa and sat rubbing my knee for a while. Why had Chantelle done that? First the single photograph, and now a whole wall full of them. What was Chantelle feeling, to have done that?

From the direction of the kitchen, something fragile could be heard smashing into pieces. To come through the manic thrashings that were somebody's idea of music, whatever it was must have been thrown. A Turin businessman could be imagined turning over in his sleep.

I saw Michael leaning against the wall and made for him. He was wearing his small rectangular sunglasses. I stood behind him, waiting until he'd finished speaking.

'People always have their backs to me at parties,' I shouted as he turned round, scratching at his scalp as he always did when something had 'blown him away'.

'I put these on,' he earnestly informed me, 'because I have been dazzled by beauty. That *guy*! Isn't he just something else? One hundred per cent pure Eurotrash.'

'Which guy?'

'My God, Frank! Are you blind? You'd know if you were on the sunny side. He brushed my tush, Frank. I swear. Have you seen the way his cuffs break over his shoes? His name's Marc. With a "c".'

Most of this was incomprehensible to me. I asked how Marc's cuffs could break over his shoes.

'Oh, you Brits are so *sweet*. So insecure, so *celibate*. Is there a tush in your shorts, Frank? Is there?'

I nodded. 'Come on, Michael,' he reprimanded himself. 'Don't be overenthusiastic. You'll only get wounded in the heart by Cupid's tender savage dart.' He sighed and clasped my hand, making me feel chilly in my spine. 'You know my problem, Frank? My problem is that I want it all *now*.'

'Hello there,' Pilar called. 'Would anybody like a stuffed olive?'

'Michael's in love again,' Michael said. 'Why oh *why* is Madrid so full of tight-assed men with wonderful personalities? See you guys later. It's been real.'

It was always the same. Despite the anticipation, the sense that tonight might be the night, I could never enjoy Chantelle's parties. I only wanted to be at them.

The problem was that I wasn't sure what tonight might be the night *for*. A blistering bout of rough and ready sex, a pair of Iberian teenage buttocks clanking against the toilet-roll holder? A deep conversation with someone on my own wave-length? A good bop? Sex, conversation and dancing were all beyond me, all ways in which you could get hurt. The thought of my having sex, or getting to know someone better than I knew her, would have terrified Auntie Beryl, driven her to her oft-cited early grave. She was always there at my shoulder, hovering. I hated myself for not feeling able to dismiss her from my mental life.

I whiled away the next hour observing, getting more and more drunk.

'Observing's my speciality,' I told a girl. 'I live my life at one remove. You don't get hurt that way. I'm English, you see. At school, whenever I was reading a book and came to a funny part, I didn't laugh. I wrote "humour" in the margin.'

All around me, people were looking at me, wondering what I was *doing* there. 'What are *you* doing here?' Mrs Stanton, my teacher, had said when I'd first run away from home, arriving at her house at 2.30 in the morning, thirteen and drenched. 'I love you,' I'd said and, like Africa, Mrs Stanton had told me not to be silly, that I didn't in fact love her. That was what it all amounted to, in life: people not believing you when you said you loved them. I avoided thinking about the miserable implications of this by counting the reproductions of Derek John Platt's face. A song came on which seemed to be called 'Holiday'.

'Listen,' the girl said. 'Do you want to dance?'

'No, thanks.'

'You think too much, *chaval*. Thinking kills.'

I wandered around hunting for another one of Chantelle's cigarettes. Someone handed me something which resembled it, but when I sucked the effect was like sulphuric acid at the back of my throat. I'd have gone back to Africa's, but to have found her with anyone else just then would have crippled me. So I stood for a while listening to Donald as he informed a different young Spanish girl from the first one that he'd had a monkey-gland operation in a Swiss hospital and that he was now, at this precise instant in fact, reaching his sexual peak.

'That's a lie,' I told the girl while Donald was fetching a drink. 'He hasn't had a monkey-gland operation. I work with him. He couldn't possibly have gone to Switzerland and back without my noticing. Unless he went on a Saturday, of course, and came back on a Sunday. I used to work in New York with Robert Mapplethorpe. The internationally renowned photographer.'

The girl looked at me. I smiled at her; she turned away and shouted someone's name across the room.

I drifted out through the french windows and on to the balcony, where I rested my arms on the cast-iron balustrade. They were disgusting forearms, mine: a butcher would have had trouble getting rid of them.

Things were quieter out here. From behind, music and laughter; from below, the low crackle of a city burning its immense energy. A city I was afraid to get to know.

Auntie Beryl's funeral would be tomorrow. In several hours,

74

in fact. For some reason, even though she was dead, the bloody woman was occupying more space in my mind than ever before. While others were mourning her passing, I'd be three thousand miles away, nursing a titanic hangover.

Then I was sick.

'Don't think about it,' a voice said, meaning suicide. 'Don't even think about it, because thinking can make it happen. And don't turn round,' and I turned round, but there was no one.

Then Brian was there. It was all right, he said. He understood. He proffered a Kleenex.

'What do you understand?'

'How you might overindulge youself on an occasion such as this.'

'Listen, Brian. I'm in control.' I mopped my lips. 'This is nothing. It's just my hair-raising lifestyle catching up with me.'

His hair was all over the place. There was a crow on the end of his nose: I wondered whether I should tell him about it. He took the Kleenex from me and blew his nose on it. I'd never thought of Brian as a disgusting, crumbly old man before.

'That night I saw you on the beach,' I said. 'I sort of thought you were getting used to it. You know . . . your wife's death.' I'd forgotten her bloody name again.

'In a way. I suppose you could be right . . . these things always do have an impact on you, don't they? They're very hard to face up to.'

'I noticed that you were very quiet when we were making the confession.'

'The confession?'

'The statement.' I hadn't said confession. Brian's hearing was going.

'It's rather a strange time, don't you think?' Brian said. 'Something's not quite right, is it? I just can't put . . . oh, gosh, my idioms. Too long in Spain.'

'My finger on it.'

'Exactly.' Brian leaned down close to me. His breath no longer smelt of pickled onions: it now smelt indescribable. 'Have you seen what Chantelle has done? Does that not strike you as a little peculiar?'

Putting one hundred and twenty-nine pictures of a dead man's face on a wall was similar to something I'd read about called immersion therapy. Perhaps Chantelle wanted to overcome her fear of her own mortality by immersing herself in it. I tried to explain this to Brian, but it came out garbled.

'There used to be something different about the youngsters who worked here,' Brian said. 'It's hard to explain. It's rather as if they used to believe in things outside themselves. I was never a great one for social causes myself, but to see them getting all worked up about CND, that sort of thing, it was quite inspiring. They were more . . . *committed*. Now, they don't seem to believe in anything except themselves, and even then not very much. No. Something is definitely not quite right . . . they think too much about how they look, the impression they give . . . I don't know . . .'

Suddenly his arm was on mine, his manner urgent.

'Have you ever read the Bible, Frank? It's very good. The greatest story ever told.'

'I tried,' I said, which wasn't true. 'My Bible's Camus's *The Outsider*, actually.'

'Oh, it's well worth persevering with. I sometimes feel that we're losing touch with the inner man, Frank. All this technology. Computers. The telephone. Do you know what I mean?'

'That's just why I'm here,' I explained, secure in the knowledge that Brian wouldn't understand. 'To lose touch with the inner man. To have a break from myself, as it were.'

'Very good. How *is* the novel going?'

'Fine.'

'Oh dear, here's Donald come to corner us.'

'What are you two depressives doing out here? Let me guess. Talking about our friend Mr Derek John Platt.'

76

'In a manner of speaking,' Brian said. 'We were just saying that it's a strange time.'

'It's always a stange time, sunshine. Death is attracted by inertia. Death *is* inertia. Have you ever noticed' – Donald hiccuped – 'have you ever noticed, that when you try to turn a light *on*, it often has to struggle? But when you turn it *off*, it always goes out immediately. It goes out like a light. That's death. We all long for it, secretly. Light itself longs for it. Bloody hell, my body may be buggered but my mind shines on.'

'And, Donald?' I said. 'Inertia?'

'And since I've never seen such an inert bunch as you lot, I'm not surprised death put on a little show for us the other week.'

'Might we talk about something else, Donald?'

'We might, Brian.' He was in unusually ferocious form tonight. 'As long as we're not going to talk about that little runt Carlos. I'll break his wee Castilian neck if I see him again.'

'Oh, Donald. The boy was only doing his duty.'

'Listen. Ever since I started that school, the idea was that everybody could come along, have a nice time and get bugger all money for doing bugger all work. A retreat for some, a limbo for others. A place where you didn't feel the future breathing down your neck.' Donald put a hand on the balustrade and looked out over Madrid. 'And now, if we're not very careful, we'll all have to go out and get proper jobs.'

'Is it that serious?' I asked.

Donald turned to look at Brian and me. Then he put his arm round my shoulder and squeezed.

'I'm afraid it is, sunshine. The real world might just have caught up with us at long last. Ach,' he said, 'don't worry. It's Uncle Donald's bread and butter too, remember. Talking of which . . .' He raised his empty glass and disappeared.

'The harvest is past, the summer is over, and we are not saved,' said Brian. 'That's the Bible, Frank. The greatest story ever – '

I escorted him to the front door.

Perhaps one day in the future I'd be ready to try my hand at a 'proper job' again. But not now, not in Spain. I wasn't here for that. Nothing, I knew, would give the ghost of Auntie Beryl greater pleasure than to see me become branch manager of a Spanish supermarket, to see me reduced to the sum of my material worth. After I'd left school, she'd set me up with a job stacking supermarket shelves. The interview had been with a man called Sidney Grimes. On the bus home afterwards, she'd uttered the immortal words, 'That'll be you, one day, poppet, if you play your cards right.' The next time I'd seen Sidney Grimes had been a month later, when he'd sacked me for reading books on the company's time. He'd become infuriated with me when I'd suggested that he use an anti-dandruff shampoo, asking me what that had to do with anything.

The number of people in the living room had decreased. Most of the healthy-minded young Spaniards I'd envied earlier were long gone to other places, to have healthy conversations, healthy sex, healthy dreams.

I went into the kitchen. The hot-water tap was running flat out. I tried to turn it off, but the faucet span uselessly in my hand. I looked for the wall clock, but there it was, in pieces, the second hand floating on the remains of the punch. 'Something's not quite right, is it?' Brian had said. The bass guitarist from Nightmares in a Damaged Brain squatted by the refrigerator, making a hole in himself with a needle; a girl swayed above him, pretty but clearly unwell, singing the tune of 'Smoke Gets in your Eyes' with the words 'Things Can Just Explode'. There were three bodies on the floor, the head of one of them positioned in what looked like a thick pool of Russian salad. There were three more bodies in the living room, and I raised the hand of one of them to see the time. 4.17.

In one of the bedrooms, evidently designed with the Italian businessman's children in mind, there was a poster of a black basketball player exhorting us to 'Be Like Mike'. In order to be like Mike, I'd have to grow eighteen inches, change colour, and be a multi-millionaire, so somebody somewhere must have had a sense of humour.

Pilar was sitting on the lower bunk with her arms around Michael's shoulders. Michael was naked to the waist, with a paunch you wouldn't have suspected. He looked extremely young at that moment, with his hairless, slippery skin. His doleful eyes peered up at me, two small wet eggs stuck in a big wet egg.

'Michael's sad,' Pilar said.

'The bastard.' Michael sniffed and blinked. 'How can a person *do* that to another person?'

'A fucking man has stolen his wallet.'

'And my haematite and diamond cufflinks. From Asprey's Fifth Avenue. My mother bought them . . . they cost a fortune . . .'

'Not that guy with the turn-ups?' I said.

'Oh, no . . . God, if *only* . . .'

'Why do you believe these people?' Pilar said. 'Why do you *trust* them?'

'Oh, sure. I know love's just a word. But I don't think it's asking *too* much just to attach a *teeny* bit of meaning to it? What do you say, Frank?'

I was hardly an expert on the subject of love and its million meanings. I did feel something for Africa, something I was sure I'd never feel again, but of course I'd had assurance that it wasn't love. I looked at Michael and wondered whether what Chantelle had told me was true after all, that he'd slept with Derek John Platt on the toss of a coin. I could never have brought myself to ask him directly.

'All I want,' Michael said, 'is someone to love, who loves me too. Everybody has it. Storekeepers have it. Kafka had it. So tell me this. Why doesn't Michael have it? I mean, life is so super*ficial* here . . . hey, do you want to hear the latest instalment of my *Book of Influences*? It's influenced by Frank Capra.'

Things were returning to normal in Michael's head: he used his paragraphs as other people used jokes, to gather us together at moments of awkwardness.

'Frank Capra? Him that did *It's a Wonderful Life*?'

'Franz Kafka. Did I say Frank Capra? It's like, Donald said that when we found Derek John Platt it was Kafkaesque, and I thought Michael, you're so dumb, here you are in a Kafkaesque situation and you've never even written anything like Franz Kafka! Ready?'

Pilar winked and smiled. But:

' "One morning, Michael Mann woke up and found that he was dead. He had never been dead before. He felt very tired, like something had sucked all the blood out from two small holes in his neck. It was a real good feeling, to know that action was impossible, that he'd never have to trust anybody any more, never have to be deceived by anybody, never have to sit waiting for a telephone call that wouldn't come, never have to worry about the opinions of his parents, or love, or happiness, or any of that shit, never have to be abandoned and feel guilt. He was free of the world. He got out of bed and pulled on his Calvin Kleins from Moholy Nagy." '

'It's good,' I said.

'It's not true, is it?' Pilar asked.

'Hey. This is pure imagination, OK? It was inspired by finding Derek John Platt. Totally invented. I just thought of it now, before you guys came in and plucked me from the edge of the abyss.'

'Any title ideas?' I liked Michael's titles. They were elegant and stylish, with an agreeable sound when you spoke them.

'I thought maybe *Death Wore Blue Jeans*. I think that says it all. What do you say, Frank? Your opinion matters to me.'

' "He was free of the world." I liked that.'

'Listen. I have to use the john, as we rednecks say. Excuse me.'

While Michael loudly hammered on the bathroom door and told Chantelle to get her sweet little ass out of there, Pilar and I stared at one another.

'He's only acting,' I said. 'He wants to give himself a tragic dimension. Did he say anything to you about sleeping with Derek John Platt?'

'What?'

'About sleeping with Derek John Platt? The night before we found him?'

I watched as Pilar struggled to comprehend this and failed. Her face broke into a smile.

'You creative types,' she said. 'I suppose you must get confused sometimes. Between fantasy and reality. Sometimes I wish *I* could do the same. Aren't I terrible?'

It was 5.14. On the floor lay several mangled, prostrate bodies, one of which was Donald's. A black mongrel which had found its way in off the street and up six floors now helped itself to salami and cheese from the Italian businessman's fridge.

Whether in the street or in a conversation, at a bar or at a party, I was generally the last to go, fighting sleep, waiting for something to happen, which never did.

My legs were apparently stapled to the floor, my brain suspended six inches above my cranium. I'd just spent twenty minutes being tutored by a Senegalese man wearing a tuxedo in the art of rolling joints, and was just about to light my fifth in a row.

Through the haze I could make out two people I'd never seen before. One, a gaunt-featured girl, wearing what seemed to be a slightly dislodged blond wig, sat cross-legged on the floor at the feet of her companion. Every so often her head lolled forwards and it took her whole body to jerk it back.

The companion, on the other hand, was wide awake and beautiful.

His beauty drew my swimmy gaze and held it. He seemed to be in his late twenties or early thirties: his hair slicked back and glistening, tied in a pony tail, a coating of stubble on his chin, he sat with one leg over the arm of the Italian businessman's black director's chair, smoking a thin cigarette and saying nothing. His turn-ups broke perfectly over his brogues.

I searched his face for imperfections and became confused when I found none. He appeared to be a carefully composed photograph hanging there on Chantelle's morbid wall, an island of glamour.

He shifted his gaze on to me, smiled and winked, as though we shared some kind of secret. A strange moment: I imagined that it was a televized wink, being broadcast into millions of homes, and that I was sitting alone in a darkened room, in a silent city, watching it. In about five minutes, I knew, I was going to be sick again.

Nobody was saying anything. Like me, they were staring at the stranger.

'That coke.' Chantelle ran her hand roughly back through her hair. 'Who brought all that nasty cocaine into my house? Was it you, Marc? Of course it was.'

Donald groaned in his sleep. 'It's not *having* it,' he said. 'It's what you *make* of it. Life's a block of wood.'

The others quietly began to rave, a multiple personality wandering in search of laughter. I kept my eyes on the stranger, allowed their words to fill my head like weird, distant music, wondered what the secret was he thought I shared with him. It was hard to find a thread through the words. Sharpened screwdrivers were mentioned, and unhappiness, and orgasms, and love, and a recipe for *gazpacho*.

Then suddenly it was everyone's turn to tell a joke. Michael started.

'What did one deaf Zen Buddhist monk say to the other deaf Zen Buddhist monk?'

'Tell us. Do.'

'What's the sound of two hands clapping?'

Nobody laughed. It seemed to be my turn. I was a great one for not understanding jokes, and telling them was harrowing. But my mind was not in its usual place.

'What's the difference between Frank Bowden and Frank Bowden?'

'What?'

I raised my voice. Were they all stupid?

'What's the difference, right, between Frank Bowden and Frank Bowden?'

'Calm down, Frank. Tell us.'

'I don't know,' I said. Then I was leaning forward in agony as a small quantity of vomit dropped from my mouth. When I looked up, everyone was laughing, which made me feel happy. I swilled out my mouth with the contents of a glass lying nearby and retired into the shadows.

'Hey, you guys!' Michael turned his attention to the stranger. 'Michael,' he said. 'We met earlier. Twenty-five. Capricorn. Ambitions: fame and fortune.'

'Marc,' said the man. 'With a "c". Good to know you all.'

'So how did you hear about the party?'

'He saw us in L'Estartit,' Chantelle said. 'And then he just introduced himself to me this evening. Isn't that right?'

'Yes. That's exactly right.'

There was more silence, although this time it was busy. 'Marc,' I murmured to myself. 'With a "c".'

'What's *your* name?' Marc said to Michael.

'Oh, wow. Michael.'

'No, it isn't. What's *your* name?' he asked me.

'This is Frank,' Chantelle said. 'He has a mysterious past, but part of it was being an artist in New York. As a matter of fact, Frank's writing a novel.'

'No,' I said. 'My name isn't Frank, actually.'

'Frank's sure in a weird mood tonight,' Michael said. 'A lost sock in the laundromat of life.'

'My name's Derek John Platt,' I said.

'Hey,' Chantelle said. 'This is your party, then. That's you on the wall.'

To say "my name's", followed by someone else's name, felt pleasant, a little dangerous. I should have thought of it before. Why did I have to be called 'Frank', anyway?

'It's good to know you, Derek John Platt. Have you played the identity game before?'

'The identity game!' Chantelle squealed with delight.

The black mongrel looked up at her, puzzled, and then went on eating.

'You'll feel better after you've played,' Marc said. 'Everyone should try to escape from themselves once in a while. If only for a few minutes. It's a mood thing. Everybody think of a person . . . now, just think, how it would be . . . actually to *be* that person . . .'

For a while, the atmosphere became pleasantly dreamy. I pictured myself sitting in a bar in L'Estartit, drunk and depressed, not knowing why I was there. I pictured myself, thin and smelling bad, being dragged down to the beach by Michael and Chantelle, and waking and telling them the story of my life, and about my greyhound, and wondering who these two people were, this young Australian and this young American with no hair . . . 'You might think,' I imagined myself saying, 'that Stanley's an odd name for a greyhound . . .' The sharpness of Chantelle's voice snapped me out of this reverie.

'What's your name, Pilar?'

'Pilar,' Pilar said, speaking more loudly than normal. 'I'm not sure I like this.'

'You can't be Pilar.'

'My name is Pilar. Identity game or no identity fucking game.' There was a tremor in her voice. She pulled her handbag up on to her knees. 'Donald,' she said, prodding him with her toe. 'Wake up.'

There was a lengthy groan from the underworld.

'What's your name, Donald?' Michael asked.

'How the fuck should I know? Leave me alone.'

'Who are you then, Michael?' Pilar asked.

'Marc,' Michael said.

'No,' said Marc. 'You can't be Marc. I'm Marc.'

The tension which this activity had caused to ripple among us had made us alert in our end of evening sleepiness. It had been a while since the dynamics of the group had been unpredictable.

'You can get your greedy eyes off him, Michael,' Chantelle said. 'Marc's mine.' She crawled across the parquet and put her arms around the stranger's calves, rested her head against them

85

and closed her eyes. The girl with the blond wig was sleeping now.

'Ugh,' Donald said. 'Some cunt's thrown up on my head.'

'So, Marc,' Michael persisted. 'What do you do?'

'I travel. You know. From one place to another.' Marc didn't say anything else. He was staring at the pictures on the wall, perhaps even counting them as I had.

'Just like a serial killer,' Chantelle said sleepily.

'I wouldn't say I was from any particular place. I'm from nowhere.'

'You must be from somewhere,' Pilar said.

'I suppose I must, yes. The thing is . . .' Marc inhaled on his cigarette and waited until the smoke had vanished. 'I haven't decided *where* yet.' He smiled and shrugged his shoulders.

'He sells drugs,' Chantelle said. 'He's a drug trafficker.'

'No he doesn't,' Pilar said quickly, lacking the imagination to recognize this. 'Don't say that.'

'Well, there are worse ways to make a living, I guess . . .' Michael seemed impressed.

'These are troubled times,' Marc said. 'You have to do what you can.' His accent was impossible to localize, but I knew now that his had been the voice on the balcony, the voice which had told me not to do it.

It was like having someone famous in the room. Someone you've been longing to meet. J. F. Kennedy. Marilyn Monroe. Lee Harvey Oswald.

I took 'Bat out of Hell' from my pocket and crawled across to the stereo, accidentally kicking Donald as I did so. He didn't seem to mind.

'Marc makes movies, too,' Chantelle murmured, her eyes still closed. 'He does all these *cool* things. Sells drugs. Makes movies. Makes love.' She hiccuped and giggled.

'What sort of movies?' Pilar asked.

'Oh, all these questions. Is there nothing else to talk about? All this polite chat. Art movies. Dealing with subjects which interest me.'

86

'Have you had anything released?' Michael asked, clearly desperate for the answer 'yes'.

'Of course.' Marc smiled patiently. 'I used to work with Robert Mapplethorpe in New York. I was part of that group. I was with him towards the end. Chantelle tells me you knew Robert, too, Frank.'

'You're *kidding*,' Michael said. 'Do you two guys know each other?'

Suddenly I felt ill and unable to speak. I'd never vomited three times in one evening before, but there was a first time for everything.

'When did you work with Robert?'

I didn't answer. I think Chantelle answered for me.

When I looked up, Marc was gazing at me like a television hypnotist. I attempted a smile which was no doubt revolting to behold.

'I was nothing but a lonely boy, looking for something new,' sang Meat Loaf.

'I like Meat Loaf,' I said weakly.

'So do I,' Marc said. 'Possibly the kitschest music ever recorded by man. Frighteningly . . . *vacant*.'

'Yes,' I said, although the fact was that 'Two out of Three Ain't Bad' was still, after all this time, capable of moving me to tears.

'I feel active,' Marc said. 'I want movement.'

'Still?' wondered Chantelle. We laughed; I laughed hysterically. The pressure was off.

'There's something burning inside me. Do you never have that?' Marc asked no one in particular. 'Those pictures. They're terribly unaesthetic. They're disturbing.'

'I don't know why I put them up. Pino'll kill me this time.'

'We should take them down.' Marc stood, sort of uncurling himself to his full height. He crouched in a corner and tore off one of the photocopies. Dumbly we watched. 'Something burning inside me.' That was it exactly.

Some material came off the wall. Paint. A small puff of plaster.

'Marc . . . do be careful . . .'

'Come on. I can't do them all alone.'

We looked at Chantelle. After staring into space for a second, she made her decision and suddenly stood, uprighted a chair, climbed on to it and began to tear down the pictures from the opposite corner to Marc's.

'All revved up with nowhere to go!' she sang. 'Come on!'

Within thirty seconds, they were all tearing at the wall, scratching at it with their fingers urgently and uselessly, as though the key to their happiness lay concealed behind the pictures of the dead man.

Derek John Platt's multiplied face lay torn into pieces on the parquet. Bits of him hung limp from the wall. His nose. His dead eyes.

'It's making my spine shiver!' Michael shouted. 'Someone please turn up the music.'

'This music's crap,' Chantelle shouted. She jumped down from her chair, went to the music centre, removed a compact disc and snapped it in half. She didn't seem surprised that the music continued as loudly as ever. The black mongrel was standing in the doorway, its tail between its legs, whimpering.

'This is building up into something,' Marc whispered into my ear. 'Don't you get involved. You're above all this, Frank . . .'

'Wow! You should try smashing a CD in half!'

'Chantelle,' Pilar warned. 'Be careful . . .'

'Oh, fuck off. You are *so* dull.'

'This music has no heart,' Marc said. 'No soul.' He removed his pale jacket, laying it carefully over one end of the sofa. Across the back of his T-shirt, in bold black lettering, was the legend: 'S T R A N G E R'. He pulled three compact discs from their boxes and snapped them, flipping them out through the balcony windows. They spun silver through the night, shearing off the heads of passing birds.

'This is *wild*,' Michael shouted, and adopted a kung-fu position. He poked with his foot at a dresser in the corner, testing the temperature of invisible water. The dresser rocked. Several items of porcelain toppled and fell. He poked again, fascinated, and more ornaments came down.

'Be careful about your heads!' Marc called. He had torn a speaker from its mounting on the wall and was carrying it aloft out to the balcony. Michael had the other speaker. He tossed it at the wall, where many of Chantelle's photographs, torn and frayed, still remained. On impact the front of it sprang away, almost decapitating the Senegalese man, who was slumped against the television. He rose and staggered out.

I crawled over to the music centre. I found a pair of headphones in a drawer and plugged them in. I put them on to watch.

'I cannot lie, I cannot tell you that I'm something I'm not . . .'

Michael punched the dresser. His body jerked in pain. He reached behind it and Marc, grinning broadly, reached around the other side. The dresser toppled and fell. There was a flash of light as one of its corners went through the television screen, millions of little sparks in my eyes. Chantelle was stamping up and down on a picture she'd taken from the wall, dancing a private dance, arms flailing. A bland seascape, it had been, part of a limited edition.

Donald stirred. He stumbled towards me, tore the headphones off.

'Arma bloody geddon,' he shouted. 'Get out of here . . .' He tripped and fell.

Nothing was clear any more. All about me people were breaking free of themselves, casting off the burden of their personalities, temporarily losing themselves in frenzy. Yet I felt incapable of joining them, scared to experiment with a new version of myself when it was easiest, when it most mattered, now. I was trembling with self-directed anger, locked inside a reinforced cage of self- consciousness, fit only to watch.

I was afraid the floor might give way. People tumbling to their deaths, dropping through one floor after another, crashing through homes. Pilar had found something small and was urgently scratching into the table top with it: even Pilar. Her lips formed words. Chantelle tore open the bookcases and started pulling out books one by one, throwing them to the floor where Michael sat, splay-legged and gaga, ripping out the pages.

Slow motion. Desperately sad music filled my head, filled up my eyes.

Then the light-bulb blew and the music cut out and we were in the darkness. I'd hardly moved. I was gasping for breath.

I hoped no one had noticed me not doing anything. There was a sweet taste in my mouth. I'd bitten my lip so hard as to draw blood.

'I've cut my hand,' Chantelle said. 'Oh, Jesus. I need alcohol.'

'I've cut my life,' Donald said, crouching, framed by the balcony windows. 'I need alcohol.'

No one laughed.

A match was struck. It flared, glowed. Mysteriously, Marc was back in the director's chair again, his leg over the arm, a cigarette dangling from his lips, his jacket across his lap. Steadily, he brought the match to beneath his chin and looked about him.

'Something has happened here,' he said, 'and we must ask ourselves what it is.'

'Marc,' Chantelle moaned from the floor. 'No matches. Please, Marc.'

'Don't worry. Thank you for one of the best films I've ever seen.'

'Wow,' Chantelle said.

'Listen to me. I was in L'Estartit at the same time as you all were. So it's only correct that you all know that I know who killed Derek John Platt.'

'What?' Michael said. 'You killed Derek John Platt?'

'No. No. I *know* who killed him.'

'Hey,' said Pilar. 'I don't like this. Who *are* you, anyway?'

'None of us like this.' Marc opened wide his eyes a moment

90

before bringing the match to the tip of his cigarette. 'And your second question, Pilar. Who do you *think* I am?' He softly blew, and we were back in darkness again.

It was quite beautiful.

'Let's get out of here,' someone said.

II

I awoke the next day at 3 o'clock in the afternoon: I'd slept through the funeral. I looked into the mirror and laughed at what I saw, although laughter hurt.

It was hilarious. One lens of my spectacles was cracked. There was blood on my left temple as well as my chin, although when I looked for a cut I couldn't find one. My head felt as though someone had tried to stick a knitting needle through it, my shoes and trousers were spattered with vomit. I had no recollection of how I'd managed to get back to the *hostal*.

But I felt exhilarated. This was the first time I could recall that something had happened to me which I hadn't been aware of at the time. The first time I'd freed myself from myself. Probably the others had pushed me into a taxi, and probably I'd banged my head and broken my glasses that way. Probably it was simply broken glass at Chantelle's party which had cut me.

But perhaps I'd spent the intervening hours flying, looking down on the lights of Madrid, the slow traffic of the Gran Vía, the vast, black expanses of the Casa de Campo. Not to know: to have lived, if only for half an hour, and to have no memory of it. That was exhilarating, liberating. It almost compensated for my self-disgust at not having abandoned myself at the party as the others had.

There was a curt note attached to the door from Sr López, the landlord, about the unpaid rent. The problem was that I had a choice between roof and food: if I continued to pay rent, I'd probably starve to death. And money was shortly going to be an even bigger problem, since I wouldn't be receiving the pittance Donald had paid.

The £1,129 I'd taken from Auntie Beryl's top drawer was disappearing more quickly than I'd thought it would, mostly into Africa's purse. My plight was hardly surprising, given that I'd never had the opportunity to organize my finances before.

I took the note from Sr López and put it under the bed with the others.

Over the course of the afternoon I lay in bed and mulled over two things in particular which Marc had said at Chantelle's party. The first was that he'd worked with Robert Mapplethorpe. His reality was my invention: there was something *right* about that, something almost frighteningly right. I thought about chance, which had never played an important role in my life. For chance to affect you, you have to come into contact with people, and I'd never had much of that.

The second thing was more troubling, and started to revive in me my obsession with the death of Derek John Platt, which had faded somewhat after I'd met Africa. 'I know who killed Derek John Platt', I thought I'd heard Marc say: but with all that punch and all those joints, I couldn't be sure, no more sure than that I'd heard a voice on the balcony, telling me not to jump. The Derek John Platt sentence had been a remarkable thing to say, and it had been uttered in such a brassy way, too, not in the fearful undertone you'd expect.

I found the figure of Marc strange and compelling. He'd winked at me: he'd told me I was 'above all this'. It was as though several strands of my life – my desire to escape from England, my invented past and my wish somehow to make it real by writing a novel, and the beach killing itself – had suddenly been woven together by this clean-cut, charismatic figure with the bright eyes and the bizarre T-shirt, who had galvanized the others into delirium, into a liberating destructiveness.

Had he really said he was from nowhere? That he 'hadn't decided' where he'd been born? What was he doing in my life? Who *was* he? I felt about these questions much the same as I often felt when I was watching a film: I asked them, I wanted to know the answers to them – but I didn't want to know *yet*, not until I'd seen what happened. It was perfect. It was thrilling. It fitted in with my philosophy, until then unformulated, in coming to Spain. Instead of being subject to the nightmare of repetition, of knowing all the answers in advance, there would now be an area of my life in which I could live to *see what happened*. That felt like an ambition achieved.

After I'd showered, I waited until I could hear Sr López snoring in front of the television and then stole out of the *hostal*. I went down to Lavapiés and stood outside the entrance to the Metro. After about forty seconds I was approached by a swaggering, skinny Moroccan with a small plastic apparatus attached to his throat.

Having awkwardly purchased a small quantity of marijuana from him, I walked to the Retiro Park to my favourite spot, by the boating lake at the edge of the shadow of the statue of Alfonso XII. I sat with pen and exercise book in hand, aware of the warmth of the concrete on my buttocks and the sound of a guitar from a group of Scandinavian youths behind me. I didn't write a word. But I smoked four joints in succession. One of the Scandinavians came and tried to chat, but I didn't react. I wasn't able to.

Auntie Beryl's funeral came into my mind. How many people had attended, how many tears had been shed? But these were a different sort of question. To this sort of question, I didn't care if I knew the answer or not. 'I'll tell you what happiness is,' she'd said once, when I'd enquired. 'Happiness is wanting to be *where* you are, *when* you are.' In that case, this was happiness I was feeling now. *'Rest in Peace,'* I wrote in the exercise book. *'Goodbye, you screwed old witch.'*

I refused to acknowledge to myself that I had, extremely quickly, actually come to need Africa. The thought was terrible to me. After all, I wasn't in Spain so that I'd have to need anybody at all, thank you very much.

97

But when I imagined life without her, without her half-deafness, her dyed eyebrows, her sunflower seeds, her weight and warmth, her failure ever to understand anything I said to her, I felt miserable. She was a counterbalance to me, keeping me more or less level inside, preventing me from either floating free or hitting the ground with a nasty bump. I was still together enough to recognize I needed something like that.

Despite my payments to her, which were causing Sr López to grow irritable, despite my attempts to maintain the statutory distance from her, I'd fallen into a very old trap.

After all, it had to be love if she was the only person in the Iberian Peninsula to have heard *Frank Bowden: the True Story*. I continued to read aloud to her my letter to Auntie Beryl as I added to it. It was now a hundred and sixty-three pages long. But although it had to be love, I was in no hurry to use that word again, to her or to anyone else. It was as though my whole life prior to having come here was a great secret, and I sometimes wondered whether it wasn't the language barrier between myself and Africa – a barrier made sometimes of tantalizing silk, but more often of frustrating steel – which had made me able to reveal it at all. After all, it was as she herself said: it was the sort of thing she *couldn't* understand.

I'd asked Africa for a photograph. She'd proudly handed me one taken thirty-five years before, of her sitting on a beach outside Cádiz, knees tight together, a parasol balanced on an altogether slimmer left shoulder.

'You wouldn't have given me the time of day thirty-five years ago, would you?' I said.

'It would have been difficult, *hijo*. You weren't even born.'

A large part of our time together was spent exchanging our histories. Being with Africa was like reading a great novel which, when you lay it down before sleep, gathers you into its papery arms and hugs you, making it a relationship with the potential for satisfying the intellect, the imagination and the body in a way I could imagine no other relationship doing.

Africa's history was like a fairy tale.

With great communicative effort, her hands and face working overtime while her tongue underachieved, she told me stories about peasant families from the provinces, from Galicia and Extremadura, migrating to Madrid and Barcelona to live in *chabolas*, jerry-built huts on the city outskirts where the *gitanos* – the gypsies – now lived. These peasants had lived in constant fear of a visit from Franco's *piquetes*, demolition men empowered to destroy your home and therefore your will to live. Stories about Spaniards, many years later, crossing the border by the thousand into Perpignan in France so they could see *Emmanuelle* on its first release, about being slapped in class for having Basque surnames, about being arrested for kissing in the street, about, until quite recently, being unable to buy the pill anywhere except under the counter at the Rastro street market. They were stories of passionate, mindless resistance to oppression, heroic tales of blood angered and spilt in indignation.

'That's how I feel,' I said. 'I'm on a heroic quest against repression. That's why I'm here.'

'Don't talk rubbish,' Africa said. 'You shouldn't joke about things like that. It's silly to compare your *historia* with the *historia* of a whole nation . . .'

Everyone has a little someone else inside them. This is the cause of what understanding there is between people. But this, in its literal-mindedness, was the first time I'd detected some Auntie Beryl in Africa. It came as quite a shock.

Occasionally we'd visit the Filmoteca Nacional in Anton Martin or, if we were feeling especially daring, take the tube to Plaza de España, to the Alphaville and Renoir cinemas. It was pleasant to sit in the muggy darkness, holding hands and munching *palomitas*, soaking up masterpieces and rubbish in a wide variety of languages. It reminded me a little of my Saturdays back in Whately when, having failed to understand the appeal of football, I'd take the train into Manchester and wander from cinema to cinema under my umbrella, sometimes seeing as many as four films in a single day, slurping Kia-Ora; sometimes, if the weather was bad, seeing the same film four times. The difference between then and now was that I was not alone.

One Sunday afternoon, arriving a little late with Africa at a showing of the film based on Truman Capote's *In Cold Blood*, I was startled to see on the screen a man with a guitar at the back of a Greyhound bus, blowing out a match to leave everything in darkness, just as Marc had done at Chantelle's party.

Then, an hour later, during one of the tedious sections when Perry – the man with the match, the killer – flashes back to his childhood, I was even more startled to see the silhouetted heads of Chantelle and Marc himself several rows in front of us. I felt a tremor of excitement, accidentally digging my nails into Africa's hand and causing her to say 'ay'. I hadn't seen either of them since the night of destruction ten days before.

Since Africa was with me, I'd have been happy to slink away at the end. Unfortunately, however, Africa had to visit the toilet, a procedure which always took at least ten minutes. As I hovered in the cafe at the front of the cinema, I heard Marc say to me, 'How's the novel going?'

I turned round. Seeing him there made me remember that I hadn't had a bath and shave before coming out. His handshake was firm and warm.

'Oh, hi, Marc. Very well, thanks.'

'A good film, don't you think?' He released my hand slowly and again observed me with the optical equivalent of a dentist's drill. He had clear, bright blue eyes. I hadn't seen them properly before, not in the semi-darkness of the party.

'I was just saying to Chantelle. Your beach killing might easily have occurred in just the same way. An accident. Unpremeditated. Wasn't I, Chantelle?'

How *did* it occur? I wanted to ask him, but couldn't: that was a night-time question, a question for a more intimate moment.

Chantelle didn't look very well at all. Her hair was no longer frazzled: it was sticking to her head in patches, and a rash seemed to be developing on her forehead. I remembered a boy called Troy Knox from school telling me that too much sex makes you look done in.

'We should get together, Frank,' Marc said. 'I'm sure we'll run into one another. Madrid's a comfortably small city.' He put his arm around Chantelle and brought her to his side. 'Why don't you two have a drink together? I'm sure you have a lot to discuss.'

Chantelle flashed him a desperate glance, evidently unhappy at the prospect of being left alone with me. But Marc sat us down at a table together and ordered us a coffee apiece before making his apologies and leaving. Africa was on her way over to us, obliviously bumping into seats with her bottom: two more strands of my life were about to come together.

I introduced Chantelle and Africa to one another as rapidly as possible, anxious that Chantelle would interrogate me about the nature of my relationship with Africa. But I needn't have worried. Chantelle's interest in those about her, always minimal, seemed to have faded still further.

'Marc's *great*,' she said in a faraway voice. 'He just is. He has enormous charisma.' She absently stirred her coffee, perhaps recalling an occasion on which Marc had displayed charisma. 'He says these great things. "My reality is your dreams." Isn't that beautiful?'

'Have you seen Pino?' I asked.

'You have to be kidding. That evening signalled a great change in my life. I knew it would, somehow.'

I hadn't told Africa about the night of destruction. It would have frightened her. For the same reason I did not now ask Chantelle about Marc's final words that night.

'I'm living with some friends of Marc's now. They're very *spiritual* people. Pino was about as spiritual as a refrigerator. It's like I'm *hiding* from him. Marc reckons,' she said matter-of-factly, 'that we caused about ten thousand pounds worth of damage.'

'How's Michael?'

'I don't know . . . If I wasn't such a kind person, I'd say Michael had a thing for Marc.'

We clearly weren't going to go too deeply into that.

'And are you still bored?'

'Frank, do I *seem* bored?' For the first time, Chantelle looked at Africa. 'I'm in love, you see,' she declared. '*Estoy enamorada.*' She rested her chin on the ball of her hand and smiled sweetly, acting as she believed people who were in love acted. '*Enamoradisima.*'

'Oh,' Africa said, 'That's nice.'

'It's the first time I've ever been in love . . . I've *loved* lots of people. But there's a difference between loving somebody and being in love with them, isn't there?'

'Of course there is.'

Chantelle, as was her wont, went on to relate her entire life story to Africa, some of which I didn't know myself. Her upbringing in Ellwood, a wealthy suburb of Melbourne, her dislike of her alcoholic father, her leaving home after college to come to Europe and broaden her education, her six months in Paris . . . I couldn't see how any of this bore on her being in love with Marc, but apparently in Chantelle's mind it did.

'And will you go back to Australia one day?' Africa asked.

'Well, I *thought* I would. But I'm not so sure, now . . . it's just so great, isn't it, when you find what you're looking for?'

'How old are you, *guapa*?'

'Twenty-one. Hey, your English is really all right.'

'That's because I'm teaching her,' I quipped, and was duly ignored.

'I'd already been married three years when I was twenty-one,' Africa said. 'Everybody runs away these days. Frank ran away, didn't you, *hijo*?'

'She means when I left home to go to New York.'

'New York?' Africa said. 'I never knew you went –' This was it. The end was nigh. But I needn't have worried. Chantelle interrupted us.

102

'I feel like I'm fifteen again,' she said.

'But you're only twenty-one,' Africa protested. I could see I was going to have to explain this to her later, how a girl of twenty-one could feel nostalgia. How lives were lived in fast forward these days, how people had generally achieved full intellectual and emotional maturity by the age of ten. 'It's nice to be fifteen, every once in a while,' Africa mused. 'I do it myself, sometimes.'

Things seemed to be working out, I explained after Chantelle had gone and we were walking towards Lavapiés so that Africa could buy some vegetables. About halfway down, outside the Avapiés bar, a man with a white beard was muttering incoherent abuse at no one in particular, spinning round as he did so. Derek John Platt as Chantelle had described him, twenty years hence. Spittle flew from his lips; his head was covered in strands of coloured bunting. A pigeon flew along the street and alighted on the orange top of a rubbish container. For a moment, I had the distinct impression that I was dreaming.

Before she'd met me, Africa had never been to the cinema. She was having difficulty in establishing why people should enjoy spending two hours in the company of other people's problems, when surely they had enough of their own. After all, the people in films weren't even *real*. Wasn't it better to sit down with someone real and spend your time trying to make them feel better?

In Cold Blood, I explained, *was* about real people. It was based on a real-life murder.

'But that film you took me to last week. That wasn't real.'

Terminator II, the film had been, starring Arnold Schwarzenegger. In the best Spanish I could muster, I reminded Africa that we were living in the nineties and, reciting from memory the words of Dr Minshull, I explained to her the importance of escape in such a helter-skelter world. Holidays abroad, videos, films, computer games, these new virtual reality machines I'd read about, drugs . . . they were all escape routes for people

103

who'd grown privately bitter about their lives, about their failure to make their dreams come true. I waxed forth. Technology allowed people relief from the humdrum. All fun these days was hysteria-tinted.

Africa was turning a lettuce in her hands.

'This one's at least a week old,' she said to the shop assistant. 'It's gone brown at the tips.' Then she turned to me.

'I have never escaped from anything in my life,' she said, 'I am proud to say. Put me a head of garlic in there, too.'

In my own list of escape routes, I could easily have included Africa. I was free to paint her as I wished, and she complied, perhaps finding it entertaining to escape into the role of lover after so many years of being herself.

This was not only a question of her dressing up for me in black stockings and suspenders – my erotic imagination being about as developed as that of an orang-utan – but also of being a teacher, sister and mother all rolled into one. Depending on my mood, I saw her in a variety of ways: when I grew bored of one version of her, all I had to do was look at her differently.

She seemed to accommodate my fantasizing without complaint. To idealize your loved one, as Dr Minshull had pointed out, is necessary and normal, but I went a little further than that. When we made love, I transformed Africa into someone else entirely – into one of the shop assistants at the Corte Inglés department store, for example, or into a student of mine called Esperanza Feijoo, or Jean Shrimpton, or even, and this required a superhuman leap of the imagination, into Chantelle Ray. I was a regular mental Houdini, Africa my coital chameleon.

'*Qué?*' she said, when I told her that.

Africa's wish to learn English, it transpired one evening, was not motivated simply by a desire to deepen her culture. It had to do with the fact that she had a son in England.

'You never told me that,' I protested.

'Yes I did. But you no want to hear, Frank. Other people have lives, too.'

'What do you mean?' Was she implying that I was self-centred or something?

'I receive a letter from him in 1979. A nice letter, for Christmas. But he no put his address. Paco is ashamed of me, I can tell, with my job.' She threw back her head in a gesture which defied shame.

'There's nothing wrong with your job. It's a public service.'

'But my son is not the public. A son no like to think of his mother doing these things. He no understand that I have no money. No education. I almost can't read, Frank.'

Out came her photograph album which, I noticed, had not been added to since Africa's waist measurement had been the same as her inside leg. The letter was folded inside it, but when I tried to read it, Africa snatched it from me like a little girl, protesting that it was private. Looking through the album made me feel as though I were looking through the archives of a library, but in fact I was looking at pictures of a family, a family later to be destroyed by historical circumstance.

These pictures, it was clear, had absolutely nothing to do with me: even had I wished to, I'd have been incapable of finding my way through the impenetrable human labyrinth which they implied. Names tripped from Africa's tongue. Carmen, Pili, Eduardo, Angela, Zaragoza, Armando, Teruel . . . were they names of people or of places? Paco, scrubbed and beaming, at his First Communion party. Paco at age eleven, holding some sort of certificate, sulking.

'I'd just hit him,' Africa explained. 'He is married now. In London. There are perhaps children . . .' Just for a moment, for the first time, she looked her age. 'How do you say "*nieto*"?'

'"Grandson".'

This wasn't *my* Africa. I felt her slipping from me, and panicked.

'It doesn't do to dwell on the past,' I told her.

'You no have a past, Frank.'

'What about my letter to Auntie Beryl? Of course I've got a past.'

It was the first time she'd been sharp with me, rather than simply direct. Her voice had been briefly rasping, like fingers down a blackboard. She sensed this, and softened her tone.

'No, you haven't. Not yet. And it is wrong to have one, at your age. You must look more at the future, Frank. You no understand things. You no know the true weight of a word.'

'Africa? What does that mean, exactly?'

'Oh,' Africa said. 'You make me angry.' Then she was silent.

'And why do I make you angry, exactly?'

'All your *psicología*. All your trying to explain yourself. Why you look at yourself so much? You are you, no?'

'I suppose so.' This was one conversation I was going to have to put out of my mind pretty quickly if it wasn't going to be torture to me. 'What are you trying to say?'

'*Ay, no sé. Tú sabrás.*' *Tú sabrás* meant, I suppose you know what you're doing. '*Es que de vez en cuando pienso que algo va muy mal dentro de ti*, Frank.'

'You think that there's something very wrong inside me. Well, thank you very much for that original insight.'

She drew a tissue from her cleavage and fingered it. 'I worry,' she said.

'Well, don't.'

If this is Africa, I thought, then give me the Hola Woman any day of the week.

'Africa, I'm not paying you so that we can have conversations like this.'

'*Muy bien.*' She shrugged her shoulders. 'As you want.'

When we met up later that evening, we argued again. Shortly before she'd met me, Africa revealed, she'd been standing outside an electronics shop in Anton Martin. There'd been a football match showing, and she'd been certain she'd seen Paco's face in the crowd.

I thought she'd suddenly gone mad, talking about seeing the faces of dead people on the television.

'He's dead,' I gently reminded her.

'No. My son Paco.'

'Oh, Africa. Come on. You must have imagined it.'

'He wear a scarf. It was red and white.'

'Oh. Well I suppose it *must* have been him, then.'

She was up on her feet, shouting, hurling a copy of *Interviú* to the floor. It fell open at a picture of a recently deceased Mexican comedian.

'Leave this house now,' she commanded me loudly, 'and never return.'

'I suppose it *could* have been Paco's face,' I said. 'I just thought – you know – the capacities of football stadiums – '

Africa simmered down. This had nothing to do, she told me, with the capacities of football stadiums. It was a question of mother and son, and it had been Paco.

She closed her eyes and sighed. In that sigh there was a depth of suppressed emotion which was frightening to see. I would never be able to sigh like that, to sigh directly from the heart.

'Africa,' I said, 'I don't feel very well.'

'Do you want a Nurofen?'

'No. I don't *feel* very well. I'm not very good at *feeling* things. Sometimes it's almost like I don't have a personality. Like I'm . . . white inside.'

'Oh, Frank,' Africa smiled and shook her head. 'Sometimes you are such a – such a –'

She went to the shelf and took down the only book she possessed, a Collins pocket dictionary. I patiently waited.

'Wally,' she said.

TEN

We gathered in Los Fernandos during the second week of July.

Nobody spoke in any detail of how they'd passed the time since Chantelle's party, apart from Brian, who had had minor surgery on his urethra. At first, after the night of destruction, what was unsaid between us counted for more than what was said. We'd revealed ourselves that night, taken an unflattering photograph of ourselves which we now wished to destroy.

Bumping into Michael in the street on the way here, I'd asked him, just idly, whether Marc had yet told him who had killed Derek John Platt: Michael replied that he had asked, just idly, and that Marc had promised to tell him when the moment was right.

'What does that mean?'

'At a guess, Frank, I'd say it meant that he'll tell me when the moment is right. It's not the sort of thing you just blurt out to people, is it? This isn't a simple thing. This is life. In all its terrible complexity.'

'Do you really think he knows?'

'Listen. If Marc says he knows, then he knows. You only have to *look* at him.'

'How well do you know Marc?'

'Well, let's say I've met him a couple of times. Which is not enough. But those couple of times have been kind of . . . *intense*. I guess absence makes the heart grow fonder . . . Chantelle is sticking to him like a *leech* . . . I guess they must have come here together . . .'

Marc was standing over by the one-armed bandit. He was territory I badly wanted to explore. But this was not the time. I'd have to control myself and wait.

We lethargically raised our glasses to the rest of the summer. Michael confessed to having put on five kilos under that baggy mauve shirt, and to being a little down, apparently just having experienced the most hedonistic four days of his life in Tangiers.

'Some *very* rough trade,' he explained, shaking his head as if disbelieving his own memory. 'A one-eyed camel driver. But I guess it could have been worse. It could have been a one-eyed camel.' We secretly smiled and winked at one another, knowing this to be another of Michael's phases.

I'd seen Chantelle more recently. Although the rash had disappeared from her forehead, I found myself thinking for the first time that she was not attractive. Unable to work out why I thought this, I watched her chatting to the others, nervously smoking and laughing more loudly than was necessary. The light in her eyes, which had once disclosed a simple delight in things, had become a little too intense. She'd become a small animal, transfixed in the headlights.

No one spoke when Donald broke the news, shattering though it was. He defensively raised his palms, one of his acquired Mediterranean gestures.

'I *told* you. I did tell you. I always warn new arrivals it isn't going to be permanent. I'm sorry. I am. I apologize. Life goes on.'

'Unfortunately,' Michael said.

'You don't appear overdistraught,' Brian said to Donald.

'No. Well, I can't say I am. The school *was* a sixties relic. This has been coming for a while now. The times they are a-changing.'

'You should have put more effort into it,' Michael complained.

Donald sipped his *pacharán* and took a deep breath. 'Listen,' he said. 'I'm not going on trial, all right? Cast your minds back. Who was it who didn't want to give classes? Sitting on that very seat not one month ago? Who were the nervous wrecks whose hands were trembling? Eh, Michael?'

'Ours,' Brian said miserably. 'Great is Truth, and mighty above all things.'

'You should have made us teach, then,' Chantelle said.

'Sometimes we need people to tell us what to do. We just do.'

'Chantelle, you're a wonderful kid, and I love you. But let me tell you that life ain't like that. Now please be quiet.'

Chantelle glanced over in Marc's direction.

'How many students have enrolled?' Michael asked. 'Hit me with some statistics here.'

'Twenty-three so far,' Pilar said. 'Not enough to cover the rent. That's the only statistic. It's never been this bad before.'

'And who's going to teach these twenty-three students how to espeaka de Eenglish?'

'Pilar is,' Donald said.

'But she's a secretary,' Chantelle said. 'She's got no more right to teach English than – '

'Than you have. Or Brian, or Michael, or Frank, or any one of the hundred and twenty-seven poor buggers who've worked for me down the years.'

'And,' Pilar said, 'I've put up with a lot more than any of you.' She plucked at the knees of her tights, embarrassed at her outburst. 'You mustn't think it's going to be easy for Donald and me. I can expect to earn thirty thousand a month, if I'm fucking lucky.' At that moment, Marc hit the jackpot on the one-armed bandit. What came out of it sounded like a fortune.

'I'll be honest with you,' Donald said. 'I'd rather wind the whole thing up as soon as possible. There are contingency plans afoot. I'm looking at other possibilities. But I'm not going to get anyone's hopes up until they've come through. Until I've got something concrete to offer you.' He leaned back and tightened his belt-buckle. 'I'm sorry I'm such a useless shit. You should never have met me.'

'Oh, Donald,' Brian said. 'There's no need to say that.'

'Yes there is,' Chantelle said.

Marc pulled up a seat and briefly adjusted the knot of his tie. 'Well,' he said. 'Now that Donald's bubble has burst, you'll all need someone to look after you.'

Donald turned to him and slowly said, 'I believe this is a

private meeting. You're only here because Chantelle saw fit to bring you.'

'No. No, I'm here because I want to be. Donald, you're a wonderful man, and I love you. But life ain't like that.'

It had been an uncannily accurate impersonation. How had Marc even heard Donald say it? It confused Donald.

'Listen to him, Donald,' Chantelle said. 'Please?'

'Why? We don't even know where he's *from*.'

'Is nationality really so important?' Marc said. 'We're all human, aren't we?'

'I'm not so sure. Christ, go on, then. We're all ears.'

'I have the impression that everyone around this table needs someone to look after them. That's the impression I have. There is lack of direction. There's nothing *happening* here.'

The lull in the conversation intensified into the shocked silence which always greets unwelcome truths.

'May I offer an opinion? May I offer the opinion that the closure of the Albion School might be – '

'Academy,' Pilar said. 'Albion *Academy*.'

'Shut up, Pilar,' Chantelle said. 'Marc's speaking.'

Chantelle thought it was love she was feeling for Marc. From where I was sitting, it looked more like hero-worship.

' – might be the best thing that has ever happened to you all?'

Donald's expression altered from confusion to surprise, as though he wished it were he who had come up with this blow-softening comment.

'You all have so much *potential*,' Marc went on. 'Chantelle with her photographs. Frank with his novel. Michael's personality is an asset in itself. Even Brian –'

Brian peered expectantly at him through watery eyes.

'Even Brian.'

'I have my *Book of Influences*,' Michael said. 'As well as my personality.'

'The Albion School was an interim. A place you came to while you were deciding what to do with the rest of your lives. Am I right?'

'I guess so,' Michael said. 'Except I haven't taken my decision yet, and I have no plans to. I have a nauseous reaction to taking decisions.'

'This moment had to come at some point. As I'm sure Donald told you it would. You can't drift for ever. The school offered no contracts' – Marc counted items off on his fingers – 'had no legal status, probably paid no taxes, and is registered as a private address. Now I doubt very much whether any of you ever sat down and contemplated the result of such a situation. But if you had . . . well, you'd have realized that it was this. It's a miracle it survived as long as it did.'

Everything he said was so patterned, so organized. I'd never heard anyone speak in this way before.

'We might be listening to you, sunshine,' Donald muttered, 'if we had a fucking clue who you were when you were at home. Pardon my Sanskrit.'

Marc closed his eyes and brought his fingertips fleetingly to his forehead. 'All this means,' he said, 'is that you have to start doing what everyone else does. Which is live. Face up to it. The holiday's over. Life begins here.'

That came as a shock to me. That was the last thing I wanted, for life to begin. I wanted excitement, not life.

I didn't say anything. Marc was leading up to something.

'That's what *I'm* always telling them,' Donald said. 'Aren't I always telling you that?' But now there was the sense that Donald's words were coming from the past and Marc's from the future.

'Life begins here,' Marc repeated. 'It's frightening. It's horrible. Worst of all, it's true. Why should life have to begin?'

A barman arrived. Marc ordered a round of drinks.

'So,' Michael said dejectedly. 'I guess my folks were right all along. I guess it's off the gravy train and into the factory. I guess it's bum a WP and write your CV. Mine covers a total of three lines.'

'Why should life have to begin?' Chantelle said. 'That's kind of romantic.'

It took a special person to walk into a situation as volatile as this one and take control. Mad you might call it, and arrogant, but such madness and arrogance were to be envied. It bespoke power and elicited admiration. Marc was speaking while the rest of us lacked useful words: he was verbalizing thoughts that were also mine.

'Isn't he great?' Chantelle said. 'He has a certain power.'

Marc ignored her.

'Michael,' he said. 'What are your plans?'

Michael made a face and looked at him a little woundedly, I thought. He started agitatedly rubbing the back of his neck and bobbing his leg up and down, suddenly plugged into his own nervous system.

'I can't go home, can I?' he said. 'I'll have to get another job, I guess.'

'And you, Frank? Will you go back to the Lower East Side? To finish your novel? Try and get some of that old New York creativity back into your blood?'

I decided that I would begin the novel that very evening.

'I don't know . . . I'll have to think about it . . .'

'OK.' Marc pushed back his seat and put his palms on the table.

'Haven't you finished yet?' Donald said.

'No, I haven't. Now I'm going to say what I came to say. How would you like to work for me?'

'I don't think,' Pilar said, 'that selling drugs is going to look very good on anybody's CV, do you?'

'I don't sell drugs.'

'That's what Chantelle said you did at the party.'

'Drugs are mess. Drugs are for little people. If Chantelle said that, it must have been her wild imagination. You don't believe me.' Marc quickly reached across the table and took Pilar's fore-arm. She flinched; he smiled and opened his eyes a little wider.

'Look at me. Tell me I sell drugs.'

'Get your fucking hands off her.'

'Look at my face, Donald.' Marc continued to smile at Pilar. His words were rushed and breathy. 'I'm smiling. Good will is on my face. But my pride has been hurt and I'm a little edgy inside. Now. Tell me I sell drugs. Tell me I sell drugs. See if I like it when you tell me that, Pilar. Go on. Sit down, Donald. Or you're dead.'

Pilar closed her eyes briefly, but didn't say anything. Marc relaxed his grip and patted her arm a couple of times. Pilar brought her arm up to her chest as though afraid it would fly off.

'She doesn't say anything because she's not in the business of lies. No, I don't sell drugs. I make films. Small art films. I do not sell drugs.'

'He doesn't sell drugs,' Donald muttered. 'Now we know. Fucking psychopath. Just go, will you?'

'No. How would you like to work for me?'

'Who?' Michael asked.

'Specifically you, Chantelle and Frank. You don't have to decide now.' He looked at his watch. 'Film work. I generally pay on signature of contract, but in this case . . . given the unusual circumstances . . .'

'Get out of here,' Donald insisted. 'Go on. This is private. We don't need you.'

'Shall I go? Shall I go, Chantelle, and you'll never see me again?' Marc made as if to stand.

'No . . .' she said faintly. 'Of course not . . .'

'Hey, don't listen to Donald,' Michael said. 'He's just jealous of your devastating good looks.'

Marc ignored him.

He relaxed back into his seat, unbuttoned his left shirt cuff and rolled it back. He held up his wrist.

Tattooed on to it was the finely wrought image of a watch.

'What time does it say?' he said. 'Michael? Tell me.'

'Midnight,' Michael whispered. 'Wow.'

'And why does it say midnight? Tell them, Chantelle.'

'Because,' Chantelle quiveringly murmured, 'it's always midnight wherever you are.'

114

'Good. It's always midnight, wherever I am. And that, Donald, is why I never leave until I want to leave, and why you will not suggest it again. What happens is this.' He stood and slowly circled the table, his hands in his pockets. 'I do not do what I'm expected to do. I do whatever the hell I like, and nobody argues. Don't get too close to me on this. I am quietly . . . deranged. Donald's right. I am a fucking psychopath. You should know this about me.' He smiled and put his finger to his lips. 'Just listen to how quietly I say it.'

Donald mouthed the word 'what', but no sound emerged. Marc rebuttoned his cuff and slid out a wallet, from which he removed a thick slice of money. I couldn't believe what I was seeing. It was a gripping performance. A thrill of disquiet made me inwardly shiver.

Marc counted off five notes and gave them to me, and then did the same for Michael and Chantelle.

'Now I'm talking,' he said.

Auntie Beryl's voice entered my head, suspicious of displays of generosity, reminding me that folks don't do something for nothing. Such negativity opened no doors, led nowhere. I took the money in silence.

'Just hang on,' Donald said. 'This is all wrong.' He sat with his whisky halfway to his mouth.

'Do you want some of my money, Donald? All you have to do is ask.'

'No, I fucking do not. And if I was ten years younger . . .'

'Well, you aren't,' Marc said. He stood. 'I can't sit here with you any longer. I've said what I came to say.'

'Hey,' Pilar said. 'Wait.'

'I'm going to work for him,' Chantelle said. 'Film work? You bet.' Marc was on his way to the door. She hurried after him.

We sat in silence. A man shouted loudly for a plate of *boquerones*.

'Now that Donald's little bubble has burst,' Donald said, attempting an unsuccessful impersonation of Marc. 'Where the fuck is he coming from?'

'You should be pleased,' Pilar said. 'He bought you a double scotch *and* gave them severance pay.'

'Yeah,' Michael said. 'I guess I'm happier at this point than I would have been if he hadn't showed up.'

'Michael,' Donald said slowly. 'Listen. I want you to go after him. I want you to stop him and I want you to give him that money back. Go on.'

'Twenty-five thousand,' Michael said. 'For doing jack. I guess money *is* power, after all.'

'He's repellent,' Pilar said. 'He made a mark on my arm, look.'

'Repellent? You have to be kidding. He has the tightest little ass this side of Miguel Bose.'

'How can you say that, Michael? Did you see what he did to me? He's like one of those James Bond villains. All he needs is a leather glove and a cat. He's watched too fucking many films.'

'I guess the sexual imagination of some people doesn't run to someone like Marc, does it, Pilar? I guess someone like Marc just threatens some people.'

Brian, who had gone to the toilet without anyone noticing, now returned with a spot of urine on his trousers. He offered the opinion that Marc did seem a little off the beaten bush.

'Oh, for Christ's sake,' Donald said. 'Yes, I'm a middle-aged Scottish alkie. Yes, I am.' He glanced at Pilar. 'But I am imploring you, begging you, to give him that money back. You come across a lot of nutters on the TEFL circuit, but this guy . . . it wouldn't surprise me if he'd killed Derek John Platt himself, except he's clearly all mouth.' He shook his head, drained his glass. 'I'll give you the money myself,' he said, which provoked sceptical smiles. 'Go on, Frank.'

'I think it's my business,' I said. 'I'm sorry.'

'There's no harm in finding out what he wants, is there?' Michael said.

'There is if it's dirty money.'

'It isn't dirty money. He said so himself.'

'Oh, right. And given that this guy is clearly Jesus Christ, I suppose you believed him.'

'The times they are a-changing, Donald,' Michael said. 'You said so yourself. Given the choice between having some money and no money, which would *you* choose?'

Donald grunted.

'I could have done with a couple of thousand myself,' Brian admitted.

When we parted, for the first time it was without knowing when we'd meet. 'See you around': as I said it, I knew it wouldn't have bothered me unduly not to see Chantelle, Michael, Brian, Donald and Pilar again. They'd always been provisional. But not to have seen Marc again would have left me feeling unfinished inside, like a power cut just before the end of a compelling film.

Five crisp 5,000-peseta notes were in my hand. If you packed them together and folded them, they felt hard, like a passport to somewhere new, somewhere I'd never been.

ELEVEN

The most exciting events of my life have taken place during sleep. It was during sleep that I first made love to Africa, for example, later foolishly trying to import that particular fantasy into the real world. In sleep, you don't bang your head against the bedstead or lose your false tooth. In sleep, you don't even *have* a false tooth. It was during sleep that I'd shot Auntie Beryl through the head using Great-Uncle Vernon's air pistol, later feeling guilty when she rushed through to comfort me after my shouting, explaining to me that it had only been a dream.

It was during sleep that I'd walked out on to a sweeping, brightly lit Hollywood stage, my pancake make-up prickling my cheeks, shielding my eyes and making witty comments into the darkness, to collect my Oscar for the best film of 1976, the consummately realized, pivotal and never actually started *A Spanish Episode*. In my sleep, a naked Jean Shrimpton had presented me with the award. In front of a television audience of millions, Jean had kissed me for a good ten minutes, which had brought Auntie Beryl through again.

'I'll tell you one thing,' I'd said sleepily. 'She doesn't wear blue curlers.'

'Who doesn't, poppet?'

'None of your business. It's my secret.'

Old dreams, tender and inflamed. When I awoke from them my heart rate was about a thousand per minute, my pillow unpleasantly cool and damp.

It would be best to stave off sleep for a while. I sat, pencil in one hand, joint in the other, notebook propped against my knees. I sensed the sun come up, watched the shadow of my wardrobe lengthen. I wondered at which instant night turns to day, feeling that such a point would reflect the shadowy state of my mind and its imaginings. I listened to the blind man at the street corner, shouting at people to buy that morning's lottery tickets.

It's always midnight, wherever I am. We allow him to entertain us, but we cannot understand him: we observe him, fascinated, but at the same time relieved for the simple reason that he is not us. He may have a wife, children and family, he may be a drifter, he may be in his youth, middle age or dotage, he may have been sexually abused as a child, orphaned, you name it. Is he criminal or victim? He is both: millions of people with such histories never even dream of doing the things he does. What always matters most is what is inside him now, which has been there since before he could speak, and which will only cease when he is no longer able to. His inner life is a mystery even to himself, especially to himself. No amount of theory can accommodate him. He escapes it all.

'It's only correct that you all know that I know who killed Derek John Platt.' He'd blown out a match; everything had gone dark. 'Let's get out of here,' someone had said. I'd never forget that.

He has this feeling, wherever, whoever he is at the time, that he does not belong. He feels impotent, rejected, spiritually small, and he retreats from these feelings into fantasy, and sometimes this fantasy life, loaded as it is with frightening and powerful charm, will become confused with the real, sometimes obliterating the real altogether. He may begin to construct a life based entirely on these fantasies, which are in turn based on the sort of person he would like to have been. Locked into this dark room of his own making, he feels violently alone, feeling also the need to assert himself, to stake

119

his own claim in the world. It is a heroic, doomed project. He has to seek out others like himself so that he can impose his view of himself on them, make it real, remind himself of that person, the one he'd like to have been. We all do it. Donald the rake at Chantelle's party, Chantelle the photographer, Michael the frenzied sexual hunter, Auntie Beryl with her constantly altering hairdo: performers. Escape artists. Fantasists, struggling to make their fantasies real. It's sad, it's awesome: we all do it. But few of us follow it through.

In his case, it is overwhelming. He seeks his people out. Perhaps he falls in love with them. As part of the natural course of things they then wish to leave him, thereby polluting the fresh air of the dream. And whereas others might kill themselves, he, while he is not himself, kills them. There is a rightness about this, a rightness which approaches beauty.

Outside, the street filled with the shouting and laughter of children as they gathered, waiting for the school doors to open. I went out on to the balcony to relight my joint. One of the children pointed up at me, laughing since I was wearing only torn underpants and spectacles. Thoughtless and cruel, utterly unconcerned with consequences, ecstatically thoughtless, sublimely cruel. Only the present mattered to them. They were evil.

Derek John Platt, sweating pure alcohol in a Costa Brava beach bar. Brightly coloured swimming shorts, a silver neck-chain with a 'D', a pathetic ice-breaker; a pallid, glistening paunch, plastic beach sandals playing hell with his ingrowing toenail. That was Derek John Platt. Last Thursday's *Sun*, yellowed and crinkled. He has come to Spain to escape, after the break-up of his marriage, perhaps, or to escape the loss of his job, or to hide from the discovery that he has AIDS: to escape from some major event, anyway, which has left him devastated and confused, knowing things about himself of which he was not previously aware, forcing him to a painful redefinition of himself, to an acceptance of the lie his life has been. And they call all this a 'holiday'! Other clients at the bar notice Derek John Platt for an instant, registering his Englishness, returning to their conversations without comment. He is too drunk for proper speech and far from home. The Costa Brava, he reflects: it seemed like a good idea at the time.

A stranger appears from the nowhere that is everywhere outside Derek John Platt's troubled thoughts. Pulls up a stool. Comments on the heat. Are you on holiday? Where are you from? Really? That *is* interesting. Derek John Platt, while aware that this interest is artificial, is nonetheless grateful for it, too far gone to want to wonder why a stranger should wish to talk to him, of all people, in a bar as full of beautiful people, of both sexes, as this one. Perhaps, he thinks, watching the stranger's mouth move and loading this insignificant event with meaning, the world is not such a bad place after all, perhaps far from home is the best place to be: he observes this good-looking stranger, and buys him a drink, and feels gratitude, gratitude which cancels all suspicion. He hears himself revealing to the stranger his feelings, his fears and frustrations, his need to break away from all of that: hearing himself speak, he is momentarily surprised at his own words, and apologizes, but the stranger tells him not to worry, and places his hand lightly on Derek John Platt's skinny thigh. Derek John Platt, after a slight English shudder, relaxes, tells the stranger that it's odd, isn't it, how it's sometimes easier to talk about these things with someone you hardly know. This, however, is only a half-truth, since Derek John Platt, in his real life, and this isn't real, knows no one to whom he could tell these things anyway. He feels, he confesses, as though they've been friends for years.

'What's your name?' he asks, embarrassed, after such talk, not to know the stranger's name.

'Marc,' the stranger says. He removes his jacket and lays it carefully down. Across the back of his jacket, in bold black lettering, is the legend: **S T R A N G E R**.

Derek John Platt is excited by this. 'Derek John Platt,' he says, wiping his hand on his shorts and holding it out. 'My friends call me Derek.'

Marc takes the hand and shakes it. They laugh together at the inappropriateness of this too-formal gesture and then Derek John Platt continues with the story of his life. Marc says little, only listens, and Derek John Platt has not noticed this peculiarity, and now he never will.

Marc silently encourages him, seduces him with sheer force of personality. Derek John Platt, though he is not aware of it, is ripe for seduction, desperate as he is to spend the evening in the arms of someone. Marc senses this also, and perhaps even knows that, before the night is out, it will be necessary to murder Derek John Platt: Derek John Platt, pathetically unaware of his own role in the drama, is shortly to step into the dark room, where he does not belong.

The word 'murder' does not feature in Marc's mind. The feeling comes only as a faint, ill-defined inner shimmer – of fear, anticipation, excitement at the promise of control. Before the night is out, Derek John Platt will – the correct word doesn't come –

Derek John Platt will no longer
be –

I was breathing faster than normal. My spectacles were steamed up and had a bead of sweat on them, so I removed them and rubbed them on a corner of the bedsheet, which made them more blurred than before.

It was surprising to me how easy it was to enter into the mind of another person like this, when you knew nothing about them. Derek John Platt, Marc. How easy, and how thrilling. It felt altogether different from my Robert Mapplethorpe fiction, since this had no repercussions in the real world, and came with no real fears attached. It was a safe area, safe from invasion and abuse, safe from perversion. It was pure and private, as private as a dark thought in a dark cinema, when the person next to you, holding your hand, is in fact as far away from you as it's possible for a person to be.

Slowly I reread my words, savouring them, wondering whether Marc had indeed killed Derek John Platt, whether Derek John Platt had indeed been the forlorn victim described to me by Chantelle.

And as I read, I realized that this was surely how it must have been, that there can have been no other way. It didn't matter that Michael or Chantelle did not figure in this version of events. After all, they couldn't: this was something private, between Marc and myself. 'This isn't good for you, poppet,' I heard Auntie Beryl telling me. 'You're playing with fire, poppet, to coin a phrase.' But I banished her, too. She didn't belong here. No one belonged here except Marc and myself.

They move to another bar. They wander along the beach, unconcerned about direction. The sand is warm underfoot: out to sea, there is the hulking shadow of an anchored yacht. Derek John Platt admits to feeling a little wobbly, so they sit. Each silently notes the romance of the setting, a silent beach at 4 in the morning. The gentle rushing of the waves. The air between them is charged, and there is little laughter.

Derek John Platt says that he has horrible-looking feet, then goes on to confess that he is totally rat-arsed.

'We could go back to my hotel,' Marc quietly suggests.

'I've got horrible feet,' says Derek John Platt, forgetting that he has already said this.

'Derek, wouldn't you like to go back to my hotel?'

It's nice to be called 'Derek' like that.

'I don't know . . .'

'Oh, come on. Live. You're on holiday . . .'

The hand is on the thigh again. Only this time, it feels right and proper that it should be there.

The hotel is three minutes away. They mount the narrow,

tiled stairs, aware of the heat gathered there. Derek John Platt, who is sweating like a pig, is still drunk but no longer cares, and because he doesn't care, he feels a sort of happiness. Any happiness will do.

He stands on Marc's balcony. The anchored yacht is still there. There is a gentle breeze: on balconies, he reflects, there always is. The suicide thought flashes through his mind, but is quickly rejected.

Tomorrow he will rise late. The dead, on their final day, have always thought about tomorrow. He and Marc will sit together under the parasols which are now rolled up below him, a yellow and red blur on the terrace. He will buy a Spanish newspaper and try to read it, asking Marc for help on the difficult words such as 'bacalao', which means 'cod'. He cannot now believe that he was feeling the way he was only – he looks at his watch – only two hours ago.

At Marc's suggestion, they shower together. Derek John Platt admires Marc's physique and cannot help but compare the size of Marc's penis to his own. There is something decadent in all this but something innocent also, which redeems it: whatever, there is pleasure in such self-abandonment. Derek John Platt worries about the size of his penis, comparing it to a chipolata sausage, and Marc asks him not to worry about anything, just to let go.

Then they have sex on the crisp, white sheets. Or perhaps they do not.

At 5 o'clock, Marc suggests they go to the beach to watch the sun rise. Again they sit side by side and Derek John Platt, not wishing to think about the implications of what has just occurred, talks about his future. He doesn't intend to be a mechanic in Macclesfield for the rest of his days. Oh, no. He doesn't know what he will do, but you can bet your bottom dollar it will be something that makes people sit up and take notice. He'll be leaving Spain in a couple of days, he says. He'll have to be getting back.

He lies down and continues to speak, aware of the fresh, soapy smell of his own body, the roughness of the sand against his cheek, the increasing incoherence of his words. Then he sleeps, anaesthetized by alcohol.

Marc watches the gaunt, thoroughly relaxed frame of Derek John Platt for a while, mentally agreeing with him that he does, in fact, have horrible feet. He doesn't want Derek John Platt to go home tomorrow. He doesn't know why, but he can't bear that thought.

At the first glimmers of the rising sun, Marc slides a razor-bade from his wallet, where it has been safely sandwiched between two credit cards. Then he skilfully draws the razor-blade against the throat of Derek John Platt, encountering a small degree of resistance from Derek John Platt's Adam's apple. His hand on Derek John Platt's chest, he feels him relax still further.

Marc sighs and lights a cigarette, closing his eyes because he can't stand the sight of blood. Like sex, like drugs, he feels better afterwards, although less so than last time. He is a little surprised at how easy it has all been. No fuss, no reaction at all: death, he reflects, ought not to come this easily, ought not to be this wished-for. As though it had already been at the door of Derek John Platt's life, patiently waiting, ready to enter at the slightest bidding. But then again, things come to you easily when you are not yourself.

It's always midnight, wherever he is. It has been a beautiful death.

Outside it was silent. There was scarcely enough light to write by. I didn't know why, but I was crying. The fact that I was crying struck me as tremendously sad, and made me cry even more.

TWELVE

One evening, Africa came out of her bathroom, informed me that she had decided not to work tonight or indeed ever again, and suggested that we go for a walk. *Dar un paseo*: considering the manner of her husband's death, it was a mystery to me how she could use these three words without becoming instantly miserable. I couldn't believe that she did not intend to work again: this was a typically African grumpy mood causing her to overdramatize.

As to the reasons for the mood, she would only say that she was unhappy and refused to go into more detail. So whether it was because I continued, against her wishes, to smoke marijuana until I was good company only for myself, or because I'd lost my job, or whether it had to do with her brooding over her son, I didn't know.

I'd have given anything to hear from Marc, who would understand. To be able to tell Africa that I was going out with friends, that I wouldn't be able to see her tonight. Only then, I sensed, would I be able to free myself of the chains I'd allowed her to wrap me in.

We paused at a travel agents' window, Africa expressing surprise at how expensive it was to go on holiday. Wise though she could be on the spiritual aspect of life, she was often less informed than a three-year-old when it came to the practical. And although this was something we shared, we did, I thought, catching a reflected glimpse of us, make an odd couple: a small, wormy, bespectacled boy looking older than his years, arm in arm with a woman thirty years his senior, plump, black-haired and heavily made-up, holding a large Chinese fan, who could only be his relative by virtue of some dark genetic catastrophe. I must have been off my trolley ever to have thought we made something whole. We were misfits inside and out.

We walked along the Calle Mayor and turned left under an archway into the vast, cobbled elegance of the plaza, pausing to watch a Japanese youth doing a portrait in charcoals of an overweight tourist with horn-rims and dyed, receding hair. In the portrait, the hairline had been brought forward, the cheekbones retrieved from beneath the flab and the horn-rims had vanished completely.

Back home in America, this woman would have to wrestle her features into all sorts of unlikely shapes if she were to bear any resemblance to her portrait. These painters were psychologists also. They knew the truth, as plastic surgeons, advertisers and film-makers knew it: that people prefer their dreams about themselves to their actual selves, that what keeps you going is not who you are, but who you'd like to be. I explained it all to Africa as we descended the steps, Africa laboriously having to bring both feet on to the same step before she was able to continue to the next one. 'You're right,' she wheezed, and I knew she hadn't understood, not even 60 per cent.

We strolled in silence down the Calle de Toledo and along the Calle Bailén.

'Do you think about your Auntie much?'

'No.'

'I know you don't like that I talk about your family,' Africa said. 'But don't you ever miss them? Don't you ever want to be with them, Frank? A family is – *un ancla*.' We paused for about three hours while the dictionary came out of the handbag. 'An anchor.'

'You're right,' I said. 'I don't like that you talk about my family.'

Just across the Suicide Viaduct, on the open area of packed earth and stones called Las Vistillas, chairs and tables had been set up. Tanned young people wearing light clothing sat with cool drinks, chatting and laughing, enjoying the long, hot night and all the promises it held. As with the people at Chantelle's party, their behaviour seemed to suggest that, if they weren't happy, then at least they had the ability to make themselves so at will. They might as well have been Martians.

A man sat on a stool in the middle of it all with a guitar and a small amplifier, strumming mournful melodies of ancient Spain. Africa paused for a moment to fan herself and hum along.

'All this life,' she murmured. 'All this human music.'

'What?'

'Human music.'

'What does that mean?'

'Do you not want to be a part of the human music?' she said, and laughed. 'Ay, *mi chico solitario* ... shall we drink somebody?'

'Some*thing*, Africa.'

'Some*thing*. Some*thing*.' Her spittle hit me in the eye.

Africa sucked at a 650-peseta cocktail she'd seen in one of her magazines. I ate the cherry and fiddled with the swizzle stick. An elderly gypsy woman with a leathery face and a lurid headscarf touched my arm and held out a rose, nodding encouragement.

'*No, gracias*.' I glanced at Africa to see whether I should have bought her one or not, but she was in another world entirely.

'What are you thinking about?'

'*El futuro*.' She raised her head and smiled sharply. Her use of Spanish was an instruction to me not to pursue her.

During the tense silence that followed, I spotted Marc standing over at the far side, at the top of the slope. I felt a small rush of exhilaration. He was with several other people, among them the girl from the party, the one with the blond wig. Seeing him also made me feel a little nervous. After all, the last time I'd seen him, he'd just murdered Derek John Platt.

Marc and someone else detached themselves from the group

and came towards us. I was surprised to see that the someone else was Michael, radiating good health, wearing a baseball cap back to front and a T-shirt displaying the image of a pistol and the words 'New York'.

'Hey, Frank,' Michael said as I stood. 'Give me five.' He put his hands up and waggled them about. I'd seen this done in films, but didn't know how to do it myself.

'Hello, Frank.' Marc held out his hand, speaking a gestural language I understood.

I introduced them to Africa. 'My *God*,' Michael said. 'She's a little bit exotic, isn't she?'

In reasonable English, Africa explained that she was not a tropical plant. I kept my eyes on Marc: he seemed edgy and unrelaxed, clenching his teeth so that the skin of his cheeks twitched. Would I ever be able to confess my beach fantasy to him? Would he ever be able to understand how a person might have a fantasy like that?

'Michael and I have been discussing our film,' he said. 'Michael's been telling me all about you, Frank. I'm intrigued.'

'Frank knows Almodóvar,' Michael said. 'That's the kind of friendships I make.'

'Really? Michael and I went to see one of his films last night.'

'*Laberinto de Pasiones*,' Michael said.

'It was very good.'

'Excellent.' Michael seemed keen to establish some sort of double act.

'Won't you sit down?' It was no good having Michael around. It had to be just myself and Marc.

'No, thanks. I love Almodóvar. What's his first film called again?' Marc's eyes were trained on me.

'Beats me,' Michael said.

'Can you remember, Frank?'

'Really,' I said. 'You should both sit down.' I gestured to an empty chair.

'I have to meet some people at one,' Marc said. 'Perhaps

Michael would like to stay and tell you our plans for a small revolution in art. Have you read Bresson's *Notes on the Cinematographer*, Frank?'

'Yes. It's excellent.'

'Come on,' Michael said. 'You can sit down for five minutes.'

'I'd love to. I can't.' Marc turned and touched a passing waiter on the arm. I wondered whether the waiter would beam and say, Ah, good evening, Mr Marc. 'What would you all like to drink? Africa?'

'What's this called again?' she asked me.

'A Harvey Wallbanger.'

'A Harvey Wallbanger, a beer for Frank . . . Michael?'

'A *vodka con tónica*, I guess . . .'

Marc handed him a few thousand pesetas. 'Pay with this,' he said. 'A pleasure meeting you, Africa. Frank, we really will have to get together some time soon. Time is always the problem. I – I always have to be somewhere else.'

'Is there no way I can get in touch with you?' I asked, trying and failing to give the impression of nonchalance.

'There is. By telephone.' Marc took out a pen and scribbled on the back of a paper drinks coaster. I folded it carefully, deciding that the best place to keep it would be inside my jacket. That way, the number would definitely not be lost at the cleaner's.

I was sorry that he was leaving us. Wherever he was that night, I knew, his presence would make it a memorable event.

The three of us sat in silence for a while. Then Michael pulled his seat up close and started to whisper conspiratorially, his left leg bobbing.

'He's great, isn't he? It's like, we've only known each other since the party, but I feel like I've known him a lifetime . . . I'm gay, by the way,' Michael said, addressing Africa.

'Very nice.' Africa coughed, rearranged her skirt and recrossed her legs. Every time she left the house, it seemed, she was destined to meet confused foreigners, telling her how deeply in love they were.

'But I'm not just gay. I'm a gay in love,' Michael said, right on cue. 'It's like, you won't believe this, Frank. But my Mom and Dad never knew I was gay . . . Marc said I had to confront them, write them a letter telling them about it. And I did . . . he's the only person could have made me do that.' He jerked his head decisively and took a rapid gulp of vodka. 'Yep. Just this afternoon, as a matter of fact . . . Hey, why am I *telling* you this?'

'Was that a very good idea?' Africa asked. 'I would not like it if I receive a letter from my son saying me he is gay.'

'Hey,' Michael said. 'It was a *great* idea. One of the great twentieth-century ideas. I'd never have done it if I wasn't one hundred per cent certain that this time it's the real thing. Look at me. I have all the symptoms. My chemicals are going crazy. I'm off my food. I'm sweating to excess.'

Africa proffered a paper tissue. Michael mopped his brow.

'Something just clicked. I thought it was going to, and it did. My sexual horizons have just been really pushed back . . . it was really a smart idea to write that letter . . .'

Only a half-wit wouldn't have seen that he wasn't convinced. But I wasn't about to get involved. We're all alone in the world, after all. We all have to take the consequences for our actions. And Michael's effusiveness, given the apparent decline of matters between myself and Africa, was making me feel awkward. I asked what they'd been saying about the film, and listened to myself asking that question, which felt strange and exciting in my mouth.

'Well,' Michael said, suddenly clicking into intellectual mode, 'Marc's a very *creative* person. He has many *radical* ideas. His mind operates slightly beyond the normal boundaries, he says. And he feels that a good subject for a film would be –'

'Yes?'

'Well, *us*.'

'Us?'

'Yeah. Us. He feels we're symptomatic of the age.'

I hadn't previously been aware that I was symptomatic of the age.

'I guess he means . . . it's a very radical and challenging concept . . . very state of the art . . .' Michael's fishy eyes stared out and a vein appeared in his forehead. He didn't know what he was talking about. 'He said something about the pathetic attempts of the bourgeoisie to become marginal . . . about wanting to participate in dangerous events without facing their real-life consequences . . . I guess I don't know what he means . . . Thank you.' The arrival of the waiter was clearly a relief to him. 'He's very interested in you, Frank. I think he feels there's a bond between you guys. To do with your shared Mapplethorpe experience . . . you guys are incredible . . .'

I hoped I was right in assuming that Africa wouldn't know what a 'shared Mapplethorpe experience' was. I felt my cheeks flush at this mention of a 'bond': it didn't matter to me that practically the only thing I knew about Robert Mapplethorpe was how to spell his name. What mattered was the bond. The rest could be dealt with later. If I'd had any money, it would have been drinks all round.

'I have to go,' Michael said. 'I'm meeting a friend in Chueca. I just can't keep *still*. Hey. Africa. I'm sorry I called you a tropical plant, OK? I love your fan.'

He banged a couple of thousand of Marc's pesetas down on the table and loped off. I caught myself hoping I'd never see him again. Several seconds later, there was the sound of car horns as Michael narrowly avoided death.

'Are these people your *friends*?' Africa said.

'Sort of. That handsome one is a film director. I'm going to work for him, Africa. We're going to make a film, I think. It'd be like a dream come true for me.'

'Well, you know what they say . . .' This was something else Africa did. She'd say 'well, you know what they say' and then not tell you what they said.

'What?'

'Choose your dreams carefully, because they might come true.'

*

We walked back through Sol. Africa paused at the twenty-four-hour news stand to buy that week's edition of *Hola*. Not having bought a newspaper since Derek John Platt's death, I looked at the front page of *The Times*, trying to find something on it which bore upon my own life. Someone called John Smith had replaced Neil Kinnock as leader of the Labour Party, which didn't bear upon my own life at all. *Mubarak. Honecker*. Words, not people. I had absolutely no idea what was going on in the world, but it didn't matter. Not to know was confirmation of the completeness of my escape.

The man in front of us was holding a magazine on the cover of which there was a picture of a woman with a dog's penis in her mouth. The woman was trying to smile at the camera.

We sat down to rest on the border of the fountain. Even at 2 in the morning, the plaza was crowded: dazed tourists, freaks, lonely men and women, young lovers, drug addicts. I thought about the old house in Whately, now that Auntie Beryl no longer lived there. In my mind I wandered from room to room, up the stairs, tripping on the piece of carpet which overhung at the top. A dark, dead house. I put my arms around Africa's waist and squeezed.

'*La música humana*,' Africa murmured. She spoke Spanish without realizing it. Years, it had been, since she'd taken a *paseo* through the streets at this late hour. She was glad she'd done it, given herself the chance to take it all in again. Madrid had become a place for the young, she said. She'd heard somewhere that 40 per cent of the population was under twenty-five: it was no longer a city for the elderly, no longer somewhere you were able to grow old at your own slow pace. All this freedom. Those two men holding hands over there: they'd have been arrested under Franco. No doubt about it.

'They're women,' I said.

'They're men, *hijo. Sí* . . . Franco turned Spain into a prison. These people are lucky. They don't even remember him . . . they don't know how lucky they are . . .' A big party, it had been like,

133

after Franco had died: a great big national party. 'That would have been the best time for you to be here, Frank. *La movida*. Everybody went crazy. I was too old for it myself, but it was so nice, to see all these people, having so much *fun* . . . that will never happen again . . . it's like America now . . . I don't want to live in America.'

She was speaking to herself, not to me. It was as though she was taking stock of something. Settling accounts in her mind.

We got back to her flat at about 2.30, holding our breath against the stench of the rubbish truck as we squeezed past it. The man from the minimarket with the knotted leg was standing smoking at the corner of Mesón de Paredes with a group of gypsies dressed in black.

'Africa! You got half an hour?'

'No, I haven't. I'm tired, José . . .'

Something was gnawing at her which she wasn't telling me. I made coffee and wondered whether I shouldn't pop across to the *hostal* for a quick joint. It was getting so that I couldn't go for more than a few hours without one. When I saw Marc again, I'd ask him for some more money.

'I'd have liked it if you'd bought me those flowers from the gypsy woman,' Africa said abstractedly. 'I'd have liked that, Frank.' Her voice sounded dull, the weary, automatic reproach of someone who no longer cared much either way.

'Are you thinking about Paco?'

'I love him,' Africa said. 'I want to be close to him.'

When Africa said that, I realized that, finally, it was not age which separated us, nor language, nor nationality, nor even sex. It was that she knew the true weight of her words, and of the word 'love'. Those dark eyes, plump cheeks, bunched-high breasts, that complexion, the colour of milky coffee. All that self-fulness, humming through her veins.

Our relationship could never be more than a game, with each of us playing to different rules. The horror of this thought caused me briefly to enter a state of shock.

It was broken by the doorbell emitting its strange rattle. Africa slapped shut the copy of *Hola*, wormed her feet into her slippers and picked up her Ducados.

'I'm going to bed. Tell him I'm tired. Tell him I'm not working any more. I feel very tired tonight, Frank.'

At the door, words failed me.

'I was waiting for you across the road,' Brian said.

His grey hair was plastered across his forehead and he reeked of stale sweat. Tissue in one hand and a book in the other, he looked hopelessly crumpled and confused. 'I hope you don't mind . . .'

'Are you all right?' It was a ridiculous question. I held the door open for him. Brian stepped inside and crossed the room like something out of *Night of the Living Dead*. He flopped into Africa's chair on top of her magazine. The knot of his tie was half hidden under his collar, as though he'd wished to start his day with dignity but had lost it along the way. His fragility, always close to the surface, seemed to have become his entire self. If I'd touched him, there'd have been dust on my fingers.

'Brian, this isn't actually my flat . . .'

'Isn't it?'

'No. I live in a *hostal*.'

'Of course you do. Yes. In a *hostal*.'

From the bathroom came the sound of running taps, of Africa knocking something off a shelf and cursing.

'I can't believe she's gone,' he muttered.

'Who, Brian?'

'Carmen. I never expected things to feel so . . . so *hollow* afterwards.' He blew his nose on a lump of tissue which had clearly already been used several times, and things became rather messy. 'It was all right for about a month, but . . . oh dear, dear. This has not been a particularly good summer for me, so far.'

'Do you want some coffee?' I didn't know why Brian had come. I couldn't see what the death of his wife had to do with me. I hoped that he'd have his coffee and then go. Picking up the book he'd let drop to the floor, I saw it was an old, dog-eared copy of the Good News Bible.

'There's no school to go back to,' he said. 'I needed the school more than I imagined.'

'I thought you wanted to go back to St Ives. This is your chance.'

Suddenly Brian became oddly energetic. He stood up and stumbled, righting himself against the dresser.

'You're still young, Frank,' he said loudly, smearing a stray lock of hair back into position. 'Perhaps you don't realize that it's your dreams which sustain you. But when you're forced into *acting* on them . . . well, it's rather frightening.' He collapsed back down on to *Hola* as though he'd suffered an internal power shortage. 'I can't go back now. An – an old man like me. I *thought* that was what I wanted – yes, I did – but now I'm not so sure . . . my life's here, now. I don't have the money, anyhow. All those hospital bills . . . so much time and trouble . . .' His eyes rested on mine for the first time since he'd come in.

'I've organized my life rather badly, is what it amounts to, Frank.'

I watched him and I felt afraid.

I was picturing myself in twenty years' time. I'd realized that there was very little to prevent me from sliding down that slope at the bottom of which Brian, lost and exhausted, was now lying. It was important that I act soon, that I take control of my life and *do* something.

This was exactly what Auntie Beryl would have wanted me to think. I recalled Marc's words: 'Why does real life have to begin?' They swelled me a little.

'I took the Albion Academy job,' Brian said, 'when things were difficult. It was the sort of job where I could devote a lot of time to Carmen. Carmen was my real job. Love was my real job, Frank.' He shook his head slowly, and for one awful moment I thought he was going to give way to tears. 'Oh, Good Lord,' he muttered. 'Good Lord, just listen to me.'

'Excuse me a moment.'

I went through into Africa's bedroom and closed the door softly behind me. She was naked, apart from her slippers, sitting on the edge of the bed, wearing her Sony Walkman and muttering the sentence 'one lump or two'? Her Ducados had burned down in the ashtray. Wearily she removed the headphones and looked at me. Something about her, just at that moment, made me think she was wondering why she'd ever got involved with me. That she simply wanted to be alone.

I couldn't stand all this. Every moment loaded with significance. Watching every single moment, wondering about it, testing it for its implications. In the weariness of Africa's gaze, I found a reflection of the weariness I felt at being myself.

'We have a visitor.'

'Who?'

'Brian. I told you about Brian.'

'The one whose wife died? What's he doing here? How did he get in?'

'He was waiting. He must have seen us coming in.'

'How is he?'

'Miserable.'

Africa sighed deeply. Then, with a supreme effort, she gathered herself and stood.

I blinked. Standing before me again was the Hola Woman, no longer a weary, overweight person in late middle age, but a woman who took pride in the vast succour contained in her naked body, who knew her vocation, which was to give pleasure, and who held absolutely no doubts with regard to her effectiveness.

'Just give me five minutes,' the Hola Woman said, 'and then tell him to come in here.'

'What?'

She went over to the mirror above the small washbasin in the corner and leaned towards it, pulling her skin this way and that.

137

'*Oh Dios* . . . look at me . . . Now. Five minutes, and tell him to come in here.'

'Ask Brian to come in here? What for?'

'For the same reason you come in here,' Africa said. '*Venga.*'

Brian was standing in the middle of the living room, all at sea.

'I think you'd better go, Brian,' I said. 'I have a lot to do tomorrow. I'll call you.'

He turned slowly to face me.

'I shouldn't imagine you will.' I went to open the door for him and he moved towards it unsteadily. 'Perhaps you'd be better not to. Thank you for the coffee.'

Then Africa was at her bedroom door. She uttered something rapidly in Castilian which I didn't catch, but her voice sounded like fingers down a blackboard.

'Hola,' she said.

'Hola,' Brian said.

Africa disappeared into her room. Brian coughed and then followed her, and I was a ghost.

Suddenly feeling extremely tired myself, I poured a glass of gin and waited. Dreadful thoughts tried to enter my mind, but I just about succeeded in holding them at bay.

Occasionally there came the sound of a nose being blown. After a couple of glasses of gin I put my ear to the door to listen, but drew back, realizing that I wouldn't like what I heard. If they weren't making love, if Brian's scrawny white buttocks weren't jerking back and forth in a grotesque parody of sexual inter-course, then they'd be talking, conversing in flawless Spanish, truly communicating, revealing, understanding.

I picked up Brian's Bible from where it lay on the floor, hoping to open it at random and find some great, redeeming insight into existence of the sort which Brian had been clinging to, evidently without success. Instead I found that about a third of the pages had been ripped out. It was hard to imagine Brian in the grip of such passionate frenzy.

I'd known it would come to this. It always did. The inevitable result of love is loneliness. The worst thing about it was that it hadn't been me who'd decided. My relationship with Africa had lasted seven weeks. The night we'd first made love had signalled the end of my relationship with the Hola Woman, which had lasted three months.

I could never have anything to do with Africa again. That much was obvious. There was no point in fighting it. No point in risking pain. I certainly didn't intend to act out the whole sorry charade of pleading with her to come back to me. I hadn't come to Spain to have to do that. The fantasy was over, and that was how it had to be. I gloried in my isolation. Fuck them all.

I drained my glass and quietly slipped away. All my anchors had gone. No family, no job, the people I knew with other things on their minds: no Africa, no Hola Woman. I was as good as dead, I reflected morbidly. There was a kind of relief in that.

THIRTEEN

'This is 445 2423,' Marc's voice said. Certain chemicals inside me reacted with one another to create a sensation which combined longing and fear. He existed more strongly in my fantasies than in my reality. 'I am somewhere else at this time. Leave me a message.'

'It's Frank,' I said. I enjoyed speaking into these things. They didn't answer back: they absorbed what you said about yourself as willingly as Michael and Chantelle did. 'Please ring me back as soon as you can. It's about the film.'

I replaced the receiver. It had gone pretty well, I thought. Then I realized that I was calling from a telephone box. I didn't want to leave the number of the *hostal*: people who had worked with Robert Mapplethorpe didn't live in *hostales*. They lived in luxury apartments, probably. Full of matt-black items which operated at the touch of a button. On Fifth Avenue or something.

'It's Frank again. I think I just asked you to ring me. I'm afraid I'm going to be away for a few days. On the Lower East Side. I'll ring you when I get back. Over and out.'

I wasn't sure why I'd said 'over and out'. I wished I hadn't.

I continued my Letter Never Sent to Auntie Beryl. She was dead. But I had to continue with it anyway.

You never understood my decision to see a psychiatrist. Psychiatrists were odd, new-fangled things, like answering machines. They weren't to be trusted. Perhaps it was hard for you to accept that the child you'd brought up was not the healthiest-minded creature ever to walk the earth. The tantrums, the escape attempts, the biannual dalliances with suicide were, in your eyes, just a part of growing up, as natural as wetting the bed or German measles. I tried to talk to you about it, to explain to you what a narcissistic personality disorder actually was, but it was all a foreign language to you.

It was good, having Dr Minshull to listen to me. I used to long for those Wednesday afternoons when she and I would sit drinking coffee in her small white room with the Paul Klee painting on the wall, looking into her eyes and knowing that she understood everything, even that I didn't particularly want to be cured, that I liked being different. That there had to be a part of myself to which I could retire, safe in the knowledge that nobody would understand me there. I have you to thank for that. After all, it was you who sent me into those dark areas, who taught me the joys of escape. Dr Minshull could never have done me any good, of course. I've heard of people leaving their doctor with a cheery 'I hope I don't see you again!' With me it was rather different. I wanted to MARRY Dr Minshull. It crippled me when she died.

Another reason I have come here is that I feel I should have the opportunity of a childhood. As you apparently failed to realize, childhood should not be a time of isolation and worry, of psychiatrists and a complete lack of freedom. It should be a time of freedom of thought and action, the child coming to his own decisions about the world, taking risks, getting hurt sometimes, but at least learning from the experience. It should be a time of love and adventure. You'd have been pleased to hear that I did find love, for a short time, and it's definitely true what they say about it. It was very nice. But it's over now. Did you ever feel love, Auntie Beryl? Did passion ever make you forget who you were?

The adventure part is about to begin. I am going to make a film with a friend. I reckon I know a bit about it, after all that time at VideoWorld. One day, perhaps, you'd have been able to see it at the Odeon. You'd have been proud of me. You'd have shed a tear as the name of Frank Bowden, Great-Uncle Vernon's famous 'dead loss', rolled across the screen.

But there was no one to read it to.

Half awake, half asleep, constantly under the influence of marijuana, I dreamed strange dreams.

I dreamed repeatedly of a beach in Catalunya, of a man called Derek John Platt having his throat cut by a man called Marc: the one an emotional mess, a disaster case who was better off dead, struggling hopelessly against the demands his past imposed on him, the other a charismatic individual, perpetually frustrated at the banality of the everyday, who lived in a state of disregard for convention, whose very existence made others twitch in discomfort, who possessed sufficient confidence to freely confess criminal involvement, cool and elegant to the depths of his soul, soaring above the human mess. A success in life who ought, by every traditional standard, to have been a failure.

The one my past, the other my future. Depending on my mood throughout that limbo period, I identified first with the one and then with the other, without ever fully becoming either. I was playing the identity game.

August was the month when anyone with money left Madrid to go to the coast or to their chalets in the relative cool of the *sierra*, leaving the city in the possession of the dispossessed. For eleven days I lay on my moist sheets, sweating, disturbed by the flies of midsummer and the fleas which had found a home in my mattress, causing bumps to come up on my arms and legs. I cautiously approached Sr López one afternoon about a new mattress, but he just laughed. He'd get his rent, I told him: I was going to start making a film soon. All being well, I'd be able to pay him six months in advance.

'Hollywood?' Sr López said. 'Greta Garbo?'

'Possibly,' I said. 'You never know.'

'Are you still seeing Africa?'

'No.'

'You know I only let you stay on here because Africa told me to?'

That couldn't be true. He had to be lying.

I was tired of people, tired of the hypocrisy they required of you. If I'd invented my past, I decided, it was only because I'd been the only one brave enough to admit my dissatisfaction and bring it to my surface.

I lay there exhausted with coughing, dull but heroic, disturbed. The noise of the others in the *hostal* as they went about their business. Arguments on the landing, keys clattering in locks, mumbled curses: had nothing altered in their lives, too? The seven-foot German woman who had come to stay with her bullfighting boyfriend. The transvestite Jehovah's Witness. The Frenchman who appeared absolutely normal in every respect.

Dust made a home on my surfaces. The rubbish reeked: white objects turned yellow. Cockroaches scattered whenever I kicked the pipe under the washbasin.

Africa was only twenty yards away, across the street. How could she have *done* this to me, I thought, forgetting that she hadn't in fact done anything to me, that it was all in my own head. But the fantasy had been destroyed. It was repellent to me that she might have brought a man with crows visible on his nose and urine stains on his trousers to orgasm. It was all too real, too squalid, too Whately for words. One day I heard Sr López shouting through the door that she had come to see me. If she wants to come again, I thought, she can, and I might see her. And apparently she did, and I didn't.

I'd bought a large quantity of Valium. I observed it through half-shut eyelids, envisaging horrendous scenes of guilt and retribution. Frank Bowden, the last glorious international love victim. The wailing of Africa, the tears coursing down her plump cheeks.

I did not dream of beautiful things, no. But at least I dreamed.

Eleven days is a long time. I became used to the rhythms of a night-time in a narrow street in a *barrio popular* of Madrid: the half-hour coughing fits of the old man who lived two doors down, something I'd spoken of with her; the *basureros*, the dustbin men in their rowdy truck; the street-cleaners, one hour later, with the tap-tap of their hydrant key and their gushing hoses; the woman who, each morning at 6, wandered down the street alone, kicking an empty, loud, soft drinks can and singing about the pain in her heart; the voice from the radio across the street, telling of the parents who had abandoned their fifteen-month-old child in a rubbish skip. One day I thought I heard a report about a gypsy being arrested for a series of murders on southern European beaches, but I was a bit out of it that day and afterwards couldn't remember if I'd dreamt it. Later, I thought I heard another presenter saying ' . . . a man called Marc has been arrested for the murder of the English tourist Derek John Platt'.

I felt hopeless when I heard that. If it were true, he wouldn't be there when I rang.

'This is 445 2423,' Marc said. 'I am somewhere else at this time. Leave me a message.'

Although it wasn't actually him, it was a relief to hear his voice. Later that day I stole a handful of 5-peseta pieces from Sr López's drawer, went to the telephone and dialled Marc's number eleven times, so that I'd be able at least to hear him.

There was hammering on the door of the *hostal* one afternoon. I lay with my eyes closed, waiting for whoever it was to leave.

'Ach, come on, sunshine. Now we've not come all this way just so we can go away again.'

Reluctantly, sleepily, I let them in, and then returned to bed.

Donald was unusually smartly dressed, in a pair of beige needlecord slacks, a short-sleeved shirt and, incredibly, a tie. It was reassuring to see that his shirt-tails were hanging out at the back.

'We've brought you some *pasteles*,' Pilar said. 'You look as though your blood sugar's low.'

'Been overdoing it, sunshine? A spot too much nightlife?' He looked into the wardrobe. 'By God, you've been taking lessons in domestic management from your Uncle Donald. What, might I ask, is' – he peered into the foil carton and recoiled – 'is a prehistoric chop suey doing in your wardrobe? Eh?'

'I probably wasn't hungry,' I said. My private territory had been invaded. If Donald had believed for a second that I'd worked in New York, then that chop suey had surely exploded his illusion.

'I don't think he has been overdoing it,' Pilar said. 'He looks puffy-faced. It's very . . . *stuffy* in here.' What she meant was that it stank to high heaven. She went to the balcony windows and threw them open. Light which had been banished now rushed eagerly in, producing temporary blindness.

'It's still summer out there,' Donald said.

'Have you been ill, Frank?'

'I've just been a bit down. You know.'

'Ain't no cure for the summertime blues. You've got to get out there and *live*, boy.'

Oh, shut up, I thought. I've tried that. I tried to imagine what Marc would have said to Donald. 'You sound like an advertisment for Pepsi Cola,' he'd have said. Some such thing. '*Get out there and live*.'

'I *mean* it,' Donald said, though I hadn't said anything. 'Fifteen years ago, people didn't lie in bed all day when the sun was shining. They were out drinking. And fucking.'

'So what you're telling Frank to do,' Pilar said, 'is go out and become an alcoholic with AIDS.' I expected Donald to fight back at that, but he didn't: he looked at her almost shyly, and smiled.

'The world,' he said, 'needs more people like me. Anyway, the future beckons.'

Looking at Pilar for support, as though he himself didn't fully believe the words coming from his mouth, Donald said that he

145

was going to get serious. He'd managed, incredibly he thought, to obtain a hefty bank loan – at a silly rate of interest – and this time he was going to do it properly. To show how serious he was, he'd bought three new Akai cassette recorders and three video systems. He'd bitten the bullet, been phoning round companies, speaking to Spanish fucking yuppies, trying to drum up business.

'"This is Donald Brightwell of the European Languages Academy,"' he impersonated himself. '"Since you're one of the major companies in your sector, I was wondering if you might be interested in having your staff take English classes at rates tailored exclusively to the current global recession . . ."'

It wasn't a very good impersonation. There was a smug smile on Pilar's lips which told me that it was she who'd been responsible for Donald's metamorphosis.

'I tell you, sunshine, it's hard for a man of my advanced years. But let's face it. The sixties are over, the nineties are here. God knows what happened to the twenty years in between. If I may be permitted a dickish phrase, technology has replaced dreams.'

'I'd never have thought it of you.'

'I'd never have thought it of myself. Donald Brightwell, hard-drinking emotional disaster, victim of heart attack, becomes tee-total businessman? My ma'd have been proud of me.'

'How are you going to get up in the mornings?'

'I'll make him,' Pilar said.

'Don't you feel you're compromising yourself?'

'Shut up, Frank,' Donald said. 'You'll put me off. Of course I feel I'm compromising myself. But I'm forced to realize that's what life's all about. So we'll be moving out of Le Shithole. Found a nice little place up by the Torre Picasso. Costs a small fortune, but it'll be jobs for the boys once we get moving. New rules, of course. More quality control . . .'

It was alien to someone like Donald to do what I was doing, to retire from the world temporarily, unless the reason be a terrible hangover. Although he might look at me and suspect that something wasn't right, he'd never be able to understand. Whenever

Donald needed to get lost, he got lost in action. It might only be the action of raising his right elbow, but it was action all the same.

'So it just goes to show,' Pilar said. 'You can teach an old dog new tricks.'

'Nice use of idiom there, from Pilar. So what's the news? Existential crisis à la Jean-Paul Sartre in a tangy sauce?'

'That's about it.'

'Do you have friends, sunshine? Have a cake.'

'A few. No, thanks.'

'How's that woman you're seeing? Chantelle mentioned a woman.' Donald picked up the Valium, looked at it and put it down again.

'She's fine.'

'Mm-hm. So you're all right, then.'

'I'll live.'

I'd become rather good at this, telling curt lies to protect my depths.

'How's the Psychosamaritan? What's his name again?' Donald asked Pilar as she put a cream cake into her mouth and rotated her jaw like a ruminating cow.

'Marc,' she said. 'But his real name's probably Gordon Smith or something.' A bit of cream was stuck to one of the hairs under her nose.

'I don't know.'

'I'm pleased to hear it.'

I wished that Donald and Pilar would go. Why didn't they just go?

'We saw Chantelle the other day,' Pilar said. 'She was all nervous and strange. She's seeing a lot of this Marc. We think she might be taking drugs.'

'Correction. We *know* she's taking drugs.'

'She had black marks under her eyes. You know. You'd say something to her and she'd take five minutes to answer. She was like somebody I met who'd just been saved from the Moonies.'

147

'When I saw her,' I said, 'she said she was happy. She said she's found what she's looking for.'

'She told us that, too. Saying she's finally realized she has a soul, or some such nonsense.'

'The trouble with Chantelle,' Donald said, standing and tucking in his shirt-tails, 'is that she doesn't *know* what it is she's looking for. She's just dissatisfied, and then anything that comes along that looks a bit exciting, she'll throw herself into it body and soul and start thinking that that's what she was looking for all the time. She's not the first, she won't be the last. I tried giving her the Uncle Donald warning routine, but she wasn't interested.'

'She told Donald to fuck off,' Pilar said, and looked at him with affection.

'I was just trying to have a word with her. You know. I told her she was a fucking idiot, and she told me to fuck off. She asked after you.'

'Well, not so much asked after you. She said you were weird.'

'Anyway, sunshine.' Donald correctly sensed that this was the right moment for a subject change. He clapped his hands and rubbed them together briskly. 'We bring good tidings. It's going to be me and the missus again.'

'She said *I* was weird? *She's* weird. When you see her you can tell her that, contrary to present appearances, things are fine with me. I've never been so happy in my life.'

'Frank, Donald and me are getting married.'

'When you see her, you can just tell her that.'

'*My* theory,' Donald said, 'is that your man on the beach pushed her into it. Intimations of mortality and all that.'

'Pushed who into what?'

'Pilar. Into marrying me. You'd have to be off your head to do it unprovoked. I'm bound to look for ulterior motives. Hey, sunshine. Are you quite sure you're happy?'

'Aren't you going to congratulate us, Frank?'

'I'm fine. Just tell Chantelle that when you see her, OK? I've made my decisions. I'm happy.'

I was aware that I probably seemed to be raving. I stared at the small crucifix on the opposite wall, not wishing to make eye contact with them. 'Congratulations,' I said. 'You've done it three times before and failed, and now you're trying again. That sounds like an excellent idea.'

'Hey, sunshine. What's got into you?'

It was heartless of them to come in here, just after I'd broken with Africa, and tell me they were getting married. Then I remembered that they didn't know I'd broken with Africa, and then I remembered further that perhaps I hadn't, in fact, broken with her. It was all becoming too complex. I didn't want to carry on like this, never quite knowing where reality stopped and appearance began.

'I *told* you we shouldn't have told him,' Pilar was saying, apparently believing that I was too far gone to know when I was being talked about.

Why didn't they just *go*?

'All right,' Donald said. 'We'll go. Jesus.'

I hadn't been aware that I'd spoken.

FOURTEEN

I pictured him sitting in a black director's chair, his leg over the arm, lighting a cigarette. The blue smoke curls. Marc watches it until it vanishes from sight. He lifts the receiver to speak to an underworld acquaintance. Issuing instructions which he knows will be obeyed, because it simply isn't *worth* disobeying an instruction from Marc. He runs a forefinger around the rim of the legendary tattooed watch. He's thinking dangerous thoughts.

Chantelle's hard, golden body, bucking underneath him last night. Her screams of pleasure as Marc does things to her, tender, savage things that she's never had done to her before. They draw her towards him, exciting her while also making her afraid of these new regions of sensation to which she's being exposed. Afterwards, while she weeps, Marc lights another cigarette and absently strokes his pony tail. He watches her with disdain. He is bored by her, disgusted by himself, by his animal descent into the human mess . . .

What an idiot I'd been, to tell him I was going to New York. It meant I couldn't now leave him a message without sounding confused and uncertain, which I didn't want to seem. I wanted to impress him.

But it was surely only a matter of time before he'd be there in person. Talking to me. Listening to me, when I spoke.

Three days later, I returned from the toilet to find Michael waiting for me on my bed. I'd forgotten to lock the door, or he'd never have got in.

'Hey, Frank. You OK? You look kind of wasted. Ex*tremely*

sexy. Allowing your true sexy self to rise to the surface. Those hollow cheeks . . .'

The good health he radiated constituted an insult to my own condition. Apart from Michael, only a chimpanzee on heat could possibly have found me sexy.

'What you just did, Michael,' I said, 'was very interesting. You saw me, and the word "wasted" came into your head. In your head, the words "wasted" and "sexy" are associated. So by a false leap of logic you called me sexy, whereas the sexy thing is in fact the word "wasted". If the word "emaciated" had come into your mind, you'd have said something else entirely. Pitied me, perhaps.'

'That's great,' Michael said. 'That's very intellectual.'

'Do you understand it?'

'No.'

'And am I sexy?'

'. . . I guess not.'

'Thank you.'

I felt tired after that. I asked Michael if he'd mind if I got into my own bed, which he was sitting on. His scalp glowed; he wore luridly coloured Bermuda shorts, and white ankle-socks which highlighted the tan on his legs. He lifted his shorts up over his buttocks to show me his tan-line, a demonstration I could have done without.

But all of this was performed in a forced, artificial way, as though there were a new, serious Michael waiting to come to the surface which the old Michael didn't feel comfortable with.

'Have you come to talk about Marc's film? Because I'll be honest with you. That's the only thing I want to talk about at the moment.'

'No. No, I've come to have a talk. An exchange of meaningful ideas.' He offered me a stick of chewing gum, which I declined. 'Is it OK if I tell you things, Frank?'

Rubbing his scalp, his left foot bobbing up and down, Michael began by telling me that his life in Madrid, and possibly the whole of his life since leaving St Paul, Massachusetts, had been an elaborate lie. ' "A tale told by an idiot", I guess you could say. Except seriously lacking in sound and fury.'

'You were happy the last time I saw you. You were ecstatic.'

'Yeah. Well, I thought I was. But I wasn't.' He observed me for a second, his brow furrowed, his cheeks puffed out. Then he reached into his shoulder-bag and took out a folder. 'I think what it has to do with,' he said, 'is . . . is style over substance. From not living from inside your own life, kind of. Can you appreciate that, Frank?'

'No.'

'Yes, you can.' He leaned forwards and, through the sheets, placed his hand on my thigh. 'I *know* you can. I have faith in your ability to understand. I look at you, and I think about what you've been through, and I *know*.'

They came to me, these people, to confess, to reveal themselves. Brian to tell me about the death of his wife, Chantelle to tell me about her boredom. And now Michael. But it was useless to confess to me. The me they felt they were confessing to had never existed, and didn't exist now.

I took some marijuana and cigarette papers from my bedside drawer and busied myself in rolling a joint.

'Listen,' I said. 'Before you start. Why do you want to tell me the things you're going to tell me?'

'You're in kind of a weird mood today, Frank.'

'Never mind that. Why?'

'I don't know . . . I guess it's because you're like . . . detached. Yeah. You give the appearance of being detached. A survivor. Like you've been through what I'm going through, and come out on the other side. You've learned the skill of how to be cold. You and Marc are the only guys I know like that . . . Any way . . . this is the very latest from *Michael's Book of Influences* . . .'

He read for about twenty minutes. What he read told the story of a young and lonely American called Martin who falls in love with an English pen pal, Roy. At the age of seventeen, Martin

152

obtains a scholarship to go to England to study 'Math'. When he arrives, romance ensues. Soon, however, Roy tests HIV positive and then gets AIDS. 'Just like Robert Mapplethorpe,' Michael said, looking at me with a pleading expression. Martin feels guilty at this turn of events, since it was he who'd suggested that Roy have his blood tested. There are harrowing scenes involving drugs called AZT and ditiocarb; a poem; a deathbed scene in hospital among transparent tubes and pieces of moulded plastic with complicated names.

After Roy's death, Martin travels to Berlin, Paris and Rome, wandering Europe in search of someone to replace Roy, to replace the 'unsullied perfection' of their few months together. Martin is essentially a timid person, uncomfortable with the urgent, desperate air of sweat-shops. What he really wants is love. A stable relationship. His desperation slowly spreads through him like a cancer, feeding off his inner emptiness.

In Madrid he meets a man called Marc. Marc compels Martin to write a letter to his ultra-conservative parents, confessing that he is gay. This is the most important decision Martin has ever taken, since by writing the letter he is throwing away the chance of seeing his family again. Things are fine with Marc, but not as perfect as Martin would have wished them: matters became confused and messy at this point, and there were lots of big, abstract words such as 'pain', 'guilt' and 'identity', rather like those tedious Woody Allen films I'd sat through at VideoWorld.

I lost interest. I was fed up of listening to stories like this one. I'd sat and listened to Africa's stories, and she'd listened to mine, and look at what the end result of that had been. Nothing.

I was snapped back to attention by Michael's voice reading out what turned out to be the final sentence at several decibels above the norm. 'Martin didn't know what to do. But he did know that he had to talk to someone. That he had to find a *friend*.'

Michael slapped shut his folder and looked at me. He was glowing beneath his tan. He sniffed.

'Well,' I said. I left a pause so that he'd think I was reflecting on what he'd read. 'It's different from your normal stuff, Michael. There's a nice air of desperation about that final line . . . are you OK?'

'Yeah, yeah . . . it's just these contact lenses . . .' He twisted a rubber band around his fingers. 'Listen,' he said. 'You know that "Martin" here is not a character in a story.'

The rubber band broke. It flew across the room.

'I'm just asking you to understand, Frank. I wish I could just have *told* you this. Like a normal person. But I had to write it down. I just couldn't have told it you without writing it down first. "Martin" is me.' He was mumbling, continuing to sniff. 'I have to tell you that it wasn't easy coming here to tell you this, Frank. None of us like to open up, because we're afraid we'll get hurt . . . we've all come to Spain for a *reason* . . .'

'What do you mean, "Martin is me"?' I liked the sound of it. I imagined myself going up to someone at a party. 'Hi. Frank is me.' Defining yourself as though you were a character, rather than a person. *Humphrey Bogart is Sam Spade. Frank is me*.

'You're performing,' I said. 'You're acting out a tragic role because you think it lends depth and interest to your personality.'

'What?'

'Listen carefully.' I drew on the joint and exhaled. I waited, watching the smoke until it had disappeared. 'You're performing. You're acting out a tragic role because you think it lends depth and interest to your personality. You're escaping from yourself. You're wearing emotional fancy dress, Michael. We all do it.'

Days of solitude had made me articulate.

'Frank, that is *weird*. Kind of graceful, but definitely weird.' Michael stood and struck a bare corner of my mattress with his folder, causing a puff of dust to rise from it. 'No. No. Martin is me, and all the things that happen to Martin in the story happened to me. I *am* Martin, Frank. Like, I can't be much more explicit than that.'

154

'Oh, come on. That isn't you.'

'What isn't me?'

'That story. You're not lonely, your sex life is great, you don't want a steady relationship, you're not tormented.'

'Great one, Frank. You just described my total opposite.'

'No. You came to Madrid in search of pleasure, remember? "A tour of all the pink monuments of Europe"? You're just going through one of your phases.'

Michael stared at me. Wide-eyed and frankly ugly.

'You really believe I'm happy, don't you? You really believe that I go to these sweat-shop places and screw ten guys in ten minutes, don't you? That I'm not interested in being loved? So what if I told you that all of that was a lie? That I'm young, and that I want people to have a certain impression of me? A certain exotic impression which has zero connection with the truth? And what would you say if I came to you today to tell you this because I thought you'd understand, and it's very brave of me to have done this, Frank . . . I never went to Tangiers. There *is* no one-eyed camel driver. I just hung out in the park. In the gym.'

He was crying now. His head was down. The lengths some people will go to. He rubbed his forehead with circular motions of the fingertips.

'I'm sorry,' he said after a while, and blew his nose on a corner of my bedsheet. 'I guess the stories I made up were just more attractive to you. I guess that style is more important than substance after all. I guess that how you're seen matters more than what you are. Andy Warhol was right.'

'Andy Warhol?'

'Yeah. "I want to live my life like it was a movie"?'

Michael stood and went over to the balcony windows, opened them and went outside. He put his back to the street, leaned on the rail, folded his arms and looked at me.

'So why don't you want to understand me, Frank?'

I had nothing to say to that, and he knew it. I felt thoroughly exhausted. I could feel Michael silently urging me to confess my own secrets to him.

But I was trying to build myself a new life, and a single word spoken from my heart at this point would have brought that fragile edifice tumbling down.

'You slept with Derek John Platt the night before he died, didn't you?' I said. 'So that just shows how . . . *lightly* you take things.'

'What?' Michael unfolded his arms and stepped forward into the room. 'Who told you that? Chantelle?'

'Yes.'

'OK. OK. Yes, I did sleep with him. He had AIDS, and I thought about Roy, and he needed comfort, and I had some condoms with me, and I slept with him. I needed it just as much as he did, Frank. There was nothing noble in it. I guess he looked a little like Roy . . . lots of guys do.'

He dropped his gaze. He unclipped his crucifix earring and fiddled with it, talking to the floor.

'When we found him, you have no *idea* how I felt. I haven't stopped thinking about it and that's why I came here today. To tell you that.' He stared at me, entirely uncomprehending. 'Jesus. I guess those years in New York really screwed you up.'

'Yes,' I said. 'I guess they did.' He was looking at me again. I held his gaze. I had to hold his gaze. We stayed like that for about ten seconds. For about ten thousand years.

Finally Michael rediscovered his old smile and put it on. He slung his bag over one shoulder, sang a couple of bars from some disco song, and went to check his appearance in the mirror over the washbasin, brushing imaginary hair from his collar. He bent down to touch his toes a couple of times. When he was at the door, I called his name.

'Have you seen Marc?' I asked him.

'He's out of town,' Michael said quickly.

'You're lying.'

'No. Marc's out of town.'

156

'What about the film? The film about us?'

'I don't know about the film. There are more important things in my mind than the film. My life, for example. See you around, Frank. Thanks for being so – *human*.'

He closed the door behind him. I sank back into the pillow and thought: there are more important things than my life. The film, for example.

I stared into the bathroom mirror for a long time. The facts were these: my complexion was white, blotched and shiny, and grazed where I had scratched myself while sleeping. My eyes were red, my teeth golden brown, apart from the false tooth, which had gone missing somewhere, leaving a yokelish gap. Liquid dribbled from my right ear.

On looking over my letter to Auntie Beryl, I found that it spoke of a different person from myself, a historical figure. This was Hemingitis: this was the identity game, and I was a serious player. I was turning into Derek John Platt.

'This is 445 2423. I am not here at the moment. Please leave a message.'

'I don't know what's happening to me,' I said. 'I just don't. Please help.'

One night I awoke at about 3 o'clock and retched. I was happy that nothing came out, since I wouldn't have to clean it up. I felt very hungry and was uncertain about when I'd last eaten. I opened my cupboard to find it occupied by several species of insect.

They crawled over blue bread, over the packet of Valium which Pilar must have hidden in there. Some of the insects were ants, some were slightly bigger than ants, and others were smaller, but had wings. They didn't really taste of anything.

There were bars open late in Lavapiés, along the Calle Argumosa. Whether they stayed open this late, I didn't know. I got it into my head that I was literally starving, and wondered whether I shouldn't root around in a rubbish bin or two. Suck the cardboard from a Tele-Pizza. Smash an old bottle of ketchup and lick the glass.

I had no money. I felt myself to be in a pure, reduced state. Everything I saw as I walked uncertainly down the Calle Calvario possessed an unusual clarity – the yellowness of the street-lamps, the blue stencilled graffiti for the Urban Evangelistic Mission, the rows of dented cars parked nose to tail, the lonely motor-bike wheel chained to a bollard.

'Hashish?' a voice crackled at me from the shadows. '*Chocolate*?'

'Give me some. *Como amigo.*'

'Ha, ha.' It wasn't a laugh: he said 'ha, ha'.

I walked the length of Argumosa almost as far as Atocha, and thought about continuing as far as the station, where I'd be able to board a train and leave. But I was feeling weaker with every step, and sat down on the ground, my back against a shut-up newspaper kiosk.

I tried to stop a young couple walking past to ask them for money, but they didn't hear me. They paused and embraced one another, trapping me against the kiosk until they'd finished, forcing me to watch them. The girl's thigh slid up and down the boy's leg. They kissed with eyes closed, as though they couldn't bear to see the happiness they were feeling.

After they'd gone, I stopped an old man shuffling along behind a dog and asked him for a *duro*. He started talking, with frightening energy for someone so small, about how my type was ruining the area. If I wanted to take drugs and beg, the man wondered, why didn't I go back to Morocco or wherever the hell I was from, and do it there instead?

The next people I met were an elegantly dressed gypsy couple carrying a mattress on their heads. They gave me exactly what I asked for: one *duro*, 5 pesetas.

If I continued at this rate, I'd have enough for a cup of coffee by 7 o'clock. It was strange that everyone assumed I was a drug addict.

I slept.

'*Hombre, pareces jodido.*'

'Yes . . . yes, I am a bit fucked, actually . . .'

I opened my eyes to see the podgy, greasy-haired girl who waylaid people for money by the automatic cashiers of the *barrio*. She wore faded, grimy dungarees and had to keep pushing her hair back out of her eyes. It it hadn't been for her little girl's voice, I'd never have given her a single peseta, but the voice had charmed me and I'd probably shelled out several pounds to her during my time in Madrid. 'You know all the money I've given you?' I said. 'Could I have some of it back?'

She smiled and leaned over, offering me her hand.

'Come with me,' she said. '*Venga.*'

'I want to sleep.'

'Later. Come with me.'

I slowly followed her on to the steps in front of the theatre on the other side of the square. I found that I was unable to read which play was showing.

'Your voice,' I said. 'It's changed.'

'That's my working voice.'

'Who's this?' a scrawny boy said. He couldn't have been more than twelve, but he looked old. His face was heavily bruised and he wore a thick denim jacket with a sheepskin collar, as though he didn't know it was summer.

'Shut up and give him some peanuts,' the fat girl said. 'This is my brother. They're honey-roasted.'

The brother's eyes darted. A baby monkey, afraid of capture.

'I'm not your fucking brother. *Joder*. Why you keep saying I'm your fucking brother?'

A tall, skinny gypsy approached us, wearing a baggy flowered top and a pair of red hot-pants. A wicker basket swung from her right shoulder. She might have been pretty, once. Now, there were pits in her skin and her voice was cracked and slurred.

All these new people. I stretched myself out and closed my eyes.

'I just sold some *caballo*.'

'*Sí*?'

'*Un macarra de Alcorcón, sabes*? Now I'm going home.'

'Encarna, why don't you take this guy with you?' the podgy girl said. This would once have provoked a panic attack, but now I lay there, indifferent. 'This is my sister,' she explained. 'Encarna.'

Encarna looked me up and down with almond eyes, swaying.

'*No te jodes*,' she said. 'I do have my standards.'

Revived somewhat by the Maybe-brother's honey-roasted peanuts, I looked about me. All around the edge of the square, leaning against lamp-posts, sitting splay-legged on car bonnets, small groups of extremely thin people disconsolately sat.

The Maybe-brother and Encarna grumbled together about something and then went away.

'I'm cold,' the podgy girl said. 'Why don't you hug me?'

'How can you be cold?'

'I'm cold. What's your name?'

'Frank is me,' I said. 'Oh, Jesus.'

'Relax, Frankie.'

'I can't. I can't. I don't belong here.' There was so much I wanted to say to her, so little I could. 'I must go.'

'Where to?'

'I don't know . . .'

She held out a small square of silver foil, the same foil that Auntie Beryl had used for cooking chickens in. Why I was thinking of that just then, I didn't know.

'You'll feel better after this. *Alegría en polvo*.' Powdered joy.

'Haven't you got any marijuana?'

'This is better for you now.'

I took it and was astonished to see that my fingers were trembling, and my hands also, and probably my whole body.

'Take away the pain, Frankie. Hug me.'

She put her arm around my shoulder and drew me in to rest against her, softly repeating the word 'relax'. The shoulder strap of her dungarees dug into my cheek. She had a weak, bitter odour, quite unlike that of Africa.

'What's your name?' I asked her.

'Winter will be here soon,' she said. 'Time to go home. Ana. *La Gorda*, they call me. *Cabrones*. The Fat One.'

I was close to sleeping again. I couldn't speak.

'Galicia is my home,' she said. 'My mother is dead. My father is an alcoholic. I am an orphan. I sell things. Drugs at night. Tissues, matches during the day. Cigarette lighters. This is my life. I can't afford to stop. Oh, Frankie . . . it's all right . . . my new brother . . . you have such a sad face . . .'

Over the following days, I came to know better La Gorda, the Maybe-brother and Encarna, as well as two or three of the disconsolate ones. They divided their time between smoking, injecting themselves, drinking cheap, bitter wine, arguing violently over trivial subjects, selling things and making love to Encarna in the back of an abandoned Seat 850 on the Calle Amparo.

I attempted to make love to both La Gorda and Encarna, but neither time did it really work. At the second attempt, memories of the Hola Woman flooded into my head and caused me to be sick over La Gorda's breasts. After slapping me in the face, three times, she forgave me, confiding that it was not the first time such a thing had happened.

I made it my business not to think too much. The powdered joy helped. I quickly learned exactly how much was necessary to lead me into a pleasant mental No Man's Land and keep me there. The sensation of not being myself, which I had felt in the Hola Woman's arms and then at Chantelle's party and after, was now multiplied and exaggerated so that whole days and nights passed by of which I had no recollection whatever. Sometimes I dreamed about the others, about Michael and Chantelle in particular, dreams brought on by my jealousy at the possibility that they were spending time with Marc.

At the back of my mind there was the sense that this was what I'd come to Spain to do: to lose myself in a lifestyle as far as possible from the Whately lifestyle. There was something romantic about this, after all: I'd read about lives like this, in books by Henry Miller and William Burroughs. I was pushing life to its limits. It was a cool, hard lifestyle, and that provided pleasure in itself.

I quickly became known to the others as Frankie Quitarme, Frankie Get Myself Out. Although I wasn't aware of it, apparently whenever La Gorda took out the silver foil and offered its contents to me, I'd take it with the comment that I'd be able to get myself out of this whenever I liked. What was strange was that I genuinely believed I could. I'd thought the same thing about Africa.

I told La Gorda about the film, and about Marc, about how he filled my thoughts, about how I knew he'd get back in touch. She listened to me and told me her own dreams, which were to be a singer. 'Life is a cabaret,' she sang, and I knew she wouldn't be going to Las Vegas for a while yet. She didn't realize that I was closer to fulfilling my dreams than she was. But I didn't tell her. It meant so much to her.

Then one night I saw Marc crossing the square, alone. I was sure it was him. His pony tail flapped against the collar of his shirt, his hands were in the pockets of his baggy trousers. He paused to raise a hand to someone; I shouted his name, but it didn't come out right, and when I tried to stand, I found I couldn't.

'That's him,' I told La Gorda.

I watched Marc as he paused by a parked car and raised a windscreen wiper to remove the flysheet which had been left under it. He glanced at the flysheet a moment before crumpling it and throwing it to the ground.

'We're going to make a film,' I said.

'You say that all the time, Frankie.'

When I was able, I wandered over to retrieve the screwed-up flysheet. 'PODEMOS AYUDARTE', it said in bold black lettering. 'SOMOS PSICOLOGOS'. We can help you: we are psychologists. Depression. Anguish. Drugs. Psychosomatic illness. Sexual problems. Problems with your studies.

I held it to my nose. It didn't smell of anything in particular.

Each night, or morning, I'd crawl up the hill towards the San Isidro, my brains on fire, and sleep for about twelve hours. I'd lie in bed after waking and resolve, Frankie Quitarme, that I would not see either La Gorda or her friends again. Despite the obvious pleasures of this lifestyle, despite the fact that I was inhabiting a paradise of mindlessness, without responsibilities or expectations, where time was unimportant and all my own, I nonetheless knew that I was balanced precariously at the top of that steep, slippery slope, and that this could not carry on for ever. It was a holiday. My body felt terrible most of the time, full of pains and aches which made it hard to move. I was doing things to it which my mind weakly wanted to forbid.

But any happiness would do: this dull, artificial happiness was better than no happiness at all. And then, when I got back to the *hostal* one night to find my few clothes in a pile in the corridor and pushed open the door to find a man who looked like Jesus Christ lying asleep on my bed, it became clear to me that the only place I had to go was down the hill, back to La Gorda and her powdered joy.

Sr López handed me an envelope. It was from Marc. I held it to my nose and sniffed it. My eyes went wet.

> I'm back in town, Frank. It would be good to see you. I saw you in Lavapiés last Wednesday night. It made me sad to see you like this. We should meet soon. We have things to talk about. Please come to the Albion Academy. If you can't help yourself, then let me help you.

I reread the letter several times before folding it neatly and replacing it in the envelope.

I went for a long walk in the Retiro Park. The sun was shining along the tree-lined avenues, dappling the packed earth with dancing shadows.

A man and a small child were dodging around a tree, the child trying to catch the man but never quite managing it. I watched them. I felt happy for them, and happy with myself for feeling that. They appeared startled when an unhealthy-looking foreigner walked up to them, apologizing, telling them that he'd have bought them an ice cream, if he'd had any money.

III

SIXTEEN

'Frank,' Marc said. 'You look terrible. I think you might have hepatitis.'

'Hemingitis?' I said.

'Down and out in Madrid. Acting out that tired old myth. Like millions of your compatriots. We'll have to get you cleaned up. Take you to a doctor.'

'That's it,' I said. 'Acting. That's what I've been doing. Trying out lifestyles.'

'That can be dangerous. You have to know how it's done.'

He was just as I remembered him: a little taller and gaunter, perhaps. More tanned. There was still all this suppressed energy inside him, making you feel that anything might happen at any moment, that a suggestion might be made which would alter the course of things.

I'd half expected to find Chantelle and Michael sitting there. When I asked about them, Marc carefully explained that they were having certain problems in relation to one another, that it was best that they stay apart for the time being. He wished to develop his own relationships with us on an individual basis. As he was sure I appreciated, it was impossible to get to know people when there were other people around. And given the subject matter of the film, it was of course important that he feel comfortable with each of us intimately.

'Why did it take you so long to get in touch with me?' I asked. 'Why didn't you say hello in the square?'

'Let's say,' Marc said, 'that I'm interested in the social dynamics of absence. Of what happens between people when – well, when they're not there.'

'So you deliberately didn't see me?'

'I wanted you to wait until making this film was the only thing that mattered to you. I wanted to test your commitment. I'm sorry if that sounds cold. It's no doubt an expression of my own insecurities. You are, of course, free to walk out of the door and never see me again.'

I felt tired. Heavy and tired, and a little ripped-up inside.

'Well,' I murmured. 'Thank you for being so honest.'

'Good. Please step into the office and sit down.'

He explained that he'd taken over the school premises, at least until it found new tenants. We were sitting in what had been Donald's opium den, on opposite sides of what had been Donald's desk. Marc had effected few changes to the décor, but now that the old clutter had gone, the room seemed spacious and airy.

All that remained of Donald were some curiously shaped stains on the desk top. New items were a black iron director's chair with a canvas back, the aroma of eau de cologne, a miniature hi-fi unit, a video recorder and a television set. Every object in the room bespoke detachment from other human beings. Every face and every voice which entered had to come in the form of electronic signals: it reminded me strangely of the old back room at VideoWorld, minus the clutter. Clarity and perfection reigned now: I, for example, did not belong.

Piano music issued from the CD player. Chopin, Marc explained it was: a very gentle sound. The blinds were down, and the occasional faint car horn from the *glorieta* below was the only sign that Marc and I were not alone together in the world.

'People make too much empty noise. Don't you think? There's no efficiency about their lives. A life should be . . . streamlined.' He offered me a glass of wine, explaining that even the King of Spain's supply of this particular wine was rationed. Vega Sicilia Unico, it was called.

Marc crossed his legs and unbuttoned the cuffs of his pale blue shirt to roll them back. Even such minor actions as this drew the eye, such was the studied grace with which he performed them.

The watch tattoo on his wrist jolted into my stomach. I felt the hairs on the backs of my hands prickling with suppressed excitement. Marc had re-entered my life. Things were going to happen. Different things, perhaps, frightening things certainly. New territory. At one time I'd have shied away, run in the opposite direction.

'You wouldn't have a cigarette, would you, Marc?'

'I'm afraid I don't smoke.'

I needed a cigarette badly. These moments were crying out to be perfected.

'Yes, you do,' I said. 'You were smoking on the night of destruction, weren't you? I always imagine you –'

'The what?'

'At Chantelle's party. I distinctly remember.'

'I don't think you do, Frank. Marc doesn't smoke. It's a filthy habit.'

'You don't?'

'I can offer you some cocaine, if you like. Far higher quality than you'd get in Lavapiés.'

He opened Donald's desk drawer and pulled out a razor-blade, a small mirror and a plastic Kodak film container.

He settled his fingertips on the table edge and turned to face the wall as I messily prepared the cocaine and inhaled it in the way demonstrated to me by La Gorda. I needed it: such had been my anticipation at seeing him that I'd become too agitated for my own good. What would have been tiny moments in the lives of others had come to acquire monumental status in my own.

'Be careful, Frank. It's not sherbert.'

I was better now.

'I did see you the other night,' Marc said slowly. 'In Lavapiés. I know I hardly know you, and you don't have to listen to what I say –'

'I want to listen to what you say.'

' – don't lose your sense of perspective. You don't belong with these people. I know them, Frank. They're different from us. Deadbeats. Babies. Allow me to say this. I feel nothing but contempt for them.'

They're different from *us*. Although I knew I was smiling, I could feel tears forming behind my eyelids. I'd come too close to becoming part of that world, too close to remaining in it. I was grateful to Marc that he should continue speaking while I recovered from this small sadness.

'It thrills you to be with me, doesn't it?' he said. 'That's nice. Did Michael tell you about the film?'

'Yes. Yes, he did.'

'What did he say, exactly?'

'He said you wanted to make a film about us. He said you thought we were symptomatic of the age.'

'And what do you think I meant by that?'

'Don't you remember?'

'Of course I do. I just want to be clear that we're all talking about the same thing.'

'OK,' I said. I was on trial. I had to react. 'This is it. You meant that we're all escaping from something. That we're kind of pursuing an identity. That we're all a bit confused about things. Stuck between the world we come from, which we hate, and the world we're going to, in which we have no faith. Which frightens us.' I was on my feet, moving round the office, punching the air, slapping the wall. 'That we're unhappy, and we'd all like to be someone else. There's all these choices, and we can't decide who we want to be. So we're acting. We're empty people, wanting to be filled.'

I was sweating. The back of my hand slipped across my forehead as I collapsed into my chair.

'That's exactly what I meant, yes. Good. It sounds *big*, doesn't it?' Marc leaned across the table and gripped my arm. His voice did not get louder, but rather increased in intensity, as though his feelings were compressing it. 'We're going to have to *talk*,

Frank. Really talk. Talk like you're talking now. Like you've never talked to anybody else.' He took a tissue from a box on the table and wiped his hands on it. 'We're going to have to go down deep if we want to make a success of this. You're going to have to let me in. You might feel uncomfortable about this, Frank. You're going to have to trust me. But I suppose you've had time to think about that already. I suppose you've already made that decision. Because I'm offering you something I think you need. I want to be your wildest dreams.'

These things he said. They left me speechless. He was unbelievable.

'Fine. Let me speak in a direct way to you.' He closed his eyes. I watched the lids trembling, as though invisible flies were dancing on them. 'I told you all I was a psychopath. I've said and done certain things to make you believe that. But I'm not. Psychopaths generally don't have as much money as I have. It was an effect I wished to create at a certain point. You think I killed Derek John Platt, don't you?'

Stunned by such directness, I didn't speak. But Marc didn't say anything, either; and after several seconds I felt compelled to.

'No. I don't know. I –'

'No, I'm sorry. I've expressed that badly. OK . . . the thought that I might have killed Derek John Platt is somehow *attractive* to you . . .'

How could he know that?

'Chantelle and Michael have told me certain things about you, Frank. I've seen quite a lot of Chantelle. She's sweet. She's just a little lost in life.'

'What did they say about me?'

'Nothing special. Just things which give me the impression that you like the idea that I might have committed a murder.'

'It sounds crazy, doesn't it?'

'No. No, it doesn't sound crazy at all. It might sound crazy to a lot of people. A lot of people would think it was mad to be attracted by having a thought like that. Fuck them. They're *limited*. What I'm saying is, I understand. That's what I'm telling you. There's glamour and danger in death, Frank. We know this.'

It occurred to me for the first time that I might actually be sitting in the same room as a human being who had killed another human being.

'You have to let me in,' Marc had said. I looked at him as he poured us another glass of wine. He was giving me time to think. He was aware of the chain of thoughts he had provoked in me. Now he was giving me time to explore them. He understood.

'I have a confession to make,' he said. He sipped the wine. 'I've stolen something from you. Do you remember when Michael came to see you?'

'Yes.'

'Well, before he went to see you, I asked him to bring me your novel for me to read. I was interested to see it. Well, he didn't bring me your novel. He brought me this. Don't blame Michael. Michael would do anything for me.'

'Why didn't you ask *me* for it?' I asked. I felt a prick of jealousy.

Marc quickly brought his fingertips to his forehead as though he'd been stung.

'Is that an accusation?'

'No. No . . .'

'Frank. We both know why I didn't ask you for it. It would have been embarrassing to both of us if I'd asked you to give me a novel which you haven't written. I understand it, though. I understand that the idea is more important than the action. That the impression given is more important than the achievement. This is the nature of things. Don't think about all that now. Just read this.'

He pushed a transparent plastic folder across the desk. I opened it and nearly died. It contained the fantasy pages I'd written about the night of the death of Derek John Platt. *'Then he skilfully draws the razor-blade against the throat of Derek John Platt.'*

'Are you angry, Frank? Are you angry that Michael took this from you? I thought that was a nice image, the razor-blade between the credit cards . . .'

My head was entirely clear of thought and feeling. I was pure. I had nothing to say, and only wanted to continue listening.

'You aren't angry. Because I think you wanted me to read this. I think you're crying out to be understood, Frank. It's that simple. You need a friend.'

'It's invented,' I said. 'It's not real.' My voice was so weak that I wasn't sure it had even reached Marc's ears.

'It isn't really important whether it's invented or real. Nobody knows what's real or invented any more. What matters is that you *want* it to be real, Frank. Don't look at me. Just listen. Listen to Marc's voice. Filling your head.'

It was impossible to get to the bottom of these matters. Nobody can go that deeply into themselves and come out sane. The only thing you find down there is confusion and black grief, and you're better off out of it.

I was aware of the piano music coming to an end. A man in the corridor yelled at his wife to help him with the shopping. A baby started crying.

'Did you kill him?' I blurted out.

'No. No, I didn't. Is that disappointing to you? Of course I didn't . . . *kill* him . . . actually, Frank, I never *do* anything . . . all my life is here.' He tapped his forehead.

'I don't understand . . .'

'You will. This conversation is too long.'

Marc took a video cassette from the desk drawer. He switched on the video machine and the television, and pushed the video cassette into the recorder.

A grainy, uncertain image of a man came on to the screen and was held there, flickering.

'I don't suppose you've seen the news lately?'

For all I knew, the rest of the earth had frazzled under the impact of a nuclear war or global warming. For all I knew, Marc and myself were the only survivors.

The man on the video screen was thin, with startled eyes and a fecund moustache. He was being hustled from the back of a police van into a white building. A reporter spoke, the tone of his voice implying absolute indifference to the events he was describing.

'José Luis Ruiz, a gypsy from Cervera, in the province of Lérida, has been arrested for the murder . . .'

'Did you know him?'

'I'd met him, yes.'

'. . . a forty-one-year-old hairdresser . . .'

'I met him in L'Estartit. I just happened to be there. He was unhappy. He told me he was going to do something very strange. He told me he was going to confess to the murder of an English tourist. People tell me these things. I don't know why. I suppose I have the air of being detached. People feel able to tell me things, because they know I'm not involved. And because I'm interested in things I know very little about. The human heart. Do you feel relieved, Frank?'

'Relieved?' It was strange: it was as though I didn't know what I felt, and wished Marc to tell me.

'Are you relieved that I'm not a murderer? That I'm just a voice inside your head?'

I opened my eyes, frightened that I might, in fact, be sitting in this room quite alone. But I wasn't. I felt myself slipping sideways from the chair and jerked myself upright.

'What we're going to do, Frank, is we're going to get you and Michael and Chantelle together and we're going to channel your energies. I do think you have potential. We're going to make sure this story has a happy ending. I am going to be honest with you, and you are going to be honest with me. And then we're going to work hard together and make a film. I want you to ask me any question you like.'

'Why are you doing this?' I asked.

'A sense of adventure. A little bit of dangerous fun.'

'Why dangerous?'

'Because fun is dangerous by definition. Fun is escape. Escape is dangerous.'

My next question carried with it the fear and nerves of an adolescent asking his first girlfriend, for the first time, his desire to know only just overriding his fear of a negative reply, whether she loves him.

'Who are you?'

'Who am I? I don't know. What have I done? I'll tell you.'

Marc explained that he'd been born in 1962 in Vienna to upper-middle-class parents. Wishing to escape their bourgeois assumptions about him and expectations of him, he'd run away from them on 13 December 1974, while they'd been in Paris doing the Christmas shopping. Homeless and penniless, he'd become a rent boy in Hamburg.

'A rent boy?'

'Rather than return, I rented out my body to cheerless geriatrics. I took a lot of drugs. Met a lot of crazy people. It sounds epic and romantic. But believe me it isn't, Frank. It scars. I paid the price for my escape.'

In 1975 he'd gone to New York to live with the ex-mistress of one of his clients. She'd committed suicide eight months later, playing Russian roulette in Hong Kong. She had left him a considerable amount of money which permitted him to do as he wished, which was work in film in New York. He'd spent most of his teens working with Andy Warhol and Paul Morrissey, and he'd slept with someone called Edie Sedgwick: apparently Jean Shrimpton was not the only beautiful woman in the world with the name of a dinner lady. He'd played guitar in a club on the Lower East Side called CBGB's. People with names like Tom Verlaine and Richard Hell had been his drinking buddies. He was still part of the scene over there, still hung out with the right people. That's what he said: 'hung out'.

They'd been mythical days. One of the saddest days of his life had been Robert Mapplethorpe's funeral. Marc said this without showing even a glimmer of sadness.

These facts were impressive to me, justifying my initial reaction to him all those hundreds of years ago, on the night of destruction. They were just the sort of things you could imagine happening to Marc. I only hoped he wouldn't dwell too long on the Robert Mapplethorpe part.

'And then, a couple of years ago, I decided that my entire life was a tired cliché and decided to cut loose.'

'I know what you mean there,' I said.

'You do?'

'About your life being a cliché. It's like you know you're living the life that millions of people have lived before you. That your own life isn't original. You have to cut loose if you want to find the life which is your life and your life only. You have to escape from your life.'

These were the thoughts I'd attempted to express to Africa, to which Africa had reacted with all the compassion of a toilet brush.

'Thank you,' Marc said.

'. . . Why?'

'A lot of people have seen me as a bullshitter. I fall outside their limits. But you don't. We understand one another. We have a shared sense of the distance between us. Which brings us close to one another.'

He'd stolen a Chevrolet in New Orleans and travelled around the southern states for a while. He'd spent a year in jail. He'd returned to Europe six months before, and become a part-time model. He had flirted with terrorism and petty crime, and at this point he considered himself to be perpetually on the run: he considered his home to be *Im Ausland*. He was in Madrid because he'd been looking for a film to make, and now he'd found it.

'In Outland. The German is so elegant, don't you think?'

He was twenty-nine years old. I recalled exchanging histories with Africa, and my frustration at feeling unable to participate in her past, and my eventual boredom, and I watched myself, comparing my reaction then with my reaction now, and I felt I *could* participate in what Marc was telling me, that I understood it, that his words made a connection with something inside me.

This was not just fairy tales. This was not just Africa and her Civil War, and her Years of Hunger; this was not just Michael, and his doomed passion with a mechanic called Roy. This was real. This was dangerous fun.

There were so many questions to ask. Every sentence Marc had uttered over the past half-hour begged about a million of them, drew you on. Had he loved the woman he'd spoken of? What was the impact of such an adolescence as his on the personality? How did it feel to be a rent boy? What had Robert Mapplethorpe actually been like? I wanted to immerse myself in these questions, lose myself in them, give myself over to the experiences of Marc and to the self-knowledge such a life had undoubtedly brought him.

'More wine? Cocaine?'

'Yes, please.'

'It's your turn now, Frank.'

'Sorry?'

'It's your turn. Tell me.'

'Oh. Right.'

I was born in 1968, I imagined myself saying, to an alcoholic bus driver called Gordon and a woman whose job was putting little plastic animals into Cornflakes packets. When they died, I was adopted by a woman called Auntie Beryl. Not much happened for the next fifteen years. I passed all my 'O' levels and had a summer job delivering newspapers until one day I fell off my bike trying to do a wheelie in Dargan Street, opposite Garvey's chippy. I had a nervous breakdown just before my 'A' levels, saw a psychiatrist called Dr Minshull for a while, who died, and that's pretty much that.

'I was born in Paris,' I said. 'Yes. I was born in Paris, and my mother was a dancer at the Moulin Rouge. My father played with Charlie Parker –'

Unfortunately, Marc had just said something in French.

'*Oui*,' I said. '*C'est vrai*. Actually, my French is a bit rusty. I left when I was eight.'

'In 1976.'

'Yes. Yes, in 1976.'

Marc nodded. I was sweating like a pig.

'I travelled abroad. I travelled round Europe. Berlin, Rome –' In the heat of the moment, no other European capitals occurred to me.

'What were you doing?'

'Oh, you know. Odd jobs. Truck driving. I drove through the Alps in my truck. With the radio on.'

'When you were eight?'

'No. That was later. My father was a diplomat. We travelled –'

'You just said he was a jazz musician.'

Being stoned wasn't helping. '*First* he was a diplomat, and *then* he was a jazz musician. No. First he was a – and anyway, to cut a long story short, one day I got a phone call from a close friend of Robert Mapplethorpe's.'

'Yes? What was his name?' Marc had picked up a pen and was tapping the table with it.

'Arthur Negus,' I said, using the name of an English television personality of whom I could be fairly sure Marc hadn't heard. 'So anyway, I went over to LA, and then me and Robert – Bob –'

'New York.'

'Sorry?'

'New York.'

'New York. Yes. So then, right, I –'

'And what did you do with Robert?'

'I . . . *helped* him. With his photographs. His work. Like an assistant.'

'The flowers, or the portraits?' I hoped that, quite soon now, Marc would put me out of my misery.

'Oh,' I said. 'You know.'

'No, Frank. I don't know.'

'The flowers, then.'

'Frank,' Marc said, and put down the pen. 'Listen. This makes me edgy inside. I spent many months working with Robert, and I don't remember you. I was there at the openings of all his New York exhibitions. He did portraits of parts of my body, Frank. He fucked me. But I don't remember you.'

My stomach was turning over. I had developed a very bad headache.

'Also, I asked you in French whereabouts in Paris you'd lived. So you can't really say, "Yes, that's true."'

'No. I don't suppose you can.'

'We're not playing the identity game now, Frank. You can't steal my fantasy and make it your reality. We're not drawing distinctions any longer. This is real. It has to be real, if it's going to mean anything. And if you're not serious, then I leave and you never saw me.'

'I'm sorry . . .' I sat in silence, wishing I could die, desperate to confess but finding it hard to. With the others, my fibs had succeeded, because they believed them or wanted to believe them, or because they'd been too sensitive to want to shatter my illusion. But it was no longer important: as Marc said, this was real.

He was looking at me rather wearily, as schoolteachers had, as Auntie Beryl had while waiting for me to break under the pressure of interrogation. His jaw muscles were twitching; he gently stroked his Adam's apple.

'I'm getting through to you, aren't I?'

I felt about in my pockets and removed my rather sorry-looking Letter Never Sent. Encarna had accidentally set it alight in a drugged attempt to demonstrate that paper didn't burn. I proffered it in slow motion: the weight of it left my fingers; something inside me sighed a deep sigh of relief.

It had been meant for Auntie Beryl. Auntie Beryl was dead.

There was no one else to show it to.

'That's the truth,' I said.

Marc quickly leafed through it.

'Is this you, Frank?'

'Yes. Yes, it is. It's me.'

'I don't think I'd better read it. It's clearly of a personal nature.'

'I want you to let me in,' I said, unsure whether I was sounding noble or pathetic.

'Perhaps I will. Thank you.'

We then discussed cleaning me up. This would involve a complete overhaul of my delightful body, from my dandruff to my ingrowing toe-nails, replacing the broken lens of my spectacles and my false tooth and trying to clear up my complexion along the way. Marc offered to write me out a diet.

'And it's clear that you're doing too many drugs, Frank. We're going to have to cut them out. Although that will mostly depend on you.' He suggested that I come to stay at the school. We'd put a mattress down in the Children's Activity Room. It was clean in there.

'What I'm going to ask you to do is not buy any more drugs. You don't know what you're getting. I'd like you to use me as your only supplier. I'm going to give it to you in ever-decreasing quantities. We're going to really clean you up, Frank. I can't work with mess.'

'Thank you.'

We talked about the film.

'Do you know anyone with any video cameras? I left all mine in Dallas.'

'No . . .' I'd try and get one. It was the least I could do. The film's title, we agreed, should be *The Holiday People*. I cried a little, and Marc comforted me with tranquillizing words.

That closeness. That strong, quiet voice. It would be all right. Everything was going to be all right, really.

SEVENTEEN

Marc gave me 50,000 pesetas to do with as I pleased, as well as some powdered joy. 'Powdered joy,' he said. 'That's a very poetic name. Better to call it that than to call it cocaine, or ecstasy, or heroin, or whatever it is. Better to keep the romance of it alive.' When I asked him why it felt different than all the powdered joys I'd taken in Lavapiés, he told me it was because it was purer: and although, never having been one for visits to the doctor, I vomited the first time I had to inject it into myself, Marc explained that it was cleaner this way, more medical. This way, it wouldn't affect my stomach.

I needed to put myself into someone's hands. Or rather, I needed someone into whose hands I could put myself.

We talked about what had sent me down to Lavapiés, what had caused me, as Marc put it, to abandon myself like that. And I didn't know. I felt stupid at not being able to explain, but I just couldn't. It felt as though I was trying to explain the actions of someone I didn't know, trying to describe the heart of Robert Mapplethorpe.

'You've lost touch with your feelings,' Marc pointed out. 'It happens. Think of it as strength.'

'I don't know . . . I've never felt very well.'

'What were your feelings when you went down to Lavapiés the first time, Frank?'

'I don't know.'

'Sadness? Were you feeling sad that things hadn't worked out with Africa?' Sadness. I told him about the evening Brian had gone into her bedroom with her, and how that had made me decide never to see her again. I told him how that had spoiled everything. I told him that, when we'd first made love, I'd believed that I would never be able to live again without having such feelings and sensations as a part of my life. Knowing that I wouldn't be able to have them again had made me sad.

Yes, I supposed that must have been it. Sadness.

'I want you to go and see her again, Frank. I want you to remember that just because she went into the bedroom with Brian doesn't mean she doesn't love you. One last chance.'

'But she told me she didn't. She hasn't come to *see* me. I only live twenty yards away.'

'People often don't know their own feelings, do they? Look at yourself, for example. Anyway, you haven't been at home.'

'Home,' I repeated, uncertain as to what the word meant.

I bought Africa an English-language dictionary, some Y by Yves Saint-Laurent and some flowers. The woman in the flower-shop looked at me sadly and told me she was sorry, which I thought was unusually compassionate of her. I wanted to write a message to her on the flysheet of the dictionary, but I couldn't think what it should be.

'Put *Que los sueños se realizaran*,' Marc suggested. '"That our dreams may become real." That's a good philosophy. She'll understand that.'

But I felt uncomfortable. I couldn't imagine myself standing there in front of her, the same person that I'd been before, with all the same insecurities, knowing that the slightest inappropriate word from her would cut me. Before I went to see her, I'd have to feel good about myself, and I felt about as good about myself as a man trying to explain to his wife why he's murdered their children.

'If you look good,' Marc said, 'you'll feel good. The impression. Not the achievement.' Michael had been given to saying the same thing, in different words. 'It sounds superficial and impossible, but it's the best we can do.'

*

I'd managed to stay out of her way for a month. Now I stood outside her door with its familiar peephole, my bowels feeling as loose as they had on my first visit, two grubby children eyeing me suspiciously from the top of the next flight of stairs.

I was wearing a beige suit and a white tie and collar. My hair was tied back in a pony tail. Unfortunately, the lens of my glasses was still cracked, but I'd spent the afternoon fashioning a false tooth substitute from chewing gum and Tippex. I had to keep my mouth slightly open to stop it falling out, which in turn caused a lot of saliva to form. It's hard to swallow with an open mouth, and makes you feel slightly sick. I wondered what would happen if we ended up kissing, but I reckoned that if it got that far, she'd forgive me a gap in my teeth.

I'd decided to try to speak as I thought Marc would speak, to learn his language. Practising: 'It's always midnight, wherever I am.' 'This is the nature of things.' This way I'd stand a better chance of winning her back, but if I failed, I wouldn't be hurt.

It was late evening, just beginning to get dark. A roughly cut slice of sky, rich in dramatic colours, made its presence felt high above the narrow cobbled steets, and was suggestive of something better.

Africa wasn't in. I returned an hour later.

She was wearing clothes I'd never seen before. Instead of the figure-hugging, tight, bright garments I always thought of when I thought of her, she was now in a sober brown skirt, a navy blue blouse and was wearing a small silver cross around her neck. She looked like Auntie Beryl's spinster aunt, and gave off a faint aroma of mothballs.

'Frank? Is that you?'

'More or less,' I said.

'What have you got all that tape on your glasses for?'

'To keep out the sun.'

We didn't kiss hello. She scratched at the back of her head and nodded me inside.

'You've certainly changed your image,' I said.

'It's no image,' she said. '*Soy yo*. I'm me. You look different, though.' She put a bit of distance between myself and her and paused with one hand on the back of the armchair, wheezing a little. It was remarkable to me that I had scratched that back with my fingernails, licked behind those knees, inserted my tongue between those buttocks. I must have been off my trolley.

She turned, and I'd forgotten how penetrating her gaze could be. These days, I felt all gazes to be penetrating. I wouldn't be taking the glasses off.

'These are for you.' I solemnly handed her the flowers, the dictionary and the perfume. '*Gracias*,' Africa said uncertainly. '*Gracias. Gracias.*'

I looked past her and saw her plant still out there on the window-ledge. In its time, it had symbolized mystery, passion and now hope. It was no wonder it was looking exhausted.

'You look very *elegante*.'

'People who make movies generally are *elegante*,' I said. 'Any chance of a coffee?'

'I suppose so . . . I didn't think I'd see you again.'

'Well, you don't seem too happy to see me.' Marc wouldn't have said that. Marc would have said, Well, you have.

'Oh, don't think that . . . I am happy you have come . . .'

She went into the kitchen to prepare the coffee. Sure enough, there was a clattering and a curse.

'Two wine-glasses on the table?' I called through. 'Are you back at work again?'

'No . . . a celebration drink. I have given up my job. I have retired. After all these years.'

'That's good,' I said. But I knew it wasn't good. I knew that something was going to happen which I wouldn't like. 'You've been studying, too. Present perfect tense. Very good.'

We come to speak about love, about the ending of love. We speak about the present perfect.

'Mr Andrews has been teaching me. Brian. He is very patient.'

'I know.'

184

'How do you know?'

'Because I'm aware of these things, Africa . . .' Already, the first hints of pain came over the horizon, black, threatening. You had to screw up your eyes to see them, but they were there. If I stayed here, I was going to get drenched, Marc or no Marc.

'Mr Andrews is a *caballero*,' she said. 'We hired a car. We had *cochinillo* in Chinchón.'

'Don't talk about Brian, please. Don't talk about Mr Andrews.'

The smell of the coffee had mixed with the smell of the drains and the smell of Africa's perfume. It caught me out. Memories: from the point of view of emotional safety, I'd have been better off with a clothes-peg on my nose.

She stood there in the doorway, the cups rattling in their saucers, and smiled sadly. I began to feel sexual towards her.

'I wonder why it's called the present perfect?' I said. 'I've often wondered that.'

'Frank,' Africa said. She put the coffee cups down and the cloth of her dress tightened across her buttocks. 'I don't want to hurt you . . . you won't be hurt, will you?'

'No.'

'Are you sure?'

'Africa, do I look like a man who can be hurt?'

'Yes,' she said softly. 'That is exactly what you look like.'

'Just tell me.'

'I am going to England, Frank. Perhaps to live.' Her coffee cup was just in front of her mouth: when I looked up, she hastily took a sip, knowing that she'd said wrong.

There they were. The first drops of sadness, flecking my face. I put my emotional umbrella up. 'Look up "present perfect" in the dictionary.'

'You never invited me to England,' she said. 'You never believe me when I say I see Paco.'

'You *have* never invited me to England,' I said. 'Look it up, please.'

She was going to England, then. She was going with Brian.

Africa and Brian were going to England together. These words, Africa. Brian. England, going . . . I watched them as they made patterns in my mind, unable to understand what they meant, not wanting to.

'Why didn't you come and visit me?'

'I did. You were never at home.'

'How long are you going for?'

'As long as it is necessary.'

She must have seen something in my eyes, heard something in my voice. Hers now had an edge to it.

'Necessary to do what?'

'To find Paco.'

'Paco . . . oh, for Christ's sake, Africa. For Christ's fucking sake.' Marc wouldn't have said this, either. I had to fight it. I picked up the dictionary, dropped it, picked it up again, riffled through its pages.

'"Perfect: denoting completed event or action viewed in relation to the present".'

I banged it shut. I threw it across the room. Africa said 'ay' and flinched. I sat there, my heart pounding. I tore at the knot of the tie, trying to loosen it, and almost pulled my neck out of joint.

'Africa, listen to me. England's a very big place. And it's more expensive than here. What are you going to do about money?'

'I have saved up the money,' she said. The money I had given her. I had given her the money to escape. If I hadn't given her the money, she wouldn't be going.

'"Saved up",' I said. 'Phrasal verb. Very good.'

'Oh,' said Africa. *'No llores.'*

'No llores' is Spanish for 'don't cry'. But she was wrong. I wasn't crying. Not this time. It was just that my eyes had gone wet.

We sat in silence. I felt redundant. Any words I'd be able to say would be redundant words. I imagined myself quietly trying to persuade her of the foolishness of her move, applying reason where reason didn't apply, and Africa vacantly nodding in agreement, understanding the words themselves, but unable to understand what they meant because her feelings ran counter to them.

I imagined myself standing up and destroying her flat, taking it apart bit by bit in front of her, knowing that I'd be able to now, and knowing that I'd feel better afterwards. I imagined scraping the liver spots off Brian's forehead with my fingernails, scraping them off, one by one, until there were no liver spots left. I imagined tantrums, threats, employed to create in Africa the fear that I would do myself some serious damage if my wishes weren't complied with, a tactic often used with Auntie Beryl.

On balance, it was probably better just to sit there and cry.

Africa was trying to explain herself. She chided herself for ever having got involved with me, for not having known the strange boy I was. She'd thought it would be nice, having a young English friend. Surely I'd known it couldn't last for ever. I'd been so lonely, she said. Best to think of it as a summer-time romance. So lonely: and then she didn't say anything else.

'But you're escaping, Africa. Running away to England.'

'I'm not escaping, Frank. Escape is when you don't know where you're going. I know exactly where I'm going. I'm going to find Paco. Escape is when what you're leaving is more important than what you're going to.'

She was careful to speak in English. There was no chance of escaping into ambiguity. She came to me and put her hand over mine, but I pushed it away. I couldn't see what Africa's hand on mine had to do with anything.

'You're the one who is trying to escape, Frank. But you know what they say.'

'No.'

'You take yourself wherever you go.'

'I'm no good without you here,' I said. That was the sort of sentence people said in these situations.

'You're not, are you . . .' She replaced her hand, and this time I left it there. 'Frank, Mr Andrews and me . . . we were talking . . .

187

would you like to come with us? Back to England?'

'No,' I said. 'I fucking wouldn't. Fuck off.'

'Think about it.'

'I've thought about it.'

'But perhaps here, you are not happy . . .' She put her arm around my shoulders.

'Africa, look at me. Do I look like a man . . .'

'Yes,' she said. 'Yes, you do.'

'Well, forget it.'

She was close to me, her breath against my cheek, the smell of sunflower seeds. Then her cheek was next to mine. I turned my head and began to kiss it, not properly understanding that it was no longer mine to kiss. My head emptied of thought and, in my senses, Africa's cheek converted itself into her bottom: when she felt this happening, she stood up abruptly and smoothed down her skirt.

'*No, no* . . . come to England, Frank. It is your country.'

'Fuck off,' I said. 'I'm from nowhere, Africa. I'm from *Im Ausland.*'

She watched me disconsolately, her fingers plucking at the waistband of her skirt.

'I have to go now,' she said.

'To England? Now?'

'No. To the dry cleaner's.'

That was it. I picked up one of the wine-glasses. Holding it by the stem, I tapped it against the table edge just hard enough for it to break.

'Frank . . .'

'You never listened to me, did you? Not a single fucking syllable of my letter went in, did it? You're stupid, Africa. You're all feeling and no fucking brain. You don't know how to lose yourself, do you?'

'Stop shouting, Frank. You have never believed I could find my son. You have never believed in *me*, Frank. You have never seen me as a person.'

'You're the *only* thing I believed in.'

'No. You only believe in your Hola Woman. Put the glass down. Put the glass down now, Frank.'

I put the glass down.

'Now. Why did you buy me those flowers?'

What a question.

'You should know that here, you give chrysanthemums when somebody has died. You didn't know that, did you?'

I stared at her.

'Now. Roll up your sleeves.'

That woke me up.

'Phrasal verb,' I said. '"Roll up".'

'Take off your glasses, Frank.'

'No.'

'You never wear a long-sleeved shirt. Roll them up.'

My mouth felt strange: I think I was smiling at her.

'Why are you wearing a long-sleeved shirt? Why have you got that tape on your glasses?'

'Fashion. Fashion.'

'*Ay, qué pena,*' Africa said. '*Qué pena.*' What a shame. She went to the doorway and said firmly, 'Wait here until I get back, *hijo.*'

'Don't call me that.'

'Don't move from here.'

'Don't go . . .'

'I'll be five minutes. You wait. We must talk.'

The door closed. I sat down and closed my eyes. I pictured myself picking up the broken glass, sticking it into my wrist and moving it about. You had to move it about if you wanted it to work. Then I saw myself destroying her photograph of Paco and throwing the wine-glass at the television set, freeing myself through tantrum, deliberately causing anarchy in my head. I was standing on Africa's bed, urinating over the sheets, creating on them a work of modern art composed of chrysanthemums, blood, urine and broken glass.

I was trembling. Marc wouldn't have done these things: they

189

were too pathetic, too tiny. There's no point in crying for help, because the only person who's ever listening is yourself.

One hour later I was half asleep in the Children's Activity Room, being watched over by the phantoms of my infancy, namely Florence, Dougal, Zebedee and, of course, Rupert the Bear.

A voice floated across the room, struggling towards me through the warm air. I didn't know whether it was real or in my head.

EIGHTEEN

Donald would have called the few September days I spent living with Marc a fucking idiot's paradise. But he'd have been wrong. It was a paradise. Utterly insulated, utterly free. It might be idiotically ironic to say that now, given what happened: but if I'm idiotically ironic, then I don't mind. After all, I'd come to regard my own life with idiot irony. In some ways, I've never asked for anything else.

Frank! There he goes. Idiotically ironic, down to the depths of the soul he hasn't got!

Cheers.

Marc rarely slept at the school, but he was always there at the door at exactly 10 o'clock, with a *café solo* in a plastic cup, freshly baked croissants and a little powdered joy. He explained that he was able to survive on two or three hours' sleep a night, depending on his state of mind: and when there was a project to be brought to fruition, as there was now, he was able to go for days with no sleep at all.

'What do you do all night?'

'When I'm not with Michael or Chantelle, I walk the streets.'

'What do you do?'

'I think.'

'What about?'

'You wouldn't want to know.'

'Yes, I would.'

'You wouldn't. The thoughts of a bored, clever boy with too much energy, too much money and a big imagination. Work it out.'

He'd bought clothes for me: three T-shirts, three pairs of boxer shorts – I'd never worn them before, having until then been a Y-fronts person – three pairs of socks, two pairs of shoes, and the suit from Cortefiel in Alberto Aguilera.

'Do you buy your own clothes from Cortefiel?' I asked him.

'No. My suits are a little more expensive. Armani. Adolfo Dominguez.'

'I could get a T-shirt like yours. Or a tattoo. I could draw it in felt-tip pen.'

'No . . .' Marc passed his fingertips over his wrist. 'There has to be something which keeps us unique. I don't suppose you'll ever be *exactly* me, Frank.'

'A cheap impersonation,' I said, smiling to indicate my humorous intention.

But out walking, we stood by a shop window piled high with thousands of sweets and, apart from the glasses, it was hard, looking at only our reflections, to tell us apart. That fact gave me confidence, allowed me to appropriate a little of the energy which flowed through Marc, which was always busy within him.

'I'd have killed myself,' I said, 'if it hadn't been for you. I'd have ended up dead in the gutter.' Marc told me not to be silly.

There was nothing to do during the daytimes but think about the film. But it was a different nothing now, less vacant and hysterical, more secure, less tormented.

I found myself actually enjoying the heat of the sun and the sounds of the street, the taste of the wine Marc bought, the simple, nourishing food he cooked. This foreign country: although I knew, after Africa, that I'd never fully engage with it, never scratch its surface, never be able to interpret it and make it matter to me. What had been true then was true now. Where I wasn't mattered more than where I was.

One to one, Marc was quite different from his social self. He was not as intense or startling in his manner, and at times he was even gentle with me – one afternoon after a particularly bad siesta nightmare, he heard my shouting and came through to wipe my brow with a damp cloth. He admitted that he was not relaxed with large groups of people, that he functioned better in intimate company. *Functioned better*: when he said that, I thought it sounded a little clinical, but quickly realized that this was how I sounded to people also. Neither of us was an ostentatiously affectionate person.

'You're a cool guy, aren't you?' I recalled Chantelle saying, although she'd meant it differently. Whatever agitation and frenzy there was at work within Marc, he kept it tantalizingly hidden beneath the cover of perfect courtesy. I appreciated that calm. I needed it. He knew me: he'd read my Letter Never Sent; and now I wanted to know him.

Whenever he was free, we'd go for long, slow strolls through the streets of Madrid. We'd relax into the conversations which people seem to have under the Spanish sun, conversations without function or direction, whose pleasure lies in the fact that they cannot be recalled afterwards. We'd walk under the trees of Pintor Rosales, Hemingway's favourite street, from Plaza de España to Moncloa, pausing at bars to drink a Coca-Cola and do some people-watching or talk about the remarkable adventure that had been Marc's life, although I did sometimes get the impression that the subject was of more interest to me than it was to Marc himself.

'You're like a little boy, Frank. Why must you try and pin me down like this?' When we were out, I was worried that he'd have thousands of friends and that I'd have to stand at the edges of groups of people, wishing to talk but not feeling able to. But when one night he offered to introduce me to some of his friends and I told him of my fear of people, Marc understood, assuring me that he felt the same these days. It was far better to have one good relationship than to have hundreds of banal ones. He always knew just the right thing to say.

Or we'd go to the cinema. We went to see a sepia-tinted film called *A Short Film About Killing*, about a young Polish vagabond who suddenly strangles a taxi driver to death and then drops a boulder on his head. It was very realistic, and it was odd to come out into the bright afternoon.

There was only one stain on this perfect lifestyle, and that was the continuing existence of Michael and Chantelle. To think of Africa sleeping with men unknown to me had not, strangely, bothered me: after all, they'd been paying for it and, as Africa had said, they'd all had to return to their real lives afterwards – just as I'd now done. But to think of Marc having sex with Chantelle and Michael was excruciating, now that I knew him, now that he was mine.

In one way, I was happy to be feeling jealousy, because jealousy was a natural human emotion, and to have normal human emotions was reassuring to me. Jealousy implied love: perhaps, I tremblingly thought, I was in love. Frank Bowden in love? With a man? But this reassurance scarcely compensated for the torture of half knowing that when he wasn't with me, he was out with Chantelle and Michael, listening to their stupid performances, feeling their silly hands exploring his body. How could he stoop so low? What did he see in them? Only sex, I hoped: occasionally I wondered whether I shouldn't ask him about it. I burned to know, as I'd burned to know whether or not he'd killed Derek John Platt.

But I was afraid to ask. The fantasy of Marc, Michael and Chantelle making love together had been exciting to me a month before, but not now. Now, it was one fantasy I preferred not to escape into.

One afternoon, sitting in the shadow of the statue of Alfonso XII in the Retiro Park, the subject of Michael and Chantelle came up when we were discussing the best moment to start making our film. In about two weeks, Marc suggested, but the sound of those names spoilt my concentration.

He seemed to read my thoughts.

'Later, Frank,' he said. 'I don't want to lose them. Ever since I saw them with Derek John Platt that night in L'Estartit, they've

194

fascinated me. This whole filmic project came to me when I saw them. When I saw their unhappiness. I'll do whatever it takes to see this thing through. I want to see whether I can. Whether I'm capable. Michael wants me, Chantelle loves me, I couldn't give a damn about either of them. That's their choice. Sometimes they get sad, I threaten to leave if they don't stop being stupid, they stop being sad. It's a simple thing. It's all a question of putting in face time. Just so that they don't forget I'm there.'

He was more forthcoming on the subject of film. He particularly liked the hi-colour, hi-action type of British television advertisement, seeing them as 'exemplary exercises in style'. They were honest art. A vacuous culture found its perfect reflection in them. No good film made at the end of the twentieth century could afford to avoid being self-consciously stylish. And the only way a film could be original was by burying into itself and finding nothing there, since everything outside, in the so-called 'real' world, had been chronicled a million times already.

'Nothingness takes a million forms,' he told me. 'Look at Wenders.' Wenders's films, apparently, were films of surfaces, bright and crisp and hard and lovely to look at: but it was the vacuum at their heart, Marc said, a different vacuum each time, that gave them their truth. 'A perfect aesthetic of perfect absence' was what he called his ideal for his own films.

'A perfect aesthetic of perfect absence.' I repeated the phrase slowly, in a doomed attempt to understand it. 'That's very good.'

'It's what I feel Robert was working towards, Frank . . . but he never got there. There was too much love for his subjects. Too much *intimacy* . . .'

I fretted a little over how cerebral he was, waiting to see in him further flickers of humanity, wishing him fallible. It came almost as a relief to me the day we went to see a film called *Cinema Paradiso*, about an Italian film director returning to his childhood village. I found that the film manipulated me into crying despite myself, just as Africa had done. I turned to see whether Marc

195

was crying too, and he was. I could never have imagined this. He resisted classification.

'Childhood,' he whispered. 'It makes me sad to see children enjoying themselves.'

'I know what you mean,' I said.

He was no longer, he told me one night as we walked back through Lavapiés, the disoriented wreck he had once been. He preferred his experiences to be by proxy these days. He no longer had the energy to confront experience in the raw: it was quite sufficient to read a book, watch a movie, listen to a conversation.

'Unlike you,' he said. 'I can see you're straining to live, Frank. There's all this energy inside you. All this untapped potential, waiting like a coiled animal . . .'

'Well,' I said, 'I'll do your living for you.'

'What did you *feel* that last night with Africa?'

'I don't know. I didn't want to feel anything. Confused.'

'Didn't you feel anger?'

'Yes. Yes, of course I did . . .' He knew all about my imagined desecration of her flat and that I hadn't carried it out because it wasn't what he would have done.

'Could you have killed her, Frank? In your wildest dreams?'

'Kill Africa?'

We continued walking. A group of gypsy children stopped their game of football to point at us and shout that we were *maricones* – queers. It was still nice to be thought something which I wasn't. Or which maybe I was. I didn't know any more. I didn't care.

'Could you be that cold, Frank?'

'Yes,' I said. 'I could. I could have killed her when I broke the glass.'

'And why didn't you?'

'I don't know. The consequences, maybe.'

'But you could have killed her.'

'Yes.'

'You should be careful, Frank. They're dangerous thoughts you're having.' Suddenly, while I was still thinking about this, Marc paused.

'That's my body,' he said. He pointed to an illuminated billboard on the other side of the street. The image was of two silhouettes on a beach at sunset, advertising a soft drink. 'That's me in that photograph, Frank. Isn't that strange?'

'*Get away from it all*', the slogan read. This image was on hundreds of billboards all over Spain. Marc's silhouetted body, on a beach, high above the mess and fuss of life on the street, lodged into people's unconscious, perhaps causing young girls to look up and catch their breath.

'Which beach was it?' I asked. 'L'Estartit?'

'It wasn't a beach at all. It was a very hot photographer's studio. Soon there'll be no beaches at all. Soon there'll only be images of beaches, and images of people will drive images of cars to them, and images of children will build images of sand-castles, and they'll sit under images of parasols under an image of the sun . . . a world inhabited by images of ourselves . . .' He was staring up at the billboard, and had become suddenly inaccessible to me.

'Well,' I said. 'We'll all get terrible sunburn.'

'Why?'

'Well, it's no good wiping an image of suncream on your legs, is it?'

'That's an idiot sentence,' Marc said, and continued to stare. I felt humiliated and small.

'Hey! Frankie Quitarme!'

I looked at La Gorda standing fatly up ahead, her arms stretched out towards me. Only a month before I had rested my head on this girl's shoulder and wept. She had absolutely nothing to do with me. It might have been Genghis Khan standing there.

'God, you've changed, Frankie. How did you manage that? Is this your brother?'

'Come on, Frank,' Marc said. 'You don't need this.'

'Can you give me some money, Frankie? How much did that jacket cost?'

'Don't call me Frankie.'

'Give me some money, Frank. I saved your life. You told me so yourself.'

'Come on, Frank.'

Looking like Marc, being called 'Frank' and 'Frankie Quitarme': who was I, and was that the ghost of Auntie Beryl, come down to call me 'poppet'?

It was not. It was the Maybe-brother, suddenly at La Gorda's side. Behind him three others like him, all twitchy, all wearing sleeveless T-shirts and tight, torn jeans. In his right hand, the Maybe-brother held a white stick with a nail at the end. He clearly had no recollection of who I was, or indeed of who anyone was. His voice sounding like sour treacle, he told Marc and me to give him all our money. Then he changed his mind and asked us to give him at least 10,000 pesetas.

La Gorda flashed a quick, sad smile around and then stepped back into the shadows.

'Listen,' Marc said, in quiet, distinct Spanish. 'You aren't part of my plans. There's no Clint Eastwood *in* my film.' He folded his arms and stood with his feet apart, solid and tall. I also folded my arms and stood with my feet apart. But I was sweating like a pig.

'*Qué dice, tío* . . . Clint Eastwood, *joder* . . .'

'Do you understand me when I speak, drug addict?' Marc said. 'Try to focus your attention on me. If you don't put down your stick and walk away, then my friend is going to cut your face with a razor-blade. One time for every second you hang around.'

'I think we should go,' I said. I thought that Marc had just told the Maybe-brother that I was going to cut his face with a razor-blade. I hoped he hadn't said that, but I thought he had.

The Maybe-brother said something in Spanish which I didn't catch. The stick hovered at the end of his raised arm. Marc took my wrist. Between my fingers there was something so light that you wouldn't have thought it could do any damage at all.

'*Joder*,' the Maybe-brother said, almost wearily. He stepped forward and brought the stick down on to Marc.

I just raised my right arm and pushed it at the Maybe-brother's face. He shouted and dropped the stick. He stumbled backwards, his hands covering his face. The others were behind him, their palms raised in entreaty. Just like terrified Hispanics in films. I watched them.

'One time for every second you hang around, drug addict,' I said, but I don't think anybody heard me. There was too much commotion.

'Let's go,' Marc said. 'This is messy.'

Back at the school, I washed the dried blood off my hands and watched the pink water spin down through the plughole. I found I had no feelings on the matter. Someone else had done it. Marc had done it. There was no blood in there. It wasn't blood. It was just pink water.

'Have you never thought about your own life as a film, a story?' Marc asked me. We were sitting one hundred miles away from Madrid, under a natural rock arch called the Devil's Window. Below us a ravine dropped away, ending in a ragged river a hundred and fifty yards below. The distances were large, the air cool and clean: this was space. An eagle hovered above us. I was stoned.

'All the time,' I said. 'Hemingitis. The identity game.' Frank would never have felt happy in a place like this. Frank had never felt very happy at all. Standing in the Devil's Window, wearing a pale suit, smoking a cigarette, the breeze picking up my pony tail and playing with it. New false tooth.

None of them would have been able to recognize me now: Sidney Grimes, Troy Knox, Auntie Beryl, Donald, Brian,

Chantelle, Michael, Africa, Pilar. They were all dead. I tried to imagine them all recognizing me, and couldn't. It wasn't that we were dealing with Frank gone strange: we were dealing with someone else.

'All the time,' I said again, and Marc smiled.

'People are stereotypes,' he said. 'Their actions are so predictable, so much of the time. As though their lives were being scripted for them. All those young boys and girls we watch in the bars. They all think they're at a party in Hollywood. At a film of a party in Hollywood.'

'Chantelle,' I said. 'Little rich Australian girl gets bored of home, wants to see the world, wants to be a photographer, comes to Europe, gets out of her depth, gets fucked up.'

'Michael,' Marc said. 'Insecure gay boy, afraid of parents, leaves America in search of love, camps it up for all he's worth, trying to cover up for his desperation, pseudo-intellectual.'

'Michael came to see me,' I said. 'He told me some story about a man called Roy who died of AIDS. I just knew he was making it up. Trying to give himself depth.'

'Of course he was. You believe what you want to believe, Frank.'

'Africa,' I said. I wanted to carry on the game. 'Twenty-two-year-old Spanish woman, husband shot by political opposition, has no money, has to go on to the streets to earn money . . .' I couldn't go on. Somehow, it didn't sound as stereotyped as the others.

A group of young Spaniards came by, carrying a ghetto blaster which emitted heavy metal music, demolishing the silence. A noisy display of *machismo*. In later life, they'd grow fat, sitting in front of televised football matches, belching and picking at their stomachs. Later that evening, they would beat their wives and then go to sleep.

'It doesn't work for everyone, of course,' Marc said. 'Not for me and you. Donald's a troubling case. But Chantelle and Michael, they see themselves as characters. When people see themselves as characters, they become self-conscious. Even deep down. They start to direct their own lives. Their actions become predictable. They conform to a certain idea they have of themselves. They're afraid to move too far beyond that idea for fear of losing control, for fear of becoming themselves. Have you never thought of that?'

If I'd known then that Marc was describing my own life to me, things would have turned out differently. But I didn't know. I didn't want to know.

'It's escaping from yourself,' Marc went on. 'That's what your Hemingitis is. You think you're being liberated, but you have to be very careful. You're probably just changing scripts. You have to go that little bit further. But we're observers, Frank. Watchers. We see these things from the outside. We detect habits. We can see the patterns of people's lives. People like us needn't be limited to directing works of art . . .'

I hadn't seen him as agitated as this. A patch of sweat had appeared underneath his right armpit. Sweat and Marc didn't go together in my mind.

'Mothers and fathers do it. They direct the early lives of their children, don't they? They bring these characters on to the film set of the world, and then they direct them . . . lovers direct each other . . . we could direct whole *lives*, if we wished, Frank.'

'The film set of the world,' I repeated slowly. 'That's so . . . *pure*.'

'That's our film,' Marc said. He hopped down from the ledge, raised his chin, put his palms on his temples and drew them slowly back, hair peeping out from between his fingers. 'That's our film, Marc.'

He called me 'Marc'.

NINETEEN

The Holiday People was to be a film which altered people's perceptions of the world and of themselves. After seeing it, people would leave the cinema with someone they'd never met before, believing themselves to be someone else. Or perhaps everyone would leave alone.

It would cause Westerners to escape from themselves in droves. It would undermine the fragile foundations on which society currently stands. It would bring people's escapism deep into their own lives, forcing them to face the consequences of it.

Quite how any of this was to be achieved, I didn't know. Marc himself seemed vague on the subject, but my enthusiasm for the *idea* of the project, the impression it gave me of myself, was sufficient for me not to notice this – as indeed I was failing to notice nearly everything else that happened to me at the time.

I was out of my head on a semi-permanent basis, and the rest of the time I was asleep. It had occurred to me that Marc might not be decreasing the quantity of my drugs as he'd said – one day I just sort of slumped across the vegetable rack in the greengrocer's and brought down three racks of potatoes – but he assured me that things were under control, and anyway I wasn't complaining. You don't. If things are happening with the giddying, powerful logic of a dream, and if you're too happy to want to wake up, you're stuck with it.

'It's like I'm watching the film of my own life,' I said. 'It's like, I'm you, watching what I do.'

'You keep saying that, Frank. I wish you'd stop saying that.'

'It is, though. I want to see what happens in it. It's exciting. It's a whole new state of mind.'

'Frank, have you taken a bath today?'

'Yes.'

'You don't smell as though you have. We don't want you turning into Derek John Platt again.'

Little had been decided. A script, for example: we didn't have one. When I pointed this out to Marc, he said that we'd be improvising, at least at first, cutting and splicing later; if we found we needed a script, then we could work one up quickly from the material he already had in his head. *Cutting*, *splicing*, *material*: these were nice words to have floating around in my mind, making me feel trendy and contemporary. The words floating around in the mind of the greengrocer whose potatoes I'd knocked over were words like *turnip*, *cucumber* and *onion*. That was why I hadn't listened to him when he'd shouted at me, and yelled at his wife to fetch a stick out of the back room.

One thing I did know was that when you saw a film at the cinema, the list of credits at the end usually lasted longer than the film itself. Our list of credits, as far as I could see, consisted of only four people. Michael as Michael, Chantelle as Chantelle, myself as Marc, and Marc as director.

'That's in the future, Frank. These things don't happen overnight.' The first thing we'd have to do, he said, was something called a pre-shoot, which meant getting hold of equipment. He reminded me that I'd promised to acquire some.

'Can you do that, Frank?' he said worriedly. 'Can you do that for me? I'm depending on you.'

I rang Donald at his new school.

'This is the European Languages Academy,' Pilar's voice came at me, tinny, echoey. Then Donald's voice, in English: 'I'm afraid neither Pilar nor I are here to take your call at the moment, but if you want to leave a message ... Pilar, how the fuck do you turn –' Then there was a bleep.

'Donald,' I said. 'This is Marc. I believe you have some video equipment. My intention is to do a pre-shoot shortly, and –'

'Hello?' It was Pilar, out of breath.

'Pilar. This is Marc. I require the use of a video camera in order to do a pre-shoot, and Frank told me that –'

'Is that you, Frank?'

'No. Why would I say I was Frank, if I was Marc? This is Marc, and I require the use of –'

There was a bit of fuss at the other end, and then Donald came on.

'Hi,' he said. Donald never said 'hi'. 'Marc? Pilar says you want to borrow some of the stuff. No problem at all. You just get round here and we'll sort it out, OK? Gutierrez Solana, 15.'

'Listen,' I said to Marc five minutes later. 'I think I'd better go as Frank. I think Donald knows I'm not you.'

'Go as Frank?' Marc said. 'What does that mean? What would you *wear*? What would you *say*?'

I thought about that for a minute. How *would* I impersonate Frank?

'Right,' Marc said. 'We move tonight. I'll meet you outside Donald's school.'

'Jesus Christ almighty,' Donald said when he opened the door.

Pilar did rather better. She showed me round the academy with the pride of a new parent, showing me what it could do. Location was everything, she explained. Nothing mattered more than where you were. They had a hundred and twenty-five new enrolments for the following term, many of them from people living less than five hundred yards away.

I watched her as she bustled excitedly about, clicking lights on and off, running her hands over surfaces. Was she happy? Had she forgotten herself as she'd been on the night of destruction, scratching words into a costly table top? Was happiness for her something as simple as one hundred and twenty-five enrolments for a language school and an air-conditioning system? Did the prospect of running a small business, of being on the telephone, talking to people she couldn't stand, of filling out tax returns, of being caught in the rush-hour traffic four times a day, really satisfy her, allow her to connect with herself?

I pitied and despised Pilar for her lack of ambition, her unthinkingness, the way she'd been herded, together with all the millions of others, into believing that the only way you could succeed in life was by doing exactly the same as everyone else, though with any luck a bit better. But Pilar wouldn't do better. All you had to do to know that was observe her for a second, note the fact that she was using make-up to conceal her tiredness, the way her tights continued to crinkle at the knees, smell the tang of exhaustion on her breath. She cared too much. Her life had been scripted, and the only escapes from it she'd ever be able to effect were the false, trivial ones of holidays on the beach or a night out with the girls. 'Oh God, I'm ready for a break,' I could imagine Pilar saying to her friends, after laughing at a comment someone had made about that nice waiter's buttocks. And she'd go and lie on the beach and go brown, and when she came back, nothing would have changed.

One day, she and Donald would have a baby, and Pilar would be ecstatic, believing that, finally, she'd discovered what it was all about. 'I feel so *realized*,' she'd say to her friends. And she would feel realized, for a short time, but then the baby would start to grow and would take on a personality of its own, and it would no longer be *hers*, and she wouldn't feel realized any more. At that point she'd have a choice: either make the child's life hell by working out her frustrations on it, or try and behave decently. She'd be weary of continual inner compromise, and there'd be no more escape routes left open to her. The horror of this would be so great that she'd have to join the rest of humanity and carry out a partial lobotomy on herself, cutting out that part of the mind which thinks and feels, leaving only that part which allowed her to carry on.

'Ooh,' she'd say to Donald, when he'd done something she didn't like, when something was happening inside her which she didn't like. 'Ooh, I could just *scream*.' And that would be the most dramatic, radical thing Pilar's poor imagination would be able to come up with by way of escape, by way of exploding out of the prison she'd realize she'd built for herself. A scream into outer space, inaudible to everyone but herself.

But Pilar wouldn't scream. She wouldn't even scream. And that was Pilar's life, and everyone except mine and Marc's. An unscreamed scream.

'You and me should have words, sunshine,' Donald said in his new office. 'I don't like the look of you one bit. She won't mind if I just have the one.'

He took a squashed Ducados and a cigarette lighter from inside a language teaching book. 'Oh, Christ,' he said as he inhaled, recalling old pleasures now forsaken.

I understood from the uncharacteristic gentleness of his voice that we were going to have a man to man talk. I'd have to be careful not to weaken. Absolute control was called for: I'd never had a man to man talk in my life. It would be an exchange of platitudes, I assured myself, the deep, sincere voices providing the illusion that something real and true was being said.

I was aware of my hands pressing the sides of my head and then running back through my hair, down to the end of my pony tail. I watched Donald, the grey hair, the red face, the vein maze, and tried to detect some absence of light in his eyes. Because surely some flame inside him must have guttered out. It was incredible that Donald should be going the same way as all the others, that he'd opted for the lobotomy.

'You're not well, Frank.' He'd never called me Frank before, either. 'We've all been through it. What you're going through. One reason I started drinking was because I thought it was romantic. Dylan Thomas, Malcolm Lowry . . .'

'This isn't the same. I'm going through it more deeply.'

'I wish I'd never said the bloody word.'

'What word?'

'Hemingitis, for Christ's sake. Just look at yourself, sunshine.'

I didn't want to do that.

'You're an intelligent kid,' he said. 'Now I'm going to ask you one question. I want you to think about it, and then I want you to give me the answer. Now I know it must sound about as interesting as watching paint dry, but in two weeks, at the beginning of October, we'll be ready. I've broken my back trying to get it into shape. So that you and the others would have somewhere . . .'

'That's not true.'

'Yes, it bloody is. There's money for you. One day in the future, when I decide I want a break, there could be a seat for you in this office . . .'

'What's the question, Donald?' I said.

'Yeah . . . the question is, do you want help?'

'Donald, do you remember my interview with you? The sort of person you were then?'

'Well . . . not really, no . . . too pissed, probably . . .'

'We're both talking to the wrong person,' I said. 'We've changed. Are you going to let me have that video, or aren't you?'

'No. No fucking chance, sunshine.'

'Now you're talking,' I said.

Marc would have said that.

Donald stubbed out his cigarette on the floor. He'd forgotten that he was stubbing it out on his own money.

'You never lived in New York, did you, Frank?' He shook his head, disbelieving the distance I'd come. 'Christ, I never thought I'd hear myself saying this . . . You never did any of that, did you?'

'Oh yes,' I said. 'I did. Believe me.'

I didn't say anything else.

At 10.30 I went to the toilet. I bolted shut the door, sat down and waited for three minutes. A small, comfortable place, warm and soft. I could have been happy in there for the rest of my life. Absolute control.

Then I stood up, flushed the chain and rattled the door.

Donald's voice.

'You all right in there?'

'The bolt's jammed.'

'Oh, fuck. You're kidding.'

'No. I can't slide it open.' I pushed the bolt in the wrong direction until my forefinger throbbed.

'Ow,' I said loudly.

'Oh, for fuck's sake . . . Pilar!'

They muttered.

'Have you really tried to get out?' Pilar said.

'Yes.'

'Kick it or something,' Donald said.

'No,' Pilar said. 'You might damage it.'

I didn't know what it was they were talking about, but it didn't seem to be a door. A life or something, perhaps. That's how clear-headed I felt. That's how profoundly I knew where I was going.

More muttering.

'Listen, sunshine. The porter's on his way up. Wiggle it about till he gets here. This isn't doing your Uncle Donald any good at all, you know.'

'Spanish craftsmanship,' I said.

The porter was at a loss to know how to deal with the problem. He explained that it was hard to open a door when the bolt had jammed. He reminded Donald that the bolt, after all, had been built into the door with security in mind.

'This do we know, José,' said Donald. 'Just get him out. He's not well.'

'*No puede ser, Señor Brightwell. Mañana.*' It was very difficult, he repeated, when it was the bolt.

They muttered.

'OK, sunshine. This is the situation. We have to wait until tomorrow morning before a guy can come. What's outside the window?'

I looked. 'About fifty yards of dirty air and some pipes. Then concrete.'

'Are you going to do anything stupid, Frank?' Pilar asked. I was about as far from killing myself as I'd ever been.

'I'll be OK. Donald. This is a nice toilet.'

'Far too nice to shit in.'

'No graffiti, please,' called Pilar.

'I'll have to come in. I'll come in at about seven. Or Pilar will.'

I imagined Pilar, as they entered the lift, telling Donald that at least the videos were safe.

An hour later it was time to go. I'd taken some powdered joy, which hadn't been a good idea. I unbolted the door, went to the video room and put a Sony Handycam video camera under my jacket, holding it in my left hand through my pocket. The Sony Handycam: so compact that it can be lifted with no trouble at all.

I went into Donald's office and pushed his computer monitor off its table. I swept the articles off his desk with my free arm, and tore the telephone cable out, and threw the telephone against the wall. Nobody could hear anything: this entire building was padded, so that life couldn't get into it. I grabbed a fistful of Venetian blind and pulled it down, tearing a fingernail. I kicked the computer printer off its stand.

In a way, I hoped the damage wouldn't be excessive. This wasn't about doing harm to Donald and Pilar, it was about showing myself what I could do. I wanted to see how far I'd come since the night of destruction, in which I hadn't been able to participate. It felt as though I'd come a long way.

I picked up a ballpoint pen from the floor and held it tight in my fist. I pushed hard into the desk top and wrote:

You've all got it all wrong, fuckwit
Adiós
It's always midnight wherever I am

I looked at the mess I'd made. It looked suitably psychopathic.

Donald would find it tomorrow. He'd look at it, and he'd sigh, and swear, predictable to the last. It would confirm his suspicions about me. But I wouldn't be here. I'd be gone. My fingers hurt.

Chantelle, Michael and Marc were standing on the corner across the street. I stood for a moment with my face up to the late September rain, making myself calm again.

It was strange to see Chantelle after all this time. She was wearing a leather jacket, a yellow cheesecloth skirt and Doctor Martens, no doubt the visual product of some odd new idea she had of herself: dirty and small, and not at all as I'd imagined her. Michael didn't look very different. We didn't say hello, although they did express the statutory surprise at my appearance.

We were no longer the same people as before. We'd come through to the truth of our situation: we were now three individuals who scarcely knew one another, standing under a tower block on a cool night in a foreign city, not knowing why they were there, but determined, whyever it was, to see it through to the end, afraid to let go of their dreams.

Nothing bound us together any more except Marc. He looked immaculate.

'This is going to be good,' Michael said dully.

'Sure,' Chantelle said. 'Just like old times.'

'Where's the car?'

'Up there,' said Marc.

We walked in silence. Silence was right. There was nothing to be said. We were going back to L'Estartit to make our film, but we knew that we were going back for other reasons, too, reasons which we didn't dare talk about, were unable to talk about. A pleasant breeze cooled our faces, and finally the summer was over.

'We hid in the shadows,' Chantelle said. 'We watched Donald trying to get it started. But he couldn't. Marc did something to the wires.' She giggled, her hand moving to her mouth just a little too slowly, her eyes meeting mine just a little too late, and although I was pretty far gone, I could see that she was further gone still. Perhaps she'd had further to fall.

Thinking about that giggle now, I feel a twinge: looking at it then, I felt nothing.

'I'm cold,' Chantelle said.

It wasn't cold. But I knew what she meant.

The VW Beetle was parked on a side street. Marc went round to the driver's door and fumbled around for several seconds. He reached in and the bonnet came free.

'Get inside,' he said. 'Michael, Chantelle, get inside.'

I sat in the passenger seat.

'This is an adventure,' Chantelle said in a monotone. 'Midnight rides, stolen cars. *Thelma and Louise*.'

'*On the Road*,' Michael said.

The engine coughed.

'Press the accelerator,' Marc called. 'Frank.'

'That's the brake, Frank,' Michael said. 'Didn't Robert Mapplethorpe teach you where the brake was?'

The engine was turning over, smoke billowing from behind as I shoved at the accelerator with my hand.

'Shit,' Michael said. 'Look.'

Marc slammed shut the bonnet and got in.

I turned my head. Donald and Pilar were behind us. They broke into a run. Behind them, a fat little man waddled along with a Corte Inglés carrier bag.

'Marc . . . hurry up, darling . . .'

'This is good,' Marc said. 'Playing it close.'

Uncertainly, we moved away.

'Keep your heads down. Just keep your heads down. We're safe in here.'

'What the *hell* do you think you're doing?' It was Donald's voice. There was a loud bang. 'Chantelle! Michael! Stop!'

'Too late, Donald,' Marc said.

The Beetle gathered speed. Another car swerved to avoid us

and tooted its horn. Donald was running alongside us; Pilar's face was an indescribable picture of anger and worry combined. Donald beat on the window, shouting the word 'stop' again and again, swearing.

'Here,' Chantelle said. She reached forward and passed a joint to me.

'Thank you, Chantelle,' I said, and inhaled.

'Shit . . .' Donald's voice trailed off.

After a few seconds, Marc pulled up. 'Look,' he said.

We turned to watch. Donald was lying on his back in the gutter. His left leg was kicking in a strange way. Pilar was on her knees beside him. The fat little mechanic gesticulated after us.

'Does anybody here want to get out?' Marc said. 'Do they? Does anybody want to go and help Donald?'

Nothing happened in my mind. So I didn't say anything.

'Dangerous fun,' Marc said. 'OK. Let's go to the beach.'

The windows of the Beetle were down. These were the dark hours, and the wind was colder now.

Michael and Chantelle, in the back, were unusually silent: I turned to look and saw them sitting side by side, each trying to resist sleep, their heads bobbing forwards and then jerking upwards like badly constructed back-shelf dogs. It was sweet, in a way, nice that they weren't in each other's arms or anything.

Marc raised his eyes to the rear-view mirror. 'They're not tired,' he said. 'They're burned out. It's exhausting to hover at the edges of what you want, without ever quite getting there . . .'

He drove with one leather-gloved hand at the top of the wheel, the other at the bottom, clenching the muscles in his jaw. Occasionally he swore to himself at the car's impotence. No doubt he'd never had the misfortune to drive a clapped-out VW before. It was the first time I'd seen him ruffled in the way that normal people are ruffled, but I didn't dare point it out.

'You've moved on, haven't you?' I heard Marc say. 'From sensationalism to sensation. From escapism to escape. The big leap.'

I felt exhausted myself, but also extremely content, a mindless happiness brought on by a mixture of relief, anticipation and drugs. To be sitting in this car, with this person, driving to L'Estartit to do what we were going to do. From escapism to escape: I'd succeeded in freeing myself from the tedium of my days.

I'd used to feel the same thing in this same car, driving to the same place, but it was a good deal more intense now, a good deal purer. On our return this time, there would not be the sense of expectations unfulfilled, but of achievement. This was first love: before, it had been all the other loves.

Motorway signs sped past above our heads. Guadalajara. Sigüenza. Cars, too, flashed by, lumps of purposeful metal. A fine rain had started falling, and the occasional street-lights made triangles of yellow haze. A lonely, baffled hitchhiker held up a piece of cardboard with the word '*France*' scrawled on to it.

'Would you like to drive, Frank? I hate night driving. This is going to take all night.'

'Drive? I can't.'

'I don't make requests, Frank.'

'Would a bit later be all right?' I was being daring now, pitching my own will against Marc's, working on his level.

I settled back, my feet against the dashboard. I don't know why it came to me then, when I was so far away: I pictured Auntie Beryl's suede boots lying crumpled on top of the radiator on a wet afternoon. Smelt the smell of burning toast from the kitchen. She'd never been a very good timekeeper. 'People like us don't fall in love, Frank,' I heard her telling me. 'People like us aren't cut out for passion.'

I thought of her funeral. The three or four rows of mourners, the women dolled up to the nines, dabbing at mascaraed eyes with paper tissues. Large, heavy-set men with blue chins and Brylcreemed hair, their hands behind their backs, singing loudly out of tune, as though increased volume implied increased love for the deceased. It would have been pointless for me to go, since I knew already exactly what it had been like. The women crying not because they were at Auntie Beryl's funeral, but because of being at a funeral, and funerals are sad, and you must cry at them; the men more prosaically thinking of who is going to get the first round in, of whether there'll be any sandwiches laid on, because they're bloody starving. My imagination of the occasion contained a good deal more truth than anything I'd have experienced had I actually attended.

This was the way you had to look at the world. You had to see that no single act meant anything in itself, that to be somewhere else, physically and in your head, was the only true response to living. Everything we do, if we just take the step of watching ourselves for a moment, is an escape from something else. Life is a lengthy series of tiny getaways. Donald, escaping from the mess of his life, trying to alter his personality to accommodate that. Marc now, altering the position of his hands on the steering wheel, because he'd grown uncomfortable with their previous position, and now wished to get away from it. Chantelle and her photographs, wishing to convert the shock of Derek John Platt's death into shiny pieces of card; Africa and Brian, escaping from their miseries to England; the Maybe-brother, hoping to abandon the condition of poverty. All the big issues: birth, love, marriage, child-bearing, divorce, death. All the small ones: every turn of every conversation, starting smoking, stopping smoking: all escapes from the horror of tedium, from the nightmare of repetition.

I looked at Marc. Here I was sitting next to him, wearing the same clothes and, I hoped, sharing the same thoughts. The purity of my own escape was something to be marvelled at. The purity of Marc, in letting me in. We were heroes. We were out on our own. Driving through the darkness on a lonely road, through the rain.

He finally had us exactly where he wanted us.

'What are you thinking about?' Marc asked me, knowing.

'That letter I was writing to my Auntie Beryl. I was wondering if I could ever really have been that screwed up. I mean, I was really writing it to try and understand myself. But maybe there's no myself to understand. When I think back to when I arrived in Spain . . . I was a mess . . .'

'I wrote similar letters,' Marc said. So he'd gone through the same confusions and unsettledness as myself and yet come out on the other side, shining like a star. 'Do you think you can trace things back in this way, though, Frank? Do you not think matters are more complex?'

It was great how quickly we'd come to be friends, how intimacy had developed between us. Our strolls through Madrid, the films, the bars along Pintor Rosales, a bit of violence to make it all feel real. Already we shared memories. And now this. We were having the perfect time.

'I'll tell you something, Frank,' Marc said quietly. 'I was also brought up by an aunt. I'm an orphan, too.'

'Really?'

'You won't tell anyone, will you? It's very private to me.'

He was staring ahead, his face half in shadow. Something approaching sadness swam in his clear eyes. I'd always assumed that people who looked like film stars had no emotional burden to carry. I'd always associated a good-looking outside with a good-looking inside.

'I promise not to tell anyone.'

'Frank, would you mind driving for me?'

At a godforsaken village near Medinaceli, we pulled up for petrol behind a ghostly juggernaut and Chantelle awoke, anxious for water which Marc handed to her. Michael's head glistened as he slept.

'Let him sleep,' Marc said. 'He's not happy.'

The time had come for me to drive. We went into the toilet behind the bar and Marc gave me an injection.

It was crazy, me driving, but then craziness had entered my life and I was happy that I no longer felt any compulsion to resist it. I'd finally reached the point I'd been waiting for since I'd stood, soaked through, at Whately railway station nine months before: the point at which there was no turning back. I didn't feel nervous about driving, even though it was pitch dark.

I hadn't taken control of a vehicle since failing my cycling proficiency test at age eleven. Marc showed me what the three pedals meant, told me to drive slowly, and even slower if there were headlights of other cars, and told me I should just follow the white lines along the edge of the road. For about ten uncomfortable miles we swapped activities, myself steering and Marc

216

pressing the pedals and changing gear, and vice versa. It was easier than I'd thought.

Then I was on my own. After ten minutes, Marc fell asleep. I was free to make my mistakes unobserved. The Beetle had a tendency to pull towards the left of the road, as if pining for England, but I quickly learned how to correct this. The first couple of cars to come past were frightening, and the several which overtook were no doubt unhappy at my dangerously slow speed, but I realized that, as long as I didn't have to change gear on my own, I'd be all right. I'd wake Marc if I had to change gear.

On a Spanish highway at night, behind the wheel, with three people asleep, and me responsible for them, driving towards the future. I experimented pressing down the accelerator, taking the speed up to eighty kilometres an hour. At this the body of the Beetle started to tremble in threatening protest.

'Night driving,' Marc said on awakening. 'There's nothing like it. The long silences. The hum of the engine . . . perhaps you could keep a little further from the edge, Frank . . .'

Marc continued to speak, careful with his words as always, leaving lengthy thought-spaces so that only the truth may emerge, and for the first time I wondered whether he wasn't struggling with the English language. He told me how he'd hated his mother and father for dying, and then how he'd hated his aunt for not being his mother. He told me how he'd felt confined, repressed by her need to love him, and how he'd felt guilty at not being able to return her love. He spoke of the intense awkwardness which this had created in his relationship with his aunt and later, after she'd died, with other people.

'There's nothing wrong in seeking to trace back your insecurities to a point in history,' he said. 'It may not be correct, but it helps people like us.'

'But you seem so assured,' I said. 'You seem to be working from such a solid base.'

'That's taken years. Years and years . . .'

He, too, had been obliged to run away, he reminded me. Born in a small village in the Salzkammergut, he'd had to leave for Vienna, tasted all the romance he'd told me about, and had not stopped being romantic since.

'A romancing mind is a form of protection. How many memories do we have? It's impossible to contain them all in your mind at once. What does that mean? It means, given that we are the sum of what we have been, that it's impossible – impossible – ever to be completely ourselves.'

After about a minute, during which Marc went on talking, I had managed to work out exactly what he meant. It was one of those ideas which manages to take *everything* into account.

Marc then told me that he'd had a relationship with an older woman which had ended badly. I listened very carefully to this part. He explained that whole weeks had gone by after that during which time he'd not felt able to face the world. He'd become heavily involved with drugs, and only by a supreme effort of will was he now clear of them.

We passed by Zaragoza in silence. A huge, black bull stood on a hilltop, silhouetted against the moonlight, and I'd been listening to my own life.

'What are you thinking about?'

'The film,' I said. 'I was just thinking . . . I was just thinking about your other films.'

'No you weren't,' Marc said slowly. 'Don't lie to me, Frank. Don't make me edgy inside. I'm watching you, little man.'

'I'm not lying . . .'

The atmosphere in the car had changed suddenly, because the atmosphere in Marc had changed. Michael must have sensed it also, because he stirred and said, 'Oh, my God.'

'I'll tell you about a film I made, Frank. Do you remember that video we watched, of the gypsy? José Luis Ruiz?'

'Yes?'

'That was a film. I didn't make it, but it was a film.' He took his

218

eyes off the road to turn and look at me. His eyes crinkled slightly, as though he were studying me.

'But that was a news programme.'

'No. It was a film. It was a scene from a cheap old Spanish film. I can't remember which one. Think about that, Frank. You're intelligent. Think about what that implies.'

The edges of the road rushed blackly towards me. I wanted to close my eyes now, to lose myself in the dull rhythms the tyres made against the tarmac.

I knew what it implied: what it implied had cracked inside me like lightning. But I didn't dare say it. I just didn't.

'I've never made a film in my life,' Marc said quietly. 'But I love people to think I have. I want to do it for real now. We're going to do it, Frank. Aren't we?'

'I hope so . . .' It didn't matter that he hadn't made a film before. He was capable. You knew that just by looking at him, just by talking to him. I understood exactly what he was saying.

'We're loners, Frank. Drifters. The journey towards self-discovery, and all that crap. Nobody can escape the script. They can try. But nobody can, in the end.'

'That film you showed me . . .'

'Listen, Frank. You watch too many films and not enough news. If you watched more news, you'd realize that eight tourists have been murdered across Europe in the past three years.' His back was rigid, his hands gripping the edge of his seat. I turned to watch his eyes. At this point, watching Marc's eyes was more important than watching the road ahead. Marc didn't blink for at least five seconds, and then he said, 'I killed them.'

'No, you didn't,' I said. I said it automatically.

'Listen. I killed them. I killed Derek John Platt. I cut his throat. I cut his throat with the very same blade you cut that kid with –'

'Why didn't you tell me?' I blurted out. Instead of revulsion, panic, despair, whatever it was you were supposed to feel

219

when someone told you they'd killed eight people, I felt self-pity. 'Why didn't you tell me?' I said again. 'I *knew*. I *imagined* it. You got Michael to steal it.'

'Slow down, Frank,' Marc said wearily. 'Your confusion will kill us all.' But I couldn't think. The muscles in my face were hurting me. I wanted to cry. 'Why didn't you tell me?'

'Slow down. Lift your right foot up.'

I did so.

'You weren't ready,' Marc said. 'You'd have left me. You'd have gone back to being your old self. Let's say that then, you were able to see the difference between fantasy and reality. I don't think you're so clear, now. I'd say that you rather *like* the idea of my being a serial killer. You *like* sitting in a car next to someone who has killed eight people for the hell of it. Driving down a lonely road, at night. Into the darkness. There's something filmic about it which turns you on. Romantic. On the edge. You're friends with the man with the razor-blade. You love it, Frank. You do. But you don't know what it *means*. You're *empty*.'

On either side of us, there lay nothing but the shadows of dark, hulking mountains. Big mountains, great big, hulking, dark, shadowy mountains, which told you nothing.

'Now let me tell you something else, Frank,' Marc murmured. 'What I just told you isn't true.'

I was taking my foot off the pedals and putting my hands to my face.

Marc reached across and took the wheel: we swerved and juddered. Michael and Chantelle were suddenly awake, shouting.

'Where are you going, Frank?' Marc said. 'Trying to get away?'

'I'm going to be sick,' I said.

'Jesus,' Michael said.

'No, you aren't.' Marc's voice had become little more than a cracked whisper in my head. 'Picture it. Standing in the ditch, puking like a little baby. That's not the sort of thing you do, is it? Is it, Frank?'

My eyes were stinging. My heart was beating. I leaned forwards, wanting my forehead against the cool of the windscreen.
The seatbelt dug into my neck; there was a vicious, sour taste at
the back of my throat.

'Just think, Frank. Maybe I'd never have thought of killing
anyone at all if I hadn't seen your little beach fantasy. Maybe I'm
just a product of your trashy imagination. Maybe I read what
you wrote and thought it sounded like an interesting thing to do.
Maybe you've *created* me, Frank . . .'

I had the uncanny sense that I was taking part in a dialogue
with myself. *That's not the sort of thing you do. Marc is me. Maybe
you've created me.* It was true, I thought with dull, overwhelming
horror: I no longer knew where Marc ended, and where I began.

'I want to die,' I said. 'I mean it.'

'Frank wants to die,' said Chantelle.

'You're not going to die,' Marc said. 'I won't let you die.'

Marc took over the driving. I wasn't capable. I couldn't bear to sit
there in silence. I spoke to aid my recovery.

'Why did you tell me that?' I asked him. 'Why did you tell me
you'd killed those people?'

'I don't know, Frank. Don't ask. Maybe I did kill them. Jesus. I
am so, fucking, *tired*.' Marc brought his gloved fist down hard on
the steering wheel.

'We're the *same*,' I said softly. 'We are. I only want to understand you.'

'Would you believe me,' Marc shouted, 'if I told you I wasn't
happy? That I am far, far from being the person you, and
Michael, and Chantelle, take me for?'

'Of course I would. Of course I would, Marc.'

The tired eyes of Michael and Chantelle shone with love and
awe. They leaned forwards to hear what Marc was going to say. I
could see that, like me, they sensed that some elemental truth
about him, the truth which his very perfection hinted at and
which had until now been beyond our reach, was about to be

revealed. As with Marilyn Monroe and Montgomery Clift, there was tragedy behind the perfection of Marc. All three of us had sensed that, all three of us had wished to touch it.

'Sometimes,' he said, 'I lie awake at night and I realize that I have nowhere, absolutely nowhere, on this earth to go back to. I could live with that once. But now I find I cannot.'

He turned to look at me. His eyes were shining too, as they had on the night we'd watched *Cinema Paradiso* together. I felt in my pocket and removed a tissue, which I passed silently across to him.

'Marc,' I murmured, 'you were never a rent boy in Hamburg, were you? Or any of that?'

'I don't know.'

'Your lover didn't die playing Russian roulette in Hong Kong?'

'I don't know, Frank. Don't ask me.' His fingers worked at the scrunched-up tissue in his palm.

'Those clothes. They're not Armani, are they? That wine was just table wine, wasn't it? You never met Robert Mapplethorpe either, did you? That was just a fantasy we happened to share, wasn't it?'

'I don't *know*,' Marc said again. 'Too many questions. You're going deep now, Frank. Be careful what you say.'

His voice was scarcely audible: I thought he was going to explode, blood and muscle strewn across the road. His jaw muscles were clenching again.

'I'm sorry,' he said. 'It must be the night.' I'd never seen a person look so vulnerable.

'I understand,' I said. 'I do. I understand, Marc. You're just a dreamer. A romantic. Playing the identity game. Hemingitis. My God.'

We drove several miles without speaking. God knows what was happening in our minds at that point.

'And you didn't kill Derek John Platt, did you?' Chantelle suddenly blurted out. 'Tell us you didn't. I couldn't bear to hear that you –'

'I did,' Marc said wearily. 'I killed him, I killed the others. People are *very* stupid.' Chantelle shrieked, shattering the holy atmosphere inside the Beetle, and then started moaning. Michael's eyes were closed and he was rocking back and forth in his seat.

'That's what you all wanted to hear, isn't it?' Marc said. 'That's why you're all in love with me, isn't it? So that's what I'm telling you.'

He pulled up and turned to face us all. He took a deep breath and exhaled.

'They're on to me,' he said. 'Police all over Europe. Intelligence networks. Satellite communications. Computerized images of my face. They know my name. It's only a matter of time. I've committed some stupid errors, and they're on to me. Do you understand? Tomorrow, I'm going to ask you all to do something for me and capture it on film. You all love me. None of you could stand to live without me. Will you do this for me?'

If I'd fully believed what Marc was saying, if I'd been capable of taking on board what it was he was doing to us, then I still might have managed to say no. But of course he was elusive, *endlessly* elusive, as elusive as a complicated idea.

He'd refined the art of escape to a far greater degree than anything I could have imagined possible. He was nothing more than a flawless construction, composed of his own observations. Style without substance.

His skill was in always being the person you wanted him to be. He had no personality and no qualities, only the image of qualities. He could tell you that he'd killed eight people, and then five minutes later, he could tell you that he'd been inventing. You didn't know what was true and what wasn't: but the terrible part was that you wanted to find out, and from him. He drew you in. He was a madman who made you want to believe him, a deranged salesman of the self. And he chose his clients with supreme skill.

Perhaps Marc was not a person at all. Perhaps he was a dead film star. Because what held Chantelle and Michael and I was that he was, quite literally, unbelievable. Everything he said might have been a lie, or it might have been the truth, but there was always the sense that, since this was a film we had found ourselves in, a film he'd scripted and was now directing, with Chantelle, Michael and myself as the actors, it didn't really matter either way. I'd become as passive before the spectacle of my own life as a cinema-goer is, deeply involved and yet finally detached, continuing to sit there on the understanding that I'd be able to get up at the end and leave.

But at the time, I didn't know any of this. I was still too deeply involved to know any of this.

We drove into L'Estartit at about 10 a.m. It was desolate, an unemployed town suspended between seasons, an abandoned film set, not of this world. A fine September rain continued to fall, the first rain of the season, causing the buildings to glisten and drawing attention to their concrete nakedness. An old woman sat under a parasol with the stars and stripes on it, surrounded by shopping bags, waiting for a bus you suspected wouldn't arrive for another eight months.

We drove slowly down the Passeig Maritim, which was just a line of cold, corrugated metal shutters, a wall of sad whitewash. A thin girl in a striped apron stood in the doorway of the supermarket, smoking a cigarette. Our fish restaurant gave no sign of life, its owner, the waiters who worked there, the tourists who ate there, all far from here, all engaged in their real lives. It was as though all the life which hummed through the place during the summer months had been extinguished by the death of Derek John Platt.

We pulled up in front of the Miramar: I gave Marc the directions, but I now suspect he knew exactly where it was anyway. Marc stayed in the Beetle while Michael, Chantelle and I went and knocked on the door.

'*Sí*?' came Freddy Krueger's voice, echoey in the hallway. '*Quién es? Es periodista?*'

'I'm not a journalist. It's me. Chantelle.'

Freddy Krueger warily opened up and peered out at us, weak eyes in a leathery, pitted face.

'Chantelle? Is that really you? Ah, Señor Michael . . .' Her pronunciation of the names was, as ever, something else.

'Could we stay here for a couple of nights, señora? I know you're closed . . .'

'But I have no rooms ready . . . who's this?'

'That's Frank,' Chantelle said. 'You remember Frank.'

'I am getting old . . . my memory isn't good . . . *encantada*,' Freddy Krueger said, holding out her hand and weakly shaking that of a person she had never met before.

'I'll come back later,' Marc said when I told him that we'd booked a room. 'I have to spend some time on my own. You understand.'

'We've booked a room for you,' I said. 'You can be on your own in your room.'

'No,' he said. 'Really on my own. I'm going to drive somewhere and sit in the car and think. If that's all right with you, Frank. You should all get some sleep. I'll be back around three.'

I went into my old room, while Michael and Chantelle took a double room further down the corridor. It was unusual to enter a hotel room with no luggage. Not even a toothbrush in my top pocket. Marc had probably packed clothes for me. I took a shower – Freddy Krueger had fixed the exploding shower-head – put three crisp, clean sheets together, made myself comfortable under them, and dozed off, my wet hair cold against the pillow, the sounds of an angry sea filling my head.

There was a voice in my room. Michael's, urgently whispering.

'Frank. Wake up . . .'

I opened my eyes and pulled myself up on to my elbows.

'How did you get in?'

'We walked in through the door. Listen, Frank. I've been thinking.' He spoke quickly, as though there were no time to be lost. 'Sit down, Chantelle.' He went back to the door, where Chantelle was standing swaying with a can of Coca-Cola in her hand, took her arm and led her to a wicker chair in the corner.

'Chantelle's in bad shape. She's been coughing up blood.' He sat on the arm of the chair and put his arm round her shoulders. 'And you're not in real good shape yourself, Frank. I think we should get out of here.'

I sat up and pulled the bedsheets around my shoulders.

'I'm not leaving, Michael. Why do you think we should leave?'

'I don't know . . . I guess I can sense danger . . .'

'That's good,' I said.

'Frank, I love him. I do. I'd do anything for him. But it's like, I'm thinking something's . . . what he said in the car was *bizarre* . . . and poor Donald . . .'

'He's just different from us,' I said firmly. 'We just have to accept that. He's the same as us, but just on a different *level*. That cool Austrian blood.'

'Austrian? He isn't Austrian. He's Swedish, Frank. He told me he was from Stockholm. Stockholm's in Sweden.'

Chantelle moaned softly from the wicker seat. 'Switzerland,' she said. She agitatedly rubbed at her right arm, spilling Coca-Cola on to the tiles.

'How did she *get* that way?' Michael said. He looked at her and shook his head, having thoughts he'd never thought before. 'She's a junkie. Look at her. We have to help her. What is *happening . . .*?'

'She didn't have to do anything she didn't want to do,' I said. 'I've never done anything I didn't want to for him.'

'He offered me drugs, too. But I didn't take any.' Michael came over to me, knelt down in front of me, placed his hands on my bare knees. 'Frank, I think you *have* to listen to me now. I don't think you can *afford* not to listen to me this time.'

I looked down into his fishy eyes, staring up at me, imploring. In Michael's opinion, I was only slightly less gone than Chantelle. For a second I thought he actually wanted to help me. But then I realized that that couldn't be possible.

I didn't know what it was that Michael wanted from me, but he wasn't going to get it.

'Chantelle was telling me the most amazing things,' Michael said. 'Like, he likes to get her to play dead, and then he screws her. Chantelle just has to lie there. If she makes a sound while he's screwing her, he slaps her. Even a little sound. Then she has to sit on him, on his stomach, and like, draw a razor-blade across his throat, just so lightly that it doesn't cut him. He says he'll kill her if she spills blood. And then she tells me she *loves* him . . . "I *love* him, Mikey" . . . oh, man . . .'

'And what about you two?' I said. 'I suppose he hangs you from a coat hook and puts on a scuba-diving outfit and sucks your willy to the tune of *Colonel Bogey*. Your fantasies are wearying to me, Michael.'

Michael flinched.

'Frank, that's just how Marc speaks. "Your fantasies are wearying to me".'

'And?'

'What I'm telling you is the gospel truth, you jerk. You have to listen to me. I'm sorry . . . I mean, everyone has different tastes, but . . .'

'And why do you love him?'

'I don't know . . . he's told me that after we've made this movie, we're going to go travelling together . . .'

'Have you ever had sex with him?'

'Oh, not yet. He says we will. He says he needs time. It's killing me, Frank . . . oh, man. What have I got myself *into*, here?'

Michael was on the point of crying. I knew I had him where I wanted him.

'Listen,' I said. 'I'll think about what you're saying. Just give me the rest of the afternoon, and if I think we should go, then I'll come and get you and we'll go. All three of us. OK, Michael?'

'How, though? Marc's taken the Beetle.'

'We'll find a way. You go back to your room. Take Chantelle with you.'

Michael led Chantelle away, the pair of them taking tiny, trembling footsteps like old people. Marc would be pleased with me when I told him how Michael had wanted to escape, and I hadn't let him.

I was standing out on the balcony, playing with the video camera, sweeping it across the dull sand, the choppy, irritable ocean, the

228

powerful sky, the shadowy humps of the Islas Medes.

The effect of the camera was to extinguish entirely the power of the scene, transform it into something tiny, black and white, and manageable: a camera such as this, I reflected, could never capture the passion, the glory of anything. It was capable only of transforming life into a depthless, monochrome joke. Only the smallest, most trivial act could ever be faithfully captured using an instrument like this. But I nevertheless felt giddy and out of control when I took it from my eye and tried to take in the scene for what it was.

'Frank,' Marc said. 'It's three o'clock. Are you ready?'

'I was waiting,' I said.

He stood in the doorway in his pale suit, gazing at me, a burning match in his hand. As I watched, he brought the match to the tip of the cigarette in his mouth.

There was something strange about that cigarette. He shouldn't have been smoking a cigarette. But I didn't say anything.

'You like it when I do that, don't you?'

'Yes.'

'Frank, look at me. Just hold my gaze.'

I did so. For about ten seconds we did nothing, said nothing, standing across the room from each other. I knew what he was doing. He was looking at my inside. Penetrating me with his blue gaze.

'Just look at me.'

I thought about a lot of things. I'd lain in bed beside Africa, doing the same thing, the two of us just staring at one another, trying to understand, locked in mutual incomprehension. But this was different. I was staring at my reflection.

'You're ready,' Marc said. 'Let's go.'

I followed him out into the silent corridor and along it as far as Michael and Chantelle's room. Marc pushed open the door. They were lying naked across the bed, tangled up in one another, sound asleep. They made a strange vignette.

'They tried to have sex,' Marc said simply. 'It didn't work.' He went to the bed, removed his jacket and hung it on the wardrobe door. Then, using two hands, he set about trying to extricate them. The dull way their limbs fell as he picked them up and dropped them made me think that they were dead.

'They're not,' Marc said. 'They're sleeping deeply. I gave them something to drink. Help me.'

He pulled Michael up so that he could clasp his hands around under his arms and across his chest. I took Michael's feet. His penis was smooth and shiny and floppy, a miniature version of Michael himself. As we were manoeuvring him through the door, Marc said, 'I wouldn't have thought that six feet of thin American would be so heavy.'

'Be careful,' he said, when I dropped one of Michael's feet at the bottom of the stairs. 'I don't want any bruising.'

I hadn't had so much physical exercise for years. Getting Michael out through the back porch, over the wet scrub and down on to the beach nearly killed me, and getting him up over a sand dune and across a hundred yards of damp, heavy sand nearly buried me. If I kept going, it wasn't because I was afraid of being seen by Freddy Krueger. I was way beyond standard, everyday fears. I kept going simply because I didn't want Marc to think me weak.

'Here,' Marc said. We set Michael down. The hue of his skin blended with that of the sand.

This was the spot at which Michael had found Derek John Platt. That realization made me say to Marc, 'Are you sure he's not dead?'

'Put your head to his chest, if you want. He's still breathing. He's just sleeping.'

I didn't do so. I remember that Marc didn't say 'he's breathing', but 'he's *still* breathing': and that 'still' made me think that it would be pointless to check whether or not Michael was alive. Quite soon now, he wouldn't be anyway.

'Go and get Chantelle,' Marc said. There were flecks of rain covering his face, wetting his hair. He stood with a gloved hand on one hip, looking out to sea. I didn't know whether I'd be able to carry out his request.

'Go and get Chantelle, Frank. Or I'll kill you.'

'You don't mean that,' I said.

He didn't turn to look at me.

'Perhaps I don't,' he said. 'Bring my jacket, too.'

Chantelle was warm. She lay on the bed with her legs apart and her mouth half open, like a sleeping model in one of her trendy photograph books. I ran my hands over her flat stomach, touched her cheeks, pinched the flesh on the inside of her left thigh. Her breasts were smaller than I remembered them.

I leaned over and kissed her on her nipples, once each, just quickly. I'd been wanting to do that ever since I'd first seen her. She smelt sweet, just as she had that night on the back porch of the Miramar. Then I kissed her on the lips and on her pubic hair, just quickly also. I'd never thought of doing that before. I'd been right not to, because it didn't taste very nice. I thought of masturbating, but unfortunately Marc was waiting, so I had to get a move on.

The bumping Chantelle's feet made as I dragged her down the stairs was terrible. Going up over the sand dune, a thorn scraped her along the leg.

'I'm sorry, Chantelle,' I said.

'Put her next to Michael,' Marc instructed me.

'Are you sure they aren't dead?'

'They aren't dead yet. Stop asking that.' Marc came to me and put his hands on my shoulders, gripping them tight. 'We're going to make our film.'

I knew what was going to happen now. I knew what I had to do. I took the camera from my jacket pocket and switched it on.

'There should be enough light,' Marc said. 'Stand behind me. I'm camera shy.'

I walked back a few paces and knelt down, the camera to my

eye. Marc closed his eyes and drew a few deep breaths. Then he stepped towards Michael and looked down on him, saying something I didn't catch. He sat on Michael's stomach and took something from his pocket. A wallet. He fumbled slightly and took something else out of it. He leaned forwards, put his fingers to Michael's throat and sort of dragged them across it.

Michael gently heaved. His legs kicked three times. His arms weakly pounded the sand. Marc had one hand over his mouth, the other squeezing his nostrils. It took about a minute.

Then he did it all over again, only this time to Chantelle. It didn't take as long.

He stood up.

'Come closer,' he said. 'Capture their heads.' I did so. But I wasn't really looking. I was just pointing the camera, making sure that everything was framed properly. Black lines ran across the necks of Michael and Chantelle.

He took the camera from me and held it up for a couple of seconds. 'Say cheese,' I heard Auntie Beryl telling me. 'Cheese,' I said.

'Perfect,' Marc said. 'Simple. Thank you, Frank. I'm going now.'

He put the video camera down on Michael's stomach and held out his hand, but I didn't take it.

'Why did you do that?' I asked him. 'Don't you feel anything?'

'I don't feel anything, Frank, no.'

'Nothing at all?'

'Why *feel* anything? I haven't *done* anything, have I? You did it. Congratulations. You just carried out a new kind of killing. An image killing. One image, murdering other images. It didn't really *happen*. It isn't *true*. It took some setting up. But I suppose it felt like the real thing.'

'Can't I come with you?' I asked him. 'Can't I?' It was all that mattered.

'Don't be silly.' He opened the video camera, removed the

232

cassette and handed it to me. 'Take this to the police station, Frank. Confess.'

'No. No. I haven't done anything.'

'Take it to the police station, Frank.' Marc yawned, a big mouthy yawn, most unlike him. 'I am *shattered*. Come on, Frank. You know you're better off away from it all.'

'No . . .'

'All right, then.' He reached down, took the camera and removed the cassette. 'I'll take it.' In his mind, the entire episode was over. Already he was somewhere else.

'But they'll arrest you.'

'No they won't. I'll pretend to be someone else. Perhaps I'll even pretend to be you. The identity game, Frank. You see, I can be anyone I want to be, but you can only be me. Who will they believe?' He looked at me with exasperation. 'Sometimes, Frank, you lead me to believe that you were born without a brain. Look at this.'

He unbuttoned his left shirt cuff and rolled it back. There was no watch tattoo.

'I drew it on each morning with a ballpoint. I liked the idea of having something like that on my wrist. It's always midnight, wherever I am. Nothing is ever quite clear.'

I stood there for a few moments, stupid. The wind, the rain. Then I sat down on the sand and looked at the video cassette in my hands. I turned it this way and that. I didn't feel anything. I didn't want to feel anything, and I didn't.

'Do you know how much you know about me?' Marc said. He stood above me, hands in pockets, talking down. 'Nothing. Do you know how much I know about you? Everything. Who did it, Frank? Who's the victor? Who's the victim? Who's escaped into whom? It's hard to tell us apart, isn't it?'

'Why didn't you kill me?'

'You're the killer here. Don't worry, Frank. If it hadn't been you, it would have been someone else. Right. Off I go. Into the sunset. It was good to know you.'

He walked away. I sat on the sand, feeling the damp come through to my underpants. I pictured Marc walking up the beach, his turn-ups flapping in the breeze, his hair slicked back with the rain. Pausing at the top of the sand dune for a last look at me.

I turned. There was no one.

I heard the engine of the Beetle coughing into life.

'Chantelle,' I heard myself saying. 'Michael.'

For several hours I sat and thought about what to do with myself. I could kill myself, for example. Just walk out into the sea and keep walking. Fat chance. Or I could take the tape to the police station and try to explain everything to them. Or I could take the tape to the police station and confess, or I could throw the tape into the sea and try to run away. All of these possibilities seemed far too difficult and well beyond my capabilities. I was inhuman, shorn of desire.

So what I thought I'd do was just carry on sitting there, to contemplate the stunning perfection of what Marc had created from nothing, created from his heart of surface and light. What Marc had done to me was so beautiful, I just couldn't take my eyes off it.

TWENTY-TWO

During the first few weeks of my imprisonment, I was very ill. In fact I tried to kill myself three times. It was hard, getting by without the powdered joy: I wouldn't recommend that to anyone.

After I got better, they brought people to identify me. Sr López, Africa and Brian, and a man I'd never seen before who Africa said was her son Paco. Freddy Krueger. Even the fat little mechanic. There were quite a few people from England as well, but I can honestly say I didn't recognize a single one of them. That man who wrote the letter, for example. Pilar came too, but she didn't seem herself.

I had to be very strong. It was difficult, telling the police that I'd never seen Africa in my life before. But I found that as long as I kept repeating the words 'My name is Marc, with a "c",' they couldn't do anything about me. 'Marc what?' they'd ask, and I'd say I didn't know.

They made me write down my life story, anything I could remember. I wrote that I'd been born in a village in the Salzkammergut, and wrote more things about Robert Mapplethorpe and an Italian countess, and a game of Russian roulette. Exciting things, but all a bit confusing, and not much use to them. So eventually, they brought me to the hospital section.

The most important thing in this place is not to open your mouth, but to watch. That way, no one knows what you're thinking and you're all right. Looking back over everything I've written, I realize it might seem a little cold, a little dislocated, but I certainly didn't intend to get too deeply involved with it all a second time. I had to write about someone else. I had to pretend that none of it was me.

235

Well, none of it was.

The last person to come and see me was a man called Frank Bowden, who said he'd met me at a party once and found me a little strange. There's been no one since him. He was wearing a pale suit, just like the one I used to wear. He looked at me for a while, and smiled, and I looked at him, and smiled, and then he apologized to the police for having wasted their time. He must have got the wrong person, he said.